Time Slips

## performance works

**SERIES EDITORS**
**Patrick Anderson and Nicholas Ridout**

This series publishes books in theater and performance studies, focused in particular on the material conditions in which performance acts are staged, and to which performance itself might contribute. We define “performance” in the broadest sense, including traditional theatrical productions and performance art, but also cultural ritual, political demonstration, social practice, and other forms of interpersonal, social, and political interaction which may fruitfully be understood in terms of performance.

# Time Slips

*Queer Temporalities, Contemporary Performance, and the Hole of History*

✦

Jaclyn I. Pryor

NORTHWESTERN UNIVERSITY PRESS
EVANSTON, ILLINOIS

Northwestern University Press
www.nupress.northwestern.edu



Printed in the United States of America

10 9 8 7 6 5 4 3 2 1

Library of Congress Cataloging-in-Publication Data

Names: Pryor, Jaclyn I., author.
Title: Time slips : queer temporalities, contemporary performance, and the hole of history / Jaclyn I. Pryor.
Description: Evanston, Illinois : Northwestern University Press, 2017. | Series: Performance works | Includes bibliographical references and index.
Identifiers: LCCN 2017003470 | ISBN 9780810135314 (cloth : alk. paper) | ISBN 9780810135307 (pbk. : alk. paper) | ISBN 9780810135321 (e-book)
Subjects: LCSH: American drama—21st century—History and criticism. | Performing arts—Social aspects—United States. | Group identity in the performing arts—United States. | Psychic trauma in the theater—United States. | United States—Historiography—Case studies.
Classification: LCC PN1590.S6 P79 2017 | DDC 306.48480973—dc23
LC record available at https://lccn.loc.gov/2017003470

*For Rebecca—*

*With nothing on my tongue but Hallelujah*

My brother and I were at Sinai
He kept a journal
of what he saw
of what he heard
of what it all meant to him
I wish I had such a record
of what happened to me there
It seems like every time I want to write
I can't
I'm always holding a baby
one of my own
or one for a friend
Always holding a baby
so my hands are never free
to write things down
And then
As time passes
The particulars
The hard data
The who what when where why
Slip away from me
And all I'm left with is
The feeling
But feelings are just sounds
The vowel barking of a mute
My brother is so sure of what he heard
After all he's got a record of it
Consonant after consonant after consonant
If we remembered together
We could recreate holy time
Sparks flying

—Merle Feld, "We All Stood Together"

CONTENTS

# PREFACE

> Perhaps, says Derrida, Freud's contribution to any theory of the archive is that there isn't one: that no storehouse, especially not the psychoanalytic archive of the human psyche, holds the records of an original experience, to which we may return. Yet psychoanalysis has been responsible for some of this trouble with archives, for it wants to *get back*: it manifests a desire for origins, to find the place where things started, before the regime of repetition and representation was inaugurated.
>
> —Carolyn Steedman, *Dust: The Archive and Cultural History*

On my desk, stuck to a plastic file folder that holds the paper contents of the outline of what would eventually become this book, is a small yellow Post-it note. "NEVER FORGET," it says. I wrote it at night. And it's a good thing, because by morning, I already had.

My friend Nicole had had me over for dinner to help me map out what was then a nascent idea for a dissertation, because, as I put it, I was desperate. And I was, and we did. And she took notes, copious ones, so that I wouldn't forget, so that I wouldn't lose it all as time slipped by. "What if I forget how it all fits together?" I panicked as I was leaving. "Will you be my witness? Will you remember for me? Can you remind me?" She sealed our notes in plastic, because of the rain, and because perhaps, too, plastic—unlike memory—is the one thing that will surely, sadly, never decompose.

As I was falling asleep, I remembered one more important piece that hadn't made it into the official archive of our conversation. I didn't want to lose it. I grabbed a pen and Post-it, wrote "NEVER FORGET," stuck it to the folder, and went to bed.

"Never Forget" was the unofficial slogan for Holocaust memorialization in the 1980s, or at least it was in my neighborhood. Skokie, Illinois, was then teeming with survivors, and so, too, with public discourse about the Holocaust. Across the street from my childhood home was an Iranian synagogue (still is), with a large, metal "Never Forget" sign staked on its front lawn. Or maybe it said "Never Forget 6,000,000," I can't remember. We didn't "belong" to that synagogue (they were Orthodox, we were not; they were Iranian, we were not), but I passed it every day on my way to school. And although the word "Holocaust" was nowhere, and although I was a kid, I somehow understood its referent and knew that it had something to do with me, with my family, with what I was doing on this side of the world.

My grandfather had a scar on his right arm, or maybe it was the left. I can't remember. And I'm not sure if he told me this or if my father did, but I knew that the scar meant that he had been tattooed with a number. And I knew that the number meant that he had been a prisoner in the camps. And I knew these things because I had learned them—in Hebrew School, or in social studies class, or at home—somewhere.

I was very good at following directions: a precocious child, and an obedient one, "Never Forget" became my childhood mantra. Often I would ask my grandmother stories about the Holocaust. Selection lines, death marches, mass graves: I wanted to hear stories that matched the stories that I heard in school. I wanted to make it all fit together, all the way back to the beginning.

I was disappointed. The stories that I wanted to hear were not the ones my grandmother wanted to tell. Before the war . . . ? ("Things were *gute*.") After the war . . . ? ("Things were *gute*.") During the war . . . ? Here, she didn't say much and, when she did, those things didn't quite make sense.

Because my grandmother's stories didn't ever seem to add up like I wanted them to, I would take what little evidence I had and invent things. After seeing *Schindler's List* in high school, I started telling people that my grandparents were "Schindler Jews": that's how they made it out alive. When I learned that my grandmother had had over a dozen miscarriages between my father's birth in Germany in 1946 and his sister's in Chicago in 1961, I decided that my grandmother must have been a prisoner at Mauthausen.[1]

The truth, of course, is that I did not know the truth, but I wanted it.

My grandfather's scar, then, was my lifeline to an otherwise invisible past. It was the most solid evidence I had of past time—a tangible record of origins and lived experience. It told two stories: one of forced inscription, and one of willful erasure. I was growing up during a time and place of public discourse and memorialization of the Holocaust but also one of denial and suspicion, which in turn spurred my own anxieties and doubts. The ocular proof of the physical scar—visible to my own eyes—gave me comfort.

Family albums, home movies, letters and diaries, heirlooms, anecdotes, land: my father and his parents had few of these to share upon arriving in the Americas. Due to the structure of the war they endured—loss of property, frequent movement, displacement and evacuation, long-term imprisonment, few surviving relatives, emigration and diaspora—they were left with very few material things by 1949 and, thus, a very small record of private life. Because there was little to no ephemera to connect me to my paternal past, my grandfather's scar became all the more crucial. Not only was it hard evidence, I reasoned, but it said as much if not more about the war than the original tattoo. Like the original, it told the story of imprisonment, but it also evidenced a desire to wipe that memory out, to carve it out—literally—to unremember the ostensibly traumatic memory that it indexed.

My grandfather died in 1993, when I was high school. We don't speak of him much. But one day about seven years ago, my grandmother and I were sitting on a park bench across the street from the Olive Garden—where she liked me to take me to lunch when I would visit—and she spoke of my grandfather. (Still precocious and obedient, I had likely been probing her about the Holocaust over our all-you-can-eat salad and breadsticks, and she had likely responded with the same few stories she liked to tell, followed by the idea that I write a book about her life.) And then she told me, rather matter-of-factly, that my grandfather had gotten his number not during but after the war—at a tattoo parlor in Germany—with a friend who also got one. And then at some point—I don't remember if she said it was before or after coming to the United States—he had gotten it removed. When I asked her why he had done this, she responded rather typically, "Who *knows*?" And then she abruptly changed the subject.

That night at dinner, I did a little research. I asked my father if he knew when his father had gotten his number. "In the camps," he replied. And then I told my parents what my grandmother had told me. My mother suspected it had something to do with reparations, with money, with greed. My father voted for guilt and shame. But we all agreed it was as fascinating in its unsolvability as it was disturbing—that no matter how hard we tried to "*get back*," to *get to the bottom of things, to sort it all out so we could just remember properly*, we could not make sense of this elusive tale.

One or so years later, when writing about Hungarian filmmaker Péter Forgás's experimental documentary about the Holocaust, *The Maelstrom*, I called my grandmother on the phone.[2]

We talked for five or ten minutes: about the weather, about the holidays, about when I would graduate and become a "*dokter*" like my "*bruder*"—the plastic surgeon equally invested in the malleability of human archives. And then I said:

"Grandma Barbara, I am writing a paper about the Holocaust for school, and I want to include a story about Grandpa Jerry."

"*Really*? I have a *lot* of stories. You want to write a *bukh* about me?"

"Well, I sort of am, Grandma Barbara. And I want to tell the story about his tattoo. Remember how you told me he didn't get his number in the camps but after the war—"

"This is not true."

"No, remember, you told me—how he got his tattoo at a tattoo parlor, with a friend. But I can't remember when you said he got it removed. Was it—"

"How could you say such a thing?"

"Grandma Barbara, I am not going to tell anyone. I am just trying to—"

"Those *Natsis* did that thing to him!"

"I thought you told me that—"

"Forget about it."

And she made me promise never to ask her this question again. And I promised. Archives shift. Truths change. Memory fails. Time slips.

## ACKNOWLEDGMENTS

I am grateful to so many for their support and wisdom during the process of writing and rewriting this book. First, I must thank my teachers. My earliest teachers were my parents (who are also teachers by profession): you have instilled in me a love of learning and of justice, which forms the core of my character and provides me with the impulse to write. Thank you also to my grandparents, whose words and images frame this book.

Thank you to those incredible teachers who have placed into my hands the books that have changed my thinking irrevocably, and to those that have transformed the way that I see, make, and write about performance: Anne Bogart, Sharon Bridgforth, Ann Cvetkovich, Garrett Duncan, Steven Hoelscher, Daniel Alexander Jones, Omi Osun Joni L. Jones, Mary Overlie, Ann Reynolds, Stephan Schindler, Katie Stewart, and the APT faculty at Pig Iron.

A special thank-you to Stacy Wolf: this project began when you clipped a *New York Times* article about the memorialization of 9/11 and slipped it to me as I was heading out your office door. That was the fall of 2002, and so you I thank for origins, and for care. To Deborah Paredez: you took me on when this was but a glint of a dissertation. Thank you for always believing in me, and for modeling how to write with elegance and live with integrity. And to Jill Dolan: you taught me queer theory, and how (and why) to write about performances that I loved. Thank you for showing me (and so many) the way. I hope that this book does justice to your pedagogy, and to your scholarship.

My greatest teachers have been my students. You have kept me honest, inspired, and on my toes. To my dear ones, I dedicate the last chapter of this book.

A heartfelt thank-you to my friends and colleagues who have read drafts, shared sources, and offered critical feedback at various stages of this writing process: Javiera Benavente, Liza Minno Bloom, Paul Bonin-Rodriguez, Berkley Carnine, Margaret Cerullo, Ari Lev Fornari, Nicole Gurgel-Seefeldt, Kelly Howe, Rayna Grace Matthews, Sarah Myers, Ezra Berkley Nepon, Thomasin Parnes, Lindsay Reckson, Irit Reinheimer, Jules Rosskam, Julia M. Smith, and Jeni Wischmeyer. To my chosen family with whom I share home and community in Philadelphia, and to those far afield: thank you for the love and tenderness that have sustained me. A special thank-you to Chrissy Swanson.

Thank you to my partners: you have listened to me read passages aloud, early in the morning and late at night, when you have wanted to, and when you haven't. You have inspired me with the joy of your presence, the sorrow of your absence, and the hope of your return—the imprints of which have found their way into the pages of this book. Most of all to Rebecca Alvarez: it is because of you that I have continued to believe that repair is possible, and with and from you that I have learned that it is love and desire which move us backward and forward through the hole, and whole, of time.

Thank you to the wise women who have attended to my body, mind, and spirit, most recently and most especially Beth Ann Corr and Erin O'Brien.

There was little more humbling and thrilling than sharing this writing aloud with smart and thoughtful listeners: your questions and suggestions have shaped the direction of this work. Thank you to my colleagues at The Five College Women's Studies Research Center, the Women and Theatre Program of ATHE, the Performance as Public Practice Program in the Department of Theater and Dance at the University of Texas at Austin, the Women's Studies Department at the University of Maryland-College Park, the John. B. Hurford Center for Arts and Humanities at Haverford College, the Department of Theatre Arts and Performance Studies at Brown University, the Gender and Sexuality Studies Reading Group in the Graduate Department of English at the University of Pennsylvania, and the Department of Women's, Gender, and Sexuality Studies at Dickinson College. Thank you also to my cohort at the PLAYA artist residency program and at 3G: A Third-Generation Retreat, Jill Stauffer and the "Revision/How Time Passes" Faculty Seminar at Haverford College, students in my "Cruising Home: Queer Kinship in Theory and Practice" and "Performance, Literature, and the Archive" seminars at Haverford College, those in my "Time, History, and Memory" seminar at Northern Arizona University, and those in my "'In a Queer Time and Place': Queer Theory and the Politics of Temporality" seminar at Hampshire College.

An earlier version of chapter 2, titled "When Elephants Are in Must: Peggy Shaw, Acts of Trans/fer, and the Present Future of Queer Desire," appeared in the special issue of *TDR: The Drama Review*, guest edited by Jill Dolan and Stacy Wolf (MIT Press, 2014). Thank you to Jill and Stacy for inviting me to contribute, and for being the absolute sharpest of editors. Thank you also to Ethan Philbrick, Mariellen Sandford, and Richard Schechner.

Patrick Anderson and Nicholas Ridout: thank you for taking a chance on me. You have been incredible series editors from start to finish. Mike Levine: thank you for shepherding me through with kindness and wisdom—you are missed. Thank you to the entire staff at Northwestern University Press who carried this project to completion: Greta Bennion, Anne Gendler, Maggie Grossman, Marianne Jankowski, Gianna Mosser, and JD Wilson. Thank you also to the anonymous readers for your extensive feedback; the copy editor, Christi Stanforth, for your precision; the indexer, Steve Moore, for your attention to detail; and the typesetter, Steve Straus, for your beautiful work.

Thank you to the photographers who have kindly lent your work to this book: Margaret Cerullo, Riko Fluchel, Blake Gordon, Lori E. Seid, Mary Ellen Strom, and Manuel Vason. A special thank-you to Patrick Montero for your help with editing images. Thank you also to the people and institutions that have opened their archives to me: Bob Ebinger and the Livingston Depot Foundation, Colorado Historical Society, Gallatin History Museum, L. Tom Perry Special Collections of the Harold B. Lee Library at Brigham Young University, Wellcome Library, and Yellowstone National Park.

A resounding thank-you to my exceptional research assistants. Zemora Tevah: you have been a key interlocutor throughout this entire process, and I couldn't imagine this book without your collaboration. You have fixed my sentences, honed my vision, and buoyed my spirit. Clara Abbott: you were a godsend in the eleventh hour. Thank you for your devotion, diligence, and good, great humor. Thank you also to Devyn Mañibo for your labor of love.

Thank you to the artists about whom I write: Ann Carlson, Mary Ellen Strom, and members of the Crow and Northern Cheyenne Nations; Peggy Shaw, Suzy Willson, and the Clod Ensemble; my *floodlines* collaborators, especially Ann Graham, Julia M. Smith, and Nathaniel Zivin; Mateo Guadalupe and Zemora Tevah; and Alison Bechdel, Lisa Kron, and Jeanine Tesori. I hope that I have paid honor to your work.

# Time Slips

# INTRODUCTION

> [T]he Greek *trauma*, or "wound," originally [referred] to an injury inflicted upon the body. In its later usage . . . the term *trauma* is understood as a wound inflicted not upon the body but upon the mind. But what seems to be suggested by Freud in *Beyond the Pleasure Principle* is that the wound of the mind—the breach in the mind's experience of time, self, and the world—is not, like the wound of the body, a simple and healable event, but rather an event that, like Tangred's first infliction of a mortal wound on the disguised Clorinda in the duel, is experienced too soon, too unexpectedly, to be fully known and is therefore not available to consciousness until it imposes itself again, repeatedly, in the nightmares and repetitive actions of the survivor. Just as Tancred does not hear the voice of Clorinda until the second wounding, so trauma is not locatable in the simple violent or original event in an individual's past, but rather the ways that its very unassimilated nature—the way it was precisely not known in the first instance—returns to haunt the survivor later on.
>
> —Cathy Caruth, *Unclaimed Experience: Trauma, Narrative, and History*

> History is what hurts.
>
> —Fredric Jameson, *The Political Unconscious: Narrative as a Socially Symbolic Act*

This book investigates how performance can transform the way we think and feel about trauma and memory, time and history. It also argues that such change is vital and possible at this historical moment. Specifically, I examine moments in performance when linear time is momentarily queered; history is disordered and disturbed; memory slips; ghosts linger; specters appear; trauma repeats—with a difference—and past, present, and future are given permission to touch one another.[1] In this regard, my project enters into a central preoccupation within the field of theater and performance studies about live performance's unique relationship to the politics of temporality, or a sense of how time passes. My analysis is grounded in performance studies' repeated claim that performance—like history—is nonoriginal, and always already haunted by improperly buried ghosts as well as liberatory futures not yet performed.[2]

In concert with scholars working in a variety of disciplines, this book adopts the view that the notion of strictly linear time—the sequential progression of past, present, and future—begins to come undone when considered in the context of trauma and survivorship. As the preface to this book illustrates, survivors of trauma bear a complex relationship to time. My desire to get to the bottom of things, to get my grandmother to remember properly, to make sense of her shifting feelings of memories, and memories of feelings, and stories of skin, was a failed attempt on my part to order her history so that it neatly aligned with those official narratives of the Holocaust that I had diligently learned in school and on which I relied to authenticate my concept of self as a diasporic subject. A well-ordered narrative, I believed, was the prerequisite for historical truth. This belief, however, belied the psychic and material effects of her trauma, which produced dis-ordered, fragmented, and conflicting narratives of past events. In other words, my desire to get her to tell a coherent story was animated by an already internalized sense of time that was linear, teleological, and *straight*.

Straight time not only negates a trauma survivor's lived experience of past events, it also reproduces the logic of capitalism: the system, that is, that creates the conditions under which racial, gender, sexual, and economic violence gets enacted in the first place. When I use the phrase "the logic of capitalism," I am building on Marxist political theorist Fredric Jameson's notion of the logic of late capitalism, which he develops in his book *Postmodernism, or, The Cultural Logic of Late Capitalism*. Among other things, Jameson argues that cultural works that we might describe as postmodern, including postmodern film, video, art, architecture, and literature, are mediated by the conditions of global capitalism. Queer theorist Jack Halberstam, in his foundational book, *In a Queer Time and Place: Transgender Bodies, Subcultural Lives*, builds on Jameson's claims, as well as those of geographer David Harvey, using the term "queer time" to describe those "unscripted" modes of life that defy the logic of capitalist accumulation, as well as the presumed naturalness of a sense of time that is governed by an imperative to own property, produce offspring, establish stability, accumulate wealth, and ensure inheritance. Halberstam writes:

> Time, Harvey explains, is organized according to the logic of capital accumulation, but those who benefit from capitalism in particular experience this logic as inevitable, and they are therefore able to ignore, repress, or erase the demands made on them and others by an unjust system. We like to imagine, Harvey implies, both that our time is our own, and, as the cliché goes, "There is a time and place for everything." These formulaic responses to time and temporal logics produce emotional and even physical responses to different kinds

> of time: thus people feel guilty about leisure, frustrated by waiting, satisfied by punctuality, and so on. These emotional responses add to our sense of time as "natural."[3]

Here Halberstam makes clear the ways in which the temporality of capital idealizes certain modes of being in time (productive, efficient, and punctual), while simultaneously masking the very process through which these ideals are constructed as norms. When straight time is naturalized, the logic of capitalism is produced as inevitable and the kinds of state and psychic violence required to uphold it seem justified if not unavoidable costs of a presumably well-functioning system. Any digression from these temporal norms is produced as aberrant, delinquent, criminal, and queer.

Queer and transgender subjectivities remind us that it is possible to live, at least in part, outside of or in opposition to the time of capital, and to challenge timelines that presume the inevitability of linear gender and sexual development. For instance, while the increased likelihood of premature death for queer and gender nonconforming people is real, queer and trans people have always found ways to extend and rewrite their own lives (a point to which I will return in chapter 2): from safer sex practices that queer people invented in the early HIV/AIDS crisis and continue to teach, to antiretroviral therapy (ART) and pre-exposure prophylaxis (PrEP) which have become central in queer public health work in more recent years; from hormone blockers and estrogen and testosterone replacement therapies, DIY or otherwise, gender-confirming surgeries, and name and pronoun changes to support gender transition, to friendship, relationship, and community structures that support gender and sexual pleasure, self-expression, and self-determination. Indeed, queer and trans people have always been at the vanguard of radical ways of working, playing, fucking, organizing, educating, parenting, making home, making art, and creating ritual that defy normative patterns of clock, biological, and nuclear family time. *Time Slips* takes these and other forms of queer and trans resistance and brilliance as the foundation for hope—a belief that in spite of the daily traumas of living in the time of capital, freedom from harm is possible through creativity and collaboration.

When invoking the language of "trauma" throughout this book, I am referring, in part, to events that register on a global or national scale—for instance, the Holocaust, which frames the problem of history and memory in this book's preface; 9/11, and the HIV/AIDS crisis, both of which I examine later in this chapter as exemplary of a national crisis in temporality, and to which I return in the book's epilogue; Native American genocide, which serves as the backdrop to my discussion of Native removal in chapter 1, and to which I return in chapter 4. But I am equally referring to ambient feelings of danger and threats of violence that characterize contemporary life in the United States (which I will address at greater length later in this chapter and throughout this book, and in close detail in chapters 3 and 4). In either formulation, what remains true is the fact that for certain individuals and populations, trauma is not as much a rupture but a way of life.

As other scholars have argued, U.S. culture is often invisibly and sometimes visibly organized around the identities and lifestyles of certain citizen-subjects, as if being human were synonymous with being Christian, white, male, cisgender, heterosexual, able-bodied, neurotypical, and class-privileged. In this current system, non-Christians, people of color, indigenous people, immigrants, women, transgender and gender nonconforming people, queers, the disabled, and the poor are rendered unhuman, their lives and deaths therefore ungrievable. They are what philosopher Judith Butler, following Julia Kristeva, has called the *abject*: the subject that is not even a subject—unreal, illegible, unrecognizable to the state. Butler and Kristeva's abjections are not *oppressed* people, they are *non*-people.

> To be oppressed means that you already exist as a subject of some kind, you are there as a visible and oppressed other for the master subject, as a possible or potential subject. But to be unreal is something else again. To be oppressed you must first become intelligible—indeed that the laws of culture and of language find you to be an impossibility—is to find that you have not yet achieved access to the human; it is to find yourself speaking only and always *as if you were* human, but with the sense that you are not, it is to find that your language is hollow, that no recognition is forthcoming because the norms by which recognition takes place are not in your favor.[6]

To be unreal, this book presumes, is a powerful form that trauma can take. As Butler notes, to be unreal is not the same as to be oppressed—rather, to be unreal is to be expelled to the margins of the category of human itself. Indeed, this is the linguistic brilliance of the current Black Lives Matter movement: Black Lives Matter alerts our attention to the fact that black lives do not matter (to the state, to white power culture) and it is this *not* mattering that creates the conditions under which black lives are able to be taken in the first place. The histories that are implied by the performances I write about index the multivalent ways in which trauma is at once both cataclysmic and ordinary, collective and individual, sudden and ongoing, and the violence that trauma does is both material and psychic, immediate and mediated, located in the past and reiterated in the present.[7]

Additionally, I argue that a feeling of trauma is intricately bound to the process by which this trauma becomes or fails to become recognized as such by the person who has experienced harm; the individual(s), group(s), or state apparatus that has inflicted harm; and the community or communities to which they are each accountable. For it is not only the "original" experience of trauma which it takes its toll in psychic and material life but also the ways in which this trauma is recognized, or not, as time slips by. Philosopher Jill

Stauffer, for instance, argues that violence that fails to be recognized as such produces a kind of "ethical loneliness" for the trauma survivor. She writes:

> Ethical loneliness is the isolation one feels when one, as a violated person or as one member of a persecuted group, has been abandoned by humanity, or by those who have power over one's life possibilities. It is a condition undergone by persons who have been unjustly treated and dehumanized by human beings and political structures, who emerge from that injustice only to find that the surrounding world will not listen to or cannot properly hear their testimony—their claims about what they suffered and about what is now owed them—on their own terms. So ethical loneliness is the experience of having been abandoned by humanity compounded by the experience of not being heard.[8]

I agree with Stauffer's articulation of ethical loneliness as the violence of original harm compounded by the violence of a harm not heard. While Stauffer's focus is primarily legal case studies of state-sponsored violence (ranging from Holocaust testimony to post-conflict trials and truth commissions in South Africa, among other places), I believe that her framework is applicable to even the most ordinary and seemingly individual of harms. A racist or sexist microaggression, for instance, is called a *micro*aggression precisely because it is an insidious form of violence and, as such, can be difficult to address.[9] Like legal and/or state-sanctioned forms of violence that register on a national or global scale, this book presumes that those forms of violence that are extralegal and/or seemingly minor or idiosyncratic are similarly redoubled when met with disbelief.

Additionally, what may appear on the surface to be a minor or individual or idiosyncratic experience—including events that may even appear at times to be disconnected from trauma and violence altogether—are often symptoms of, connected to, and/or animated by larger social histories. Queer theorist David Eng, borrowing from psychoanalysts Nicolas Abraham and Mária Török, calls this phenomena the "encryption of trauma."[10] Here Eng is developing a theory of intergenerational trauma and/as affect, writing about filmmaker Rea Tajiri's experimental documentary about her family's internment during World War II, *History and Memory*.[11] Tajiri's film examines the intergenerational impact of Japanese American concentration camps—specifically, the ways in which this trauma has produced traumatic memories for Tajiri that are and are not her own. Citing trauma theorist Marianne Hirsch's notion of "postmemory," Eng writes, "Hirsch has written about the phenomenon of postmemory as it applies to children of Holocaust survivors. These children have an uncanny relation to their parents' experiences, in which images of the Holocaust continually reprised are so powerful that they come to constitute (virtual) memories in their own right."[12] One of the central motifs in *History and Memory* is the recurring "postmemory" of a young woman in a blue dress filling a canteen from a well in the desert: ultimately Tajiri discovers that this woman is her mother, and that Tajiri has carried the burden (and anger) of remembering their family's traumatic past in part because her mother has had to forget it. "[I]ntergenerational strife and gendered discord," Eng writes, "become the displaced sites of national history, serving to obscure the politics of race and nation. Indeed, such an encryption reduces political conflict to cultural questions of filial struggle and opposition."[13] Thus, Tajiri's memory of a woman at a well may seem innocuous, and her conflict with her mother may seem personal rather than political, but in actuality it is a symptom of a history of racial and national violence that she has psychically incorporated. In other words, the very ontology of trauma is that it encrypts in uncanny ways, often suturing itself to the most prosaic of details. Trauma is and is not what is seems.

Here I am reminded of the foundational work of trauma theorist Cathy Caruth, whose *Unclaimed Experience: Trauma, Narrative, and History* makes clear the ways in which the traumatic repetition is an expression of the psychic desire to recover a moment of history that the individual has lost or failed to fully experience in the first place as a result of a variety of factors, including but not limited to shock, terror, and dissociation. As cited at the opening of this introduction, Caruth writes, "Trauma is not locatable in the simple violent or original event in an individual's past, but rather the ways that its very unassimilated nature—the way it was precisely not known in the first instance—returns to haunt the survivor later on."[14] Extending Caruth, one could argue that what Sigmund Freud calls "traumatic neurosis"—the patient's relentless return to the moment of injury—is not pathological at all. When read through a queer and feminist lens, the traumatic repetition can be read as a normal and necessary attempt at reparation in a culture of harm. It is a remembering of injury (including but not limited to one's own) in a culture of forgetting. Placed, as well, within a framework of intergenerational and ongoing trauma and violence, it becomes all the more clear that the traumatic repetition is an attempt—successful or not—to "listen well," or at least better, to trauma's ghosts the second (and third and fourth and four hundredth) time, to *get back, to get to the bottom of history, to sort it all out so we can just remember properly*.[15] Trauma is and is not what it seems.

## Time Slips in Performance

This book asserts that performance can function as a necessary site of repetition, recognition, and reparation—an embodied methodology for "claiming" experience. Each case study in this book offers a different example of an artist using performance as a tool to make history visible, trauma recognizable, and transformation possible, exposing the systems of violence that are so deeply embedded in our society so as to appear natural. The performances I write about engage and reimagine violent and/or forgotten histories related to race, religion, class, gender, and sexuality, while also tracing a related history of capitalist development and neoliberal progress—which, I argue, provide the foundation on which all forms of identity-based structural violence take shape.

For the purposes of this project, I coin the term "time slips" to denote moments as a performance spectator (or maker) in which I experienced time queerly. When, because time was given permission to do those deviant things it is not supposed to—move backward, lunge forward, loop, jump, stack, stop, pause, linger, elongate, pulsate, slip—I was given recourse to feel the violence of linear time and historical "progress" *and* a way out of this narrow view of history. In other words, time slips are moments in live performance in which normative conceptions of time fail, or fall away, and the spectator or artist experiences an alternative, or queer, temporality. In this regard, a time slip reveals a previously unseen aspect of either the past, present, or future (while complicating the presumably linear relationship among and between each)—with an eye toward hidden histories, buried traumas, unclaimed experiences, invisible structures, and previously unimaginable futures. Time slips call capitalism into question, disrupting the logics of linearity, progress, and cultural amnesia. A time slip "flashes up in a moment of danger,"[16] awakening the dead, the living, and the not yet born. In so doing, time slips beckon the spectator away from the monolithic experience of time as a machine marching ever forward and into a subaltern landscape of slanted knowledge, where traumatic injury is visible and "another world [and another time] is possible."[17] Time slips pull back the curtain on systemic forces of injury, allowing them to be validated as real in the public forum that is live performance.

In using the term "time slips" as the project's moniker, I mean to invoke both the complete clause, "time slips" (*noun verb*), as well the incomplete relative clause, "time slips" (*adjective noun*). In the former, I attempt to highlight the ways in which the present of performance—like everyday life—is in a constant state of disappearance (time, that is, is always *slipping* by). Or, as performance theorist Peggy Phelan succinctly puts it, the ontology of performance is that it "becomes itself through disappearance."[18] In the latter, I aim to invoke the paranormal phenomena known as a "time slip" (or "timeslip") when a person, or group of people, travel through time through unknown means. In other words, the other ontology of performance is that it exceeds the present by calling past (and sometimes future) histories into being. As performance theorist Elin Diamond argues, "Every performance . . . embeds features of previous performances: gender conventions, racial histories, aesthetic traditions, political and culture pressures that are consciously and unconsciously acknowledged. . . . [E]ach performance marks out a unique temporal space that . . . contains traces of other now-absent performances

[and] now-disappeared scenes."[19] Reading Phelan's and Diamond's definitions of performance in tandem, this book concerns itself with those moments in performance in which both the ephemeral and the citational nature of history and people—as well as the stories they like to tell about each other—was made palpable for its audiences.

Implicit within this project about time slips are the theoretical frameworks known as "straight time" and "queer time," frameworks that have become central in the field of queer studies, particularly since its turn toward affective life and the object world. As literary and queer theorist Jord/ana Rosenberg puts it in their exquisite essay "Gender Trouble on Mother's Day":

> My particular interest—don't worry I won't go on about this—had something to do with why gender and sexuality studies seems to be so concerned with the object world these days. I can't explain this at great length here but suffice to say that all kinds of things seem to be queer these days—including dust, dna, certain kinds of worms and maybe also time itself?—and there is a part of me that still doesn't understand how that is possible because in order to be gay don't you kind of have to love/hate your mother?[20]

While Rosenberg's tone is sardonic, their point is well taken: the field of gender and sexuality studies has, in recent years, turned away from theories of sex and relationality and toward larger cultural studies claims about, among other things, the politics of temporality. A quick search of postdoctoral fellowships at major institutions of higher education, for instance, will show "time" among the past ten years' popular themes, and its notable queer theorists are often at the helm of its convening. That dust, DNA, worms, and time itself may in fact be queer, and that queers and queer time have found their way into mainstream academic discourse, tells us something about the importance of temporality to political theory. It also reveals the allure of queer theory within the academy—but, as I will detail in the book's final chapter, "Teaching Time," in no way suggests the acceptance of queer studies as an academic discipline nor that of queer people as rightful members of the academy.

When using the phrase "straight time," I mean to suggest a sense of time that is constructed as linear (progressing in a straight line), produced through the logic of capitalism as well as heteronormativity, and resulting in feelings of exclusion for those who live on its margins. My notion of straight time is akin to what queer theorist Elizabeth Freeman terms *chrononormativity*:

> Both the state and the market produce biopolitical status relations not only through borders, the establishment of private and public zones, and other strategies of spatial containment, but also and crucially through temporal mechanisms. Some groups have their needs

> and freedoms *deferred* or *snatched* away, and some don't. Some cultural practices are given the means to continue; others are *squelched* or allowed to die on the vine. Some events *count* as historically significant, some don't; some are choreographed as such from the first instance and thereby *overtake* others. Most intimately, some human experiences officially *count* as a life or one of its parts, and some don't. Those *forced* to wait or *startled* by violence, whose activities do not show up on the official time line, whose own time lines do not synchronize with it, are variously and often simultaneously black, female, queer.[21]

*Deferring, snatching, squelching, forcing, waiting, startling, overtaking, counting*, and *discounting*: why do social practices that "do not synchronize" with dominant cultural beats get marginalized, how is this marginalization produced through temporal mechanisms, and in what ways can performance redress this problem? Straight time produces impossibly limited frameworks for queer and trans life. As Freeman has similarly argued, because not only the workday but the entire life cycle is plotted and periodized, certain kinds of events and relationships get historically recorded, such as births, marriages, and deaths, while others, such as coming outs, friendships, caretaking, casual sex, separations, gender transitions, nonmonogamous relationship structures, illness, ritual, and contact with the dead, do not. This is tautology at its worst: those whose life experiences neatly fit into a socially constructed notion of time get recognized, while those that cannot be made to fit, because they require a different understanding of time or history to make sense, are rendered invisible.

In working on this project, I have been profoundly influenced by German Jewish philosopher Walter Benjamin, whose theory of "historical materialism" critiques the ways in which the traumas of the "past" are ignored in the name of forward-moving "progress." In his prescient "Theses on the Philosophy of History," Benjamin writes:

> A Klee painting named "Angelus Novus" shows an angel looking as though he is about to move away from something he is fixedly contemplating. His eyes are staring, his mouth is open, his wings are spread. This is how one pictures the angel of history. His face is turned toward the past. Where we perceive a chain of events, he sees one single catastrophe which keeps piling wreckage upon wreckage and hurls it in front of his feet. The angel would like to stay, awaken the dead, and make whole what has been smashed. But a storm is blowing from Paradise; it has got caught in his wings with such violence that the angel can no longer close them. This storm irresistibly propels him into the future to which his back is turned, while the pile of debris before him grows skyward. This storm is what we call progress.[22]

Benjamin uses Klee's painting of the "angel of history" to illustrate an alternative historiography in which the historical actor (symbolically represented by the angel)—though blown forward through time—has his eyes perpetually fixed on the cataclysmic ruins of the past.[23] For Benjamin, time is not linear but rather palimpsestic: past, present, and future coexist in the infinite now. Like two adjacent stars in the sky that may in fact be thousands of light-years apart, disparate historical events must be read side by side. What's more, in pressing "minor" and "major" histories together, the "historical materialist" creates what art historian Ann Reynolds calls "morphological networks [that] sweep against history's hierarchical and chronological grain and restore apparently negligible phenomena to view."[24] In other words, this "messianic" view of time aims to resuscitate forgotten past events from the historical waste bin; place them in present focus; and counteract the constant drive to create newer, better futures.

Benjamin's theory of historical materialism—which was written while Benjamin was in exile in France during the Holocaust—resonates with contemporary trends in queer studies toward rethinking the hegemonic logic of straight time. In this field formerly known as lesbian and gay studies, queer studies can be described as a "subjectless critique." In other words, queer theory is a poststructuralist project that aims to question not only the logic of heteronormativity—"heterosexual culture's exclusive ability to interpret itself *as society*"[25]—but all regimes of normalization. As queer theorist Michael Warner asks in the introduction to his landmark *Fear of a Queer Planet*:

> What do queers want? This volume takes for granted that the answer is not just sex. Sexual desires themselves can imply other wants, ideals, and conditions. And queers live as queers, as lesbians, as gays, as homosexuals, in contexts other than sex. In different ways queer politics might have implications for any area of social life. . . . Every person who comes to a queer self-understanding knows one way or another that her stigmatization is connected with gender, the family, notions of individual freedom, the state, public speech, consumption and desire, nature and culture, maturation, reproductive politics, racial and national fantasy, class identity, truth and trust, censorship, intimate life and social display, terror and violence, health care, and deep cultural norms about the bearing of the body. Being queer means fighting about these issues all the time . . . Organizing a movement around queerness also allows it to draw on dissatisfaction with the regime of the normal in general. Following Hannah Arendt, we might even say that queer politics opposes society itself.[26]

Bearing this ambitious framework in mind, the growing interest within the field to interrogate the politics of "time" is not surprising, particularly given its intersection with a multiplicity of areas of social life. In other words, queer studies functions as an intersectional mode of analysis that may or may not have sex as its singular object of study. As David Eng, Jack Halberstam, and José Muñoz put it in their 2005 essay "What's Queer about Queer Studies Now?": "Sexuality is intersectional and not extraneous to other modes of difference." They add that "considerations of empire, race, migration, geography, subaltern communities, activism, and class are central to the continuing critique of queerness, sexuality, sexual subcultures, desire, and recognition," and they rightly assert that "some of the most innovative and risky work on globalization, neoliberalism, cultural politics, subjectivity, identity, family, and kinship is happening in the realm of queer studies."[27] Here the authors are building on the work of, among others, queer theorist Roderick Ferguson, whose queer-of-color critique attempts to recenter questions of race and transnationalism—key frameworks that have historically been marginalized in the white and Western-dominated field of queer studies.[28]

*Time Slips* applies an intersectional feminist, queer theoretical, and queer-of-color critical lens to case studies of live performance, asking what these performances do to, as well as teach us about, the politics of temporality and the writing of history. I argue that these works are queer not (only) because they deal with sexual life, not (only) because they were created by lesbian, queer, and/or transgender artists, but because they *queer*, or question, spectators' internalized, straight senses of time. While the artists under investigation are American citizens and the performances were enacted in the United States, the work (and my analysis of it) grapples with the relationship between this nation-state and those ongoing legacies of settler colonialism, global imperialism, and transatlantic diaspora that produce(d) it. In other words, this project simultaneously focuses on the construction of U.S. nationalisms while remaining attentive to the transnational flows of bodies, capital, and ideologies that make this nation and/as empire possible and profitable in the first place. Following queer theorist Jasbir Puar's imperative, I read these performances "sideways"—across sexual and racial, private and public, national and transnational trauma cultures.[29]

In tracing time slips in performance, this book attempts to make visible how American ideals of racial and sexual citizenship are produced through linear, teleological, progress narratives—or "straight time"—and how the conditions that produce these master narratives commit social violence against queer and trans people, people of color, and other subaltern subjects. In offering performance as the site of resistance, I invoke performance's unique capacity to transform the way audiences feel about history. Here it is important to note that while other scholars working in the field of queer studies have made it clear that straight time is oppressive, and some work has been done to chart alternative possibilities in film, video, literature, and visual art, surprisingly little attention has been given to the time-based medium of live performance. As a time-based medium, performance is uniquely situated to produce "time consciousness, even historical consciousness,"[30] making audiences feel, see, hear, and sense the passage of time and the production of history—and to glimpse how we might live our lives in relation to them differently, queerly, and unapologetically.

## HIV/AIDS and the Affective Turn

Central to my project is the belief that the normalizing impulses of the LGBTQ movement—which demand that queer people live in straight time—bear strong ties to the HIV/AIDS epidemic and the various "no future" rhetorics that this global health crisis has catalyzed in its wake. This pandemic literally gone viral has not only decimated the most vulnerable social groups (queer and trans people, the poor, women, people of color, sex workers, people addicted to drugs, people experiencing homelessness), it has also produced a reactionary LGBTQ politics that seeks, by any means necessary, to secure the distinction between the "good gay" subject—healthy and partnered, normatively gendered, educated and affluent, willing to marry, reproduce, purchase property, and participate in civic life—from the "bad gay" subject—sick, single, promiscuous, disabled, dying, dirty, poor, black, brown, gender nonconforming, addicted, unemployed, uneducated, hypersexual, and refusing the norms of civic life. Obviously, this normalizing move is not only produced by the gay subject attempting to "distance [himself] from disability," as queer and crip theorist Robert McRuer has eloquently put it; it is manufactured by the state.[31] When given the right to marry, for instance, the state is producing a literal and symbolic structure through which future gay and lesbian subjects will be read as compliant (or noncompliant) within a paternalistic system that aims to save them from themselves.

In this regard, it seems that the rapid shift from what was once a discourse of sexual liberation, to what is now one of equality and civil rights, must not only be read as an assimilationist turn within the mainstream LGBTQ movement but as a biopolitical crisis that has meted itself onto queer bodies in temporal ways. Building on political philosopher Michel Foucault's theories of biopower and Puar's theory of homonationalism, Native studies scholar Scott Morgensen puts it this way: "Foucault argued that modern sexuality acts as a biopolitics when national institutions enhance normative sexuality as life while regulating racial and sexual populations marked for death."[32] What appears, then, as a collective desire to be incorporated into the nation-state as future subjects of life, rather than death, can also be read as a form of biopolitical regulation on behalf of the state. This is not to suggest that queers are cultural dupes. Rather, I mean to highlight the ways in which a system of reward, or "enhancement," is in place for those queers deemed compliant; and, for the noncompliant queers who for whatever reason refuse the state's offer of public dignity, this refusal only further evidences their depravity as well as their death drive. After all, who wouldn't want to be *normal*? Who wouldn't want a *future*? Who wouldn't want to *live*?[33]

Many queer and trans activists and theorists reject the assimilationist tendencies of the mainstream movement. Perhaps most notoriously, queer theorist Lee Edelman asserts, "Fuck the future," adding "*Queerness* names the side of those *not* 'fighting for the children,' the side outside the consensus by which all politics confirms the absolute value of reproductive futurism."[34] Pointing to the ways in which mainstream discourse takes futurity as an unquestioned social good, radical queer critiques of futurity ask what it would look like to build a movement around sentiments of antifuturity, antifamily, antireproduction, antichildren—in a future-, progress-, production-, and reproduction-oriented culture.

Here it is important to note that I do not situate myself within Edelman's "no future" camp. On the contrary, I am skeptical of the white and ablest privileges embedded in discourses of radical antifuturity, and I question the virulently antifuturist sentiments of queer studies. I, like many queers, want a future for us all, and I am alert to the ways in which radical antifuturism is a privileged discourse for those whose lives are not deemed "expendable" in the first place. Building on foundational critiques by feminists and people of color, including political theorist Cathy Cohen and queer and performance theorist José Muñoz, and taking white queer theorist Lee Edelman to task, Elizabeth Freeman asks:

> [I]s radical antifuturity . . . the new postmodernity, that is, the conceptual privilege of white middle-class male subjects who are always already guaranteed a future and so can afford to jettison the idea of one[?] . . . The imperative toward "no future" aligns too neatly with social policies that cause actual children of color to die. [José] Muñoz reminds us that the antifutural doctrine is complicit . . . in the cultural inability to imagine people of color, queer and otherwise, having or contributing to a collective fate.[35]

In this regard, my project is aligned with queer-of-color critiques that, while skeptical of reproductive futurism, are vigilant to the ways in which discourses of antifuturity reify the notion of the racialized, sexualized, and disabled other as disposable. Such a discourse is not only "complicit" in the actual deaths of people targeted for systemic violence, it also highlights the linear logic that animates necro- and biopolitics in the first place. As critics of the school-to-prison pipeline have noted, certain populations are earmarked for jail (or the clinic, or the grave) from the start, while other populations are earmarked for freedom—headed *straight*, as it were, to a life of health, wealth, and vitality.

The tensions inherent among futurity, radical antifuturity, and anti-antifuturity schools of thought reflect broader trends in public and academic discourse. Since the late 1990s, there has been a shift in academic discourse—what has come to be known as an "affective turn" in cultural theory. Scholars working across the disciplines—primarily in the humanities—began drawing heavily from philosophers such as Baruch Spinoza, Gilles Deleuze, and Félix Guattari in order to develop contemporary theories that account for sensations and bodily experiences of culture not reducible to critiques of representation, rhetoric, or semiotics—including feelings of joy, pain, pleasure, sorrow, and desire. Affect theory converged generatively with the concurrently developing discourses in queer theory, some notable participants being Judith Butler, Lauren Berlant, Sara Ahmed, Kathleen Stewart, and Ann Cvetkovich. Cvetkovich and Stewart, for instance, in collaboration with Berlant, began what they called a Public Feelings "Feel Tank"—first at the University of Chicago and later at the University of Texas, where I first came into contact with affect theory as a graduate student. From the start, the affective turn not only had inextricable ties to queer theory, people, and politics but also to what has since come to be called "queer negation," a form of antisocial queer theory and politics defined by its opposition to positive affects such as joy, optimism, and hope.[36] For instance, the Public Feelings group in Austin formed in part as a response to the rigged 2000 U.S. presidential election, which put George W. Bush into the White House, and the feelings of "political depression" that it elicited in many of the Left.[37] Its first public event was a protest of the election in which the protesters were encouraged to come in their pajamas—the message being: we are tired of hope; we are tired of caring about everything so damn much.

Within the field of performance studies, negative affects are difficult to maintain. This is due, in part, to the fact that theater, dance, and performance are, arguably, inherently acts of hope: we labor to make it with the hope that it will be good; we buy a ticket with the same. There are no guarantees, and, as Phelan reminds us, no leftovers, either. Written from the vantage point of a believer in performance's capacity to do cultural work, this project attempts a critical intervention into discourses of negative affect that seem to pervade queer and affect theory. This book directly engages in a critique of violence—discursive and material—while making a case for a politics of hope. Here my project resonates with other scholarship in the field of performance studies that asserts that performance has the potential to forge new social structures of belonging. In *Utopia in Performance*, for instance, queer and performance theorist Jill Dolan describes in compelling detail her affective experiences as theater spectator and critic, arguing that performance can bind us, move us, and allow us to imagine what a more socially just world might look and feel like.[38] Dolan draws from Frankfurt School philosophies of utopia as well as radical humanism, and she builds on similar arguments about *communitas* developed by anthropologist Victor Turner—namely, that live events can forge new kinship structures and social relations built on shared feelings of connectedness across difference. In a similar vein, Muñoz's *Cruising Utopia* provides a framework for thinking about how performance and visual culture can offer blueprints for subaltern subjects to negotiate their relationships with dominant culture, transcend seemingly fixed structures of the state, and temporarily inhabit utopia through feeling.

Sometimes mistaken as political naïveté, queer optimism runs the risk of critique. Dolan, and to a lesser extent Muñoz, for instance, have had their share of skeptics. While the roots of this skepticism are undoubtedly gendered—positive affects (and, by extension, their proponents) are read as feminine and therefore critically unsophisticated—the critique is not entirely unfounded, as it relates to a politics of social location. Is it enough, a critic might ask, for an academic to argue from the sidelines of the stage that performance is doing radical work when "actual" people are experiencing injury and harm outside the theater's doors—particularly when that academic is often (white and) class-privileged and the people experiencing harm are often not? As Gary Younge observes in his essay for *The Nation*, "Those born white and wealthy should not be slammed for developing a social conscience, becoming activists and trying to make the world a better place. But neither should the nature of their involvement be above critique."[39] I am sensitive to the material realities of privilege and critical of any scholar's or artist's capacity (regardless of identity)—mine included—to undo centuries of structural violence. Yet I remain committed to performance as a potential site of social transformation, as well as to feminist scholarship that willfully asserts the intellectual and political value of a kind of queer optimism at the heart of social justice work.

The performances under consideration in this book engage the ongoing and interconnected violence of settler colonialism and genocide; racism and antisemitism; and transphobia, homophobia, and misogyny. I believe that if there is any way toward justice and freedom, it is through human imagination and collective action. Here I am reminded of the words of the late poet Sekou Sundiata, who argued that among the most endangered species in U.S. culture at this contemporary moment, "[i]magination is at the top of the list."[40] Building on similar arguments made by Elaine Scarry and Albert Einstein, Sundiata states:

> The imagination is our field of operation. Just to be clear: when I say imagination, I am thinking of both the private realm of the individual mind and the social realm of public life: how one shapes the other and vice versa. I think of the imagination as a necessary and sacred space, a space in which "if not probable, all is possible." And although it exists within material borders and is shaped, to a large degree, by the material world, it can transcend those borders and conjure infinite possibilities of being.[41]

And while it is the selfsame human imagination that has designed instruments and regimes of violence beyond all imaginings, I remain faithful to performance's ability to create new worlds and, in tandem, make visible the untold failures of past and present ones. This book enters into that space between radical utopianism and social critique.

## "Homeland" Security States

Throughout this book, I situate my analysis against the ambient backdrop of what I call a post-9/11 "homeland" security state. The contemporary United States is defined by the regulation—implicit and explicit—not only of borders, checkpoints, nodes of transmit, sites of commerce, consumption, labor, education, and domesticity, but also through the heightened regulation of bodies and populations marked as out of place, out of sync, and out of time. As others have similarly argued, we have managed to leverage the catastrophic failures of the Bush administration in the service of ostensibly positive social change in the United States, including the first black family in the White House, LGBTQ legal victories, the Occupy Wall Street movement, Black Lives Matter, the youth-led Dreamers movement, mass mobilizations at Standing Rock Indian Reservation, and the first woman to win a major party nomination (and the popular vote) for president. But it has also, and not unrelatedly, been a period marked by war and racial and sexual violence, including a rise in hate crimes and hate speech directed at Muslims, Jews, people of color, queer and transgender people, and women—including white supremacist and rape culture rhetoric and policy put forth by the forty-fifth president of the United States himself.[42] For the purposes of this project, then, 9/11 becomes a useful flashpoint not only because it shifted my own understanding of the relationship between and among trauma and narrative, militarism and nationalism, but because the laws, codes, norms, cultures, ideologies, public feelings, surging affects, social relations, and public cultures that emerged in its wake reify hegemonic conceptions of not only race and gender, space and place, but also, as I will argue, of time—a normalizing project that continues to shape the cultural landscape and will, I believe, do so well into the "future."

In calling it a post-9/11 "homeland" security state, I mean to invoke the "U.S. Department of Homeland Security," which was established in the immediate aftermath of 9/11 to "protect" this nation-state from "terrorist" violence—a project that continues to unevenly target racialized and sexualized bodies that are out of sync with normative time. That is, I mean to invoke both the literal policing and disciplining of bodies by the U.S. government, the military, and the police, as well as the ways in which such biopolitical acts of securitization, surveillance, and violence produce a Foucauldian "disciplinary society" to which citizen and noncitizen subjects—subaltern or not—must adhere as a strategy of survival. In this regard, "security state" functions as a sliding signifier, referring both to the nation-state and the heightened, *affective states* of fear to which minoritized people are subjected in contemporary U.S. culture, which I will discuss at more length in chapters 3 and 4. Finally, in setting "homeland" in quotation marks, I mean to draw attention to the failure of the United States to acknowledge how this nation-state is also a settler colonial state, how the so-called U.S. "homeland" in fact occupied land of over five hundred sovereign nations, and how the dispossession of indigenous people is a central part of the project of U.S. capitalism, imperialism, and empire—a point that I will take up directly in the first chapter of this book, and return to again in the book's final chapter.

As I will argue in the pages that follow, the events of September 11, 2001, momentarily ruptured the linear continuity of "business as usual" in the United States and its global empire, a rupture that was all too quickly "returned to normal." As other scholars have observed, this expedient "return to normal" mobilized ambient fears of racial and sexual difference in the United States, calling on "citizens" to assist the state in policing the literal and symbolic boundaries of this nation-state from "terrorist" threat and contamination. This post-9/11 "homeland" security state in which we now live reifies the ideal citizen as white, Christian, and heterosexual, and, in turn, produces an increasingly homonormative gay/lesbian subject, further marginalizing the most nonnormative queers, and rendering their lives unlivable and ungrievable.[43]

Framing my project after 9/11 might, at first glance, seem to reify September 11, 2001, as a kind of watershed moment or reproduce a narrative that adheres to the very "paradigms of past, present, and future, a before and an after" that I attempt to dismantle. It might appear on the surface to collude with American exceptionalist portrayals of 9/11 as somehow unique even though, for most poor people, people of color, women, transgender people, and queers—in the global South and North alike—terror and violence have never been the exception but the rule.[44] However, I follow Puar in invoking "September 11 . . . cautiously, as an event in the Deleuzian sense, privileging lines of flight, an assemblage of spatial and temporal intensities, coming together, dispersing, reconverging."[45] For the purposes of this project, 9/11 functions as a flashpoint that acknowledges the spatial and temporal intensities of those events and their long aftermath while also remaining attentive to the U.S. imperial policies and capitalist ideologies that continue to produce the conditions for such ruptures in the first place.

Because I had just moved to Lower Manhattan from Chicago in August 2001, 9/11 was acutely disorienting for me. It was my first somatic experience with random and sudden death, with a psychic break from reality as I knew it, with mourning, with melancholy, with public memorials, with the difficulties of representation as it relates to trauma and grief. "We are a nation at ease with grievance," writes Anne Cheng, "but not with grief."[46] Because I lived below Fourteenth Street—the "threshold separating the living from the dead"—my neighborhood was gated and guarded, the streets closed off like a crime scene.[47] The air was filled with smoke, and dust, and the smell of burning flesh—yet we were told to shop, eat out, hang flags, and "return to normal."

I had not yet heard of Michael Warner or Judith Butler, Pierre Bourdieu or Michel Foucault, but I was becoming alert to the labor of normative citizenship and the mechanisms of power and fear that support it. I noticed when millions of flags, suddenly and seemingly simultaneously, went up all over the city, the nation, the world—T-shirts, banners, posters, lapel pins, face paint, tattoos—not always signifying in similar ways. The Pakistani shopkeeper on my block who hung a giant flag on his door and sold many more inside may very well have been struck by patriotism in a post-9/11 moment, but he may, too, have been using the flag as a cloak of protection against mounting anti-Arab and anti-Muslim racism and violence. Patriotism, like gender, was a performance, with survival as its aim. I began collecting photographs of what, following postcolonial theorist Homi Bhabha, I called "colonial mimicry": people of color, women, poor people, immigrants, and children waving the flag, or wearing it, or learning to draw it.[48]

Unemployed, queer, first-generation American, and decidedly unpatriotic, I, like many New Yorkers, did not hang a flag. I did not go shopping. I did not stop having nightmares, and night sweats, and recurring dreams of lesbian weddings interrupted by nose-diving jets. I did not, that is, return to normal. I did not know why at the time, but I was drawn to Union Square, and Tompkins Square, and Washington Square Park, where makeshift memorials, altars, shrines, and public gatherings unfolded over many months; as well as to synagogue, to theater class, to the idea of graduate school in a faraway state called Texas. The repeating, patterned logic of my ordinary life was permanently, irrevocably altered. Not only did I not know how to return to normal, but I began to question the "structuring structures" of this normal, of this nation, and to notice the "trouble" with it in the first place.

In her contribution to *Theatre Journal*'s special issue "Tragedy," published shortly after 9/11, performance theorist Diana Taylor writes:

> Tragedy cuts catastrophe down to size. It orders it into comprehensible scenarios. . . . Ultimately, tragedy assures us, the crisis will be resolved and balance restored. The fear and pity we, as spectators, feel will be purified by the action. . . . I think that using tragedy and its aesthetic connotation not only structures the events [of 9/11] but also blinds us to other ways of thinking about them. Take tragedy's organizational timetable: beginning, middle, and end.[49]

The narrativizing of 9/11 as a national tragedy reframed what was, for many, a traumatic event into a tragic event—a discursive move that was essential in consolidating a host of national affects, including racism, Islamophobia, patriotism, and militarism. As Judith Butler points out, "President Bush announces on September 21, 2001 that we have finished grieving and that *now* it is time for resolute action to take the place of grief. When grieving is feared, it seeks to resolve itself quickly, to banish itself in the name of action that is invested with the power to restore loss or rectify the world."[50] In this regard, the official narrative of 9/11 as a national tragedy worked to both forestall grief and urge resolution—and, in tandem, provide an excuse for global violence.

Put differently, the abrupt move to war in Afghanistan and Iraq could be read as evidence of a national crisis in temporality. If to stay in grief is to hold on to melancholic attachments—to obsess over the past, to psychically repeat, to refuse to move forward, or onward, or away from the pain of loss—then grief is the antithesis of official national affect. This is precisely why the fireman, the policeman, and the rescue worker emerged as our new national heroes: they represented fearlessness, resilience, productivity, and progress—not fear, grief, weakness, and depression. They represented a resolutely "American" (and masculine) sense of time.

Shortly after 9/11, the *New York Times* began publishing daily obituaries, which they called "Portraits of Grief." Here the obituary was used as an instrument for nation building to reinscribe dominant notions of straight time, dominant power, and normative subjectivity. Again and again, these narrative précis of a life—a grievable life, that is—reiterated the most normative affiliations and accomplishments. "The queer lives that vanished on September 11th," Butler reminds us, "are not publicly welcomed into the idea of national identity currently being built into the obituary pages."[51] While there is nothing wrong with being a "loving father" or "devoted wife," having "just graduated" or becoming "recently engaged," these portraits evidenced the difficulty of articulating, representing, and even imagining life outside the margins of straight time.

After 2001, the political landscape—contrary to what Dan Savage would have us believe—did not get better for queers. Racial paranoia and terror became official national affects; individuals, ethnic and religious groups, and borders were increasingly policed. After 9/11, the flow of bodies within the United States as well as transnationally became more and more difficult. Immigration in general, and immigration for queer subjects, in particular, became increasingly fraught.

The Family Reunification Act (2010), which claims to make entry into the United States easier for migrants, explicitly favors those heterosexual, married, and childbearing prospective citizens who maintain kinship ties—wife, husband, son, daughter—that the state already knows how to recognize. Queer migrants often resort to seeking citizenship through asylum status, which at once requires that they frame their country of origin as homophobic and violent (whether or not this is the case) and frame the United States as benevolent father, who will "save" them from danger. That is, these policies force queer migrants to produce racist and colonialist narratives about their homelands in order to gain entry into the United States. This demonization of the East, the global South, the nonwhite, and the foreign as backward and homophobic, in tandem with the valorization of the West, the global North, the white, and the American as a liberal, forward-thinking safe haven for queers, is what Puar has cleverly termed "homonationalism."[52]

Two years after 9/11, the Supreme Court explicitly overturned *Bowers v. Hardwick* (1986) with their ruling in *Lawrence v. Texas* (2003), which found the Texas antisodomy statute unconstitutional. While hailed by liberals as good for the gays, a close reading of *Lawrence* reveals its ongoing infringement on human rights, as well as its hidden investments in straight time. Writing *Lawrence*'s majority opinion, Justice Kennedy argued that the Texas antisodomy law was unconstitutional on the grounds of due process and extended the (heterosexual) right to sodomy to "same-sex couples" engaging in "private" and "consenting" sexual behavior. In framing *Bowers*'s unconstitutionality in terms of due process, *Lawrence* overlooks the fundamental human rights violation of the statute; in framing the right to sodomy for couples and in private, *Lawrence* suggests that for queer sex to be acceptable by national standards, it must be monogamous and domesticated. Of note, Lawrence was a white, fifty-five-year-old man and Garner was his black, thirty-one-year-old lover, and the interracial (and intergenerational) aspect of the sex act was central in motivating the original arrest—and yet the majority opinion also overlooks the centrality of race in the criminalization of Lawrence and Garner, as well as in the subsequent ruling.[53]

The normalizing logic of this ostensibly liberal ruling comes as little surprise. The idealized heterosexual family has—particularly since the collapse of the welfare state under Reagan—increasingly come to stand in for nation itself. In her groundbreaking essay "My Dangerous Desires," writer and activist Amber Hollibaugh outlines the gay and lesbian liberation movement's long-standing critique of normalcy that will later be picked up by queer theory. She writes:

> In the last twenty-five years of struggle, we have moved from gay liberation as a freedom struggle, a struggle for sexual, economic, and social justice, to a movement for gay legal rights. This struggle now parodies and duplicates a heterosexual middle class/upper class agenda based on recreating the rights of heterosexuals for gay people, with all the implicit and explicit pieces of class and race prejudice that go with it. The freedom struggle of our movement, once committed to sexual liberation, has become, instead, a movement for gay nuclear family rights and for serial monogamy. It represents the entire movement as a sort of tame civil rights challenge: one of judicial battles in the courts and referenda in the towns, cities, and states. The gains have been significant. But, looking at the bigger picture, we have gone from a movement that was full of sensibility and humor,

> powerful difference and sexual contrast, a world of camp and butch and femme, of leather communities, drag queens and kings, flamboyant girls and effeminate gay boys, a movement full of our sexual cultures and creative, erotic dreams, to a movement that chooses only those representatives who may sit politely in the president's office, gender-appropriate gay representatives who work for gay inclusion and try very hard to show everyone else that "we are just like them."[54]

While legalizing acts of sodomy for same-sex couples, then, *Lawrence v. Texas* is emblematic of this move from gay liberation struggles to gay legal rights, while also reproducing the troubling logic that defines queer citizenship only and always in terms of "respectability politics": gay and lesbian partnership, monogamy, recognizable family units, gender normativity, and sexual restraint. In this regard, LGBTQ legal victories, like *Lawrence*, and the gay American Dream that such victories promise, come at a price, including the condition that queer subjects learn to synchronize their lives to the predictable beats of straight time.

Similarly, the federal repeal of the Defense of Marriage Act (1996) in the United States, and the legalization of gay marriage on a national scale that followed suit, draws understandably mixed responses from the Left (to say nothing of the homophobia of its right-wing opponents). The Human Rights Campaign, the lead advocacy group for the federal repeal of the Defense of Marriage Act and the legalization of gay marriage in the United States, asserts:

> At its core, the push for marriage equality is simply about making the day-to-day lives of same-sex couples and their families manageable and secure. All families deserve the ability to protect themselves with basic legal rights and safeguards such as social security, health insurance and unquestioned hospital visitation. Only marriage can provide families with true equality.[55]

Like *Lawrence*, the rhetoric of gay marriage re-creates rather than deconstructs a sexual hierarchy, in which the "day-to-day lives" of lesbian and gay "families" are guaranteed what Margaret Somers calls "the right to have rights" (in the form of hospital visits, Social Security, and health insurance), while those queers with lives that do not neatly fit into normative notions of "family" are left unprotected and unimagined, by an organization that in name alone claims to "campaign" on behalf of all humans' rights.[56] Not only it is deplorable that health insurance be contingent upon employment status in the United States, the fact that an individual (queer or otherwise) can only confer employment benefits to a *marital* spouse leaves those queers without one—either because they are single or refuse to marry or exist in an unrecognized relationship structure (e.g., polyamory)—unprotected. In this regard, gay marriage—while perhaps something that "we cannot not want," to borrow postcolonial theorist Gayatri Spivak's influential turn of phrase—continues to reinforce the conservative notion of marriage as the marker of respectable citizenship (gay or otherwise), and typical family as the official unit of nation building.[57] In this sense, the 2015 Supreme Court ruling that extends the right of marriage to all couples regardless of gender expression and sexual orientation may in fact be equitable, may in fact be just, and may in fact be good for many gays—but it does not inherently bring us closer to freedom. Here I must agree with David Eng, who argues that the legalization of gay marriage provides false evidence that the "project of human freedom" has been "completed."[58] Make no mistake, unlike many on the far Left, I support all forms of queer self-expression and self-determination, including the desire to marry.[59] However, as Eng also notes, "we need to remind ourselves that decriminalization and social belonging are not coterminous."[60] First, I do not believe that the legalization of gay marriage in the United States has much to do with #love winning (perhaps #Ruth winning?). And while I would like to believe that the legalization of gay marriage on a national scale will open resources for addressing vital issues of systemic violence, injustice, and disenfranchisement affecting queer and trans people (police brutality, mass incarceration, HIV/AIDS, health care disparities, poverty, homelessness, employment and housing discrimination), I am left wondering what other logics win with marriage, and how these logics might, ultimately, do us harm.

Perhaps "progress" itself is the misguided gay agenda. It certainly was for Brandon Bitner, Tyler Clementi, Raymond Chase, Seth Walsh, Asher Brown, Billy Lucas, Justin Aaberg, Cody Barker, and Carl Joseph Walker: teen boys who killed themselves—one after the next—in 2009 and 2010. Some shot themselves in the heads, others jumped from bridges and hung from trees, one threw himself in front of a tractor-trailer. This crisis in masculinity caught the attention of "openly gay" syndicated journalist Dan Savage and his partner Terry Savage, who launched a motivational campaign called "It Gets Better." From YouTube to Facebook, "It Gets Better" relays a message of hope to an "imagined community" of depressed queer and trans teens from the nation's "hippest" mainstream celebrities: Barack Obama, Margaret Cho, Sarah Silverman, Ellen Degeneres, Kate Bornstein, Tim Gunn, Neil Patrick Harris, Jewel. Almost always citing college, marriage, family-making, and career building as examples, the "It Gets Better" campaign aims to reassure young people that the future is brighter than the past, that the promise of the American Dream is in sight—if only they just hang tight (rather than hang themselves). As the campaign picked up traction in social media, noncelebrities (mostly gays and lesbians) began voicing and circulating their own "it gets better" stories, many of which are archived on the project website and in Savage's *It Gets Better* book. Again and again, seemingly well-adjusted and assimilated gay subjects narrate their lives in terms of the predictable markers of happiness and repeatedly frame "coming out" as the catalyst for emancipation from oppression, repression, depression, and death. The ubiquitous coming-out narrative, like the discourses of same-sex marriage or national tragedy, plots life on a singular and ascending trajectory. It also elides the fact that, in a hetero- and cissexist culture that reproduces itself every day, queer and trans people come out not once but repeatedly—to the new boss, doctor, cousin, clerk—anyone and everyone who will presume their heterosexuality and cissexuality and attempt to make sense of their life accordingly. What's more, it equally elides the fact that queer and trans subjectivities are ongoing processes of becoming and rebecoming, as people's sexualities, gender identities, and understandings of self and desire shift as they move through time. As my former student and activist Mateo Guadalupe—who began transitioning from lesbian to trans man between high school and college—succinctly puts it, "I will be transitioning my whole life."[61]

If a "paranoid reading" of the "It Gets Better" campaign critiques its focus on futurity, a "reparative reading" of the teen suicides reveals the ways in which those teens were victims not of gay bashing per se but of the very futuristic rhetoric that attempts to save them. In an article published in the October 2010 issue of *Ms. Magazine*, titled "Gay Bashing Is About Masculinity," sociologist Michael Kimmel astutely points out the relationship between these suicides and gender violence. He writes:

> It's true that gays and lesbians are far more often the target of hostility than their straight peers. But it's often true that anti-gay sentiments are only partly related to sexual orientation. Calling someone gay or a fag has become so universal that it's become synonymous with dumb, stupid or wrong. And it's "dumb" or "wrong" because it isn't *masculine* enough. To the "that's-so-gay" chorus, homosexuality is about gender nonconformity, not being a "real man," and so anti-gay sentiments become a shorthand method of gender policing.[62]

What Kimmel's argument suggests is that these boys were killing themselves not necessarily because they were "gay," but because they were being perceived as feminine. As sissy boys, that is, they had failed to develop according to a chronologic that narrates the progression from boyhood into manhood as the natural order. To get stuck in boyhood or, worse, to deviate into girlhood or womanhood is not only a (queer) failure of masculinity but a failure to follow a normal, linear, sequence of gender development. Like the hundreds of young trans women whose suicides have (finally) caught the attention of the mainstream media in recent years, LGBTQ youth—particularly those who are femme presenting and of color—are dying not because they fail to realize that the future is "better" for queers, but perhaps because they know it is not.

In June 2016, forty-nine queers—mostly Latina/o—were gunned down in a gay bar in Orlando, Florida, appropriately named "Pulse."[63] The shooting captured the attention of President Obama, the mainstream media, and social media in unprecedented ways. Being called the greatest massacre in American history, the Orlando shooting at once diminishes the long history of violence against queer/trans/people of color in the United States, while reifying normative logics of race, gender, and nation. Because the shooter was Muslim, the official narrative of the event was quickly turned into one of terrorism, even though he had no ties to any terrorist group, and even though it was very clear that he, a queer of color himself, suffered from internalized racism and homophobia. While it is true that many people died that day and that this event is horrific, what is also true is that for queers, especially queers of color, this violence is business as usual. The grief within the queer community is not lessened but compounded by the erasure of this fact. When Hillary Clinton or, worse, Donald Trump, use the shooting in Orlando to prop up their neoliberal and neoconservative agendas of Islamophobia, militarism, and war—as well as their own political careers—queer Latinos are not being remembered: they are being used as an instrument of state power and violence, redoubled.

I would like to pause here for a moment to closely consider what the "homeland" security state has to do with the politics of trauma and memory, in general, and queer temporality, in particular. As I've been arguing throughout this introduction, the policing of bodies by the state bears particular ties to 9/11 and its aftermath. In her important book on U.S. surveillance culture, *Our Biometric Future: Facial Recognition Technology and the Future of Surveillance* (2011), media studies scholar Kelly Gates compellingly outlines the ways in which current facial recognition technologies that originated during the Cold War period are being developed and deployed as antidotes to a nation that sees itself in a security crisis after the failure of such technologies to prevent the 2001 terrorist attacks in New York City and Washington, D.C. Citing feminist theorist Pat Gill, Gates refers to this phenomena as "techno-nostalgia," which manifests as a cultural feeling that certain tragic events could have been prevented—that is, if only surveillance and security technologies had not failed to work. Gates, for instance, begins her book with a still image of suspected hijackers Mohammed Atta and Abdulaziz Alomari taken from the security cameras at the Portland, Maine, airport on the morning of September 11, 2001, where they allegedly caught their commuter flight to Boston.

In the image, Atta and Alomari are dressed in casual business attire; Atta carries a shoulder bag. Another man, presumably an airport security officer, is shown in the far left corner of the still frame; above him, the words "SCREENING" are overlaid onto the video surveillance tape. Below, a date stamp: 9-11-01 24H, and below this, a time stamp: 5:45:13.

The technonostalgia that this image invokes is multivalent. First, it serves as evidence of a crime—alleged terrorists Atta and Alomari rendered visible, alive, and boarding an aircraft in the hours before the attack. Simultaneously, it serves as evidence of a failure to stop a crime—surveillance protocols captured their images in advance, yet failed to capture *them*. To the post-9/11 viewer, this technonostalgia is heightened by our recognition of not only Atta and Alomari—whose faces, along with video loops of airplanes crashing into buildings, would circulate ad nauseam in the months after the attacks—but also our recognition of the date stamp: 9-11-01. For the post-9/11 spectator, this date reverberates as a historical flashpoint while, at same time, we recognize that at 5:45 A.M., when the footage was taken, this date and time meant nothing, just two men catching a commuter plane to Boston on a Monday morning in September: business as usual. In a theater studies framework, this is what we call dramatic irony.

This archive of criminality and failure, historicity and banality—along with the eerie surveillance videos capturing the would-be hijackers at an ATM, a gas station, and a Wal-Mart hours before the men boarded this Portland flight—was later used as justification by the U.S. government for deploying facial recognition technologies in the service of what would become known as "the global war on terror." The logic was that with smarter technologies and heightened surveillance standards, we could divert any future acts of terrorism and thereby secure our "national safety." Put differently, we had entered a national crisis in temporality: unlike the past, to which we had arrived too late on the scene, the future could be safe, and the future could be saved.

A decade later, the same technologies used to "prevent" and "avert" crime are increasingly being used by the (police) state as evidence of the criminality of certain "improperly" gendered and racialized bodies, further justifying acts of violence as necessary strategies of securitization and control. For instance, the previously mentioned Black Lives Matter movement—founded by a small collective of black lesbian, queer, and transgender activists—was born in the aftermath of the 2013 acquittal of white civilian George Zimmerman in the 2012 murder of black teenager Trayvon Martin in Sanford, Florida, and picked up significant traction the following year, after the 2014 murder of black teenager Michael Brown in Ferguson, Missouri, by white police officer Darren Wilson. Brown's body was shot at least six times while his hands were up in surrender, it was left on the ground for four and a half hours without medical care or transport, and a grand jury decided not to indict Wilson for the murder, spurring local riots and activist uprisings around the country. Of particular note is how surveillance technologies were used, once again, as "evidence," although to slightly different ends. In a convenience store surveillance video, which circulated widely on social media in the weeks following the murder, we see a young man purchasing cigarillos just prior to the murder. In the upper left hand corner of this three-minute video, we see a date and timestamp: 2014-08-09 11:52:57, and counting. As protests and riots unfolded in real time in Ferguson and across the nation in the year(s) following the murder, so, too, did speculations and debates as to whether this footage was evidence of a crime, or not; whether the person in the video was Brown, or not; whether he stole a box of Swisher Sweets, or not; whether

Wilson even knew that Brown was a suspect when he approached Brown for "walking in the middle of the street," or not; and, of course, whether shoplifting and/or walking while black is justification for police brutality and murder. Like the airport surveillance footage, the visual archive of the moments before Michael Brown's murder haunts the viewer. In the case of the Ferguson surveillance video, it offers evidence not of the failure of technology to prevent crime but of what I would like to call a "tauto(techno) logical" argument about the inherent criminality of black bodies and the right of the state to dispose of them.

The history of social movements in the United States illustrates the varied ways in which individuals and social groups have appropriated the very technologies aimed to control them to redefine and reimagine the world. In the aftermath of the Brown murder, for instance, we see a proliferation of performances of dissent circulating on social media and in the mainstream and alternative press. In one salient example, Howard University sophomore Khalil Saadiq, the director of student advocacy for the Howard University Student Association, in collaboration with executive vice president Ikenna Ikeotuonye, decides to stage a counterprotest with second-, third-, and fourth-year students prior to freshman orientation—a site strategically chosen because Michael Brown was scheduled to begin college at Howard a mere week after he was gunned down. In the action, hundreds of incoming students at this historically black college stand together in a crowded auditorium, their hands raised in solidarity, while Ikeotuonye snaps the photograph—at once archiving this performance and anticipating the serial performances it would inevitably enact and reenact on social media. Howard junior Megan Sims, with the handle @The_Blackness48, tweets the photograph with the hashtag #dontshoot, a moniker that will become one of the defining gestures and slogans of the movement. This staged performance then goes viral, with nearly ten thousand retweets in less than twenty-four hours.

This performance for the camera enacts and refuses the ways in which state violence metes itself unevenly onto racialized bodies. It also instructs us as to how memory and countermemory work within the post-9/11 "homeland" security state. When Howard students throw their hands up in protest and Ikeotuonye snaps the picture for all the world to see, and when five African American players for the St. Louis Rams (Jared Cook, Kenny Britt, Stedman Bailey, Chris Givens, and Tavon Austin) do the same a few weeks later on live TV, what we are seeing is the "[transformation] of the visual sign of surrender into one of political resistance."[64] Particularly when performed by a black, brown, female, queer, and/or transgender body, this gesture invokes the countless bodies, like Brown's, gunned down—the protester's gesture citing the innocent dead's final "hands up" moment before the resounding shot. It also invokes the specter of the police state itself—the (ostensibly white) officer on the other side of the frame—gun pulled, trigger ready, whose absent presence haunts the scene. At the same time, the gesture also invokes the specter of surveillance culture itself—the man behind the camera, as it were, who literally steps into the selfsame position as the officer prepared to "point and shoot." And then there is us, millions of viewers who, in and through our act of looking, adopt the gaze of the photographer and the officer alike—some, depending on social location or political framework, with a Butlerian kind of difference. As literary theorist Lindsay Reckson puts it in her compelling essay about #handsup which appeared in *Avidly* in December 2014:

> To perform for the camera might be to insist—as [Frederick] Douglass and [Sojourner] Truth did—on the unfixing of the photograph's complicity with state power, with objectification, and with death. The camera is not neutral and cannot save us, as it did not save Eric Garner, or secure justice for him. But hands up for the camera calls attention to America's long history of conviction and punishment on site/sight. Transmuted from a gesture of surrender to a gesture of solidarity, hands up refuses the logic of racial enforcement.[65]

#handsupdontshoot, and the Black Lives Matter movement writ large of which it is a part, also reminds us that even (or especially) in this security state, social actors find ways to use the very logic and technology that is meant to contain them to refuse state violence through the staging of political performances in public. To do so is to cite our vulnerability, our rage, and most of all our knowledge—about how power and violence work, about the relationship between the camera and the gun, and about the central role that performance can play in the reworking of trauma in a culture of violence.

No, the camera cannot save us, nor can the stage, nor the page, but acts of reperformance in public such as these, as well as the ones I will write about in the pages that follow, do render visible the ways in which "differently" racialized, sexualized, and gendered bodies are targets for violence. To say "#dontshoot" is also to refuse a narrative that insists that you must be shot, to insist instead on a right to living in a culture of dying. At the same time, it lays bare the chronologic that animates such a narrative in the first place. As queer and crip theorist Alison Kafer puts it:

> Queer kids, kids of color, street kids—all of the kids cast out of reproductive futurism—have been and continue to be framed as sick, as pathological, as contagious. . . . The statistical likelihood that young, black men living in particular . . . neighborhoods will be paralyzed (if not killed) by gunshot wounds serves to push them out of time, facing a future of no future, and a no future best embodied by a wheelchair. Disability, in other words, becomes the future of no future, with "dead in jail or in a chair" recognized as all the same, all signs of no future. . . . [L]oss is not the defining frame because there was nothing to "lose."[66]

There is "nothing to lose" because death, disability, and/or incarceration are figured as the inevitable outcome of being born poor, and/or a racialized and/ or sexualized other, with no future to begin with: out of place, out of sync, out of time.

And so, in this fifteen-year period (2001–2016) of public culture that I trace, of rapid "developments" in the LGBTQ movement coupled with ongoing war and violence, I find myself longing to hear public discourse and see artistic work that resists a simple progress narrative, and that reflects the actual temporalities of many queer and trans lives, mine included: nonlinear, multiplicitous, cyclical, spontaneous, delayed, defrayed, destroyed, deferred, derailed, disjointed, erratic, melancholic, and ecstatic. This book is a record of that longing fulfilled in performance, as well as a polemic for life on the margins of time.

## Following the Ghosts

This project is indebted to scholarship in a variety of disciplines that deal with the politics of archives and historical memory.[67] If "the irrevocable tie"[68] between heterosexuality and capitalism is what produces the logic of straight time, a kind of "archive fever" is what maintains it. In using the term "archive fever," I mean to invoke both philosopher Jacques Derrida's *Archive Fever* and historian Carolyn Steedman's *Dust: The Archive and Cultural History*, both of which inform my thinking and analysis. Steedman writes, "Derrida had long seen in Freudian psycho-analysis a desire to recover moments of inception, beginnings and origins which—in a deluded way—we think might be some kind of truth, and in 'Archive Fever,' desire for the archive is presented as part of the desire to find, or locate, or possess that moment of origin, as the beginning of things."[69] According to Steedman, the archive is feverish, or sick, because it is used as an instrument of state power that reifies the facticity of certain historical events and actors while dismissing others. The archivist is equally sick: driven by a desire to locate truth and search for origins, the archivist feverishly combs through the archives in search of a story with a clear beginning, middle, and end. As the preface to this introduction illustrated, there is no real beginning (or middle, or end), only the feverish drive to locate and order it. How can performance allow us to feel the natural bends in time, and to see the perversity of our desires to straighten them?

Part of my research agenda into discourses of temporality within the fields of queer and performance studies stems from my abiding interest in archives of trauma, grief, and loss. As such, all of the works under investigation in this book deal in one way or another with the politics of death and ghosting. Mary Ellen Strom's *Geyser Land*, which she conceived and directed in collaboration with Ann Carlson and members of the Crow and Northern Cheyenne Nations, and which I discuss in chapter 1, examines the buried history of racial genocide in the "American West" by literally reanimating archival photographs and cinema of the period *in situ* (on site), as a form of site-specific "ghosting." Peggy Shaw and Clod Ensemble's *Must* (dir. Suzy Willson), which I discuss in chapter 2, exposes an aging, butch lesbian "dying on stage"—literally. I draw on Herbert Blau's observation that "theater stinks . . . of mortality" because the actor is dying "in front of your eyes," and I argue that this performer's "dying" is made particularly palpable by her actual illness and frailty that haunt the performance throughout.[70] *floodlines*, which I conceived and directed in collaboration with the local community in Austin, Texas, and which I discuss in chapter 3, stages imaginary ghosts—haunting an idealized middle-class America with ambient scenes of terror.[71] In the final case study, I examine a certain kind of social death, which I frame as a "loss" of faith in the neoliberal academy as a place to do radical culture work, and I cast this analysis against the ambient backdrop of the birth and death of the Occupy/Decolonize movement. The book's epilogue (re)turns to 9/11 in New York City—on the eve of the fifteen-year memorial of September 11, reading the ways in which history haunts the closing production of the Broadway production of Lisa Kron and Jeanine Tesori's musical, *Fun Home*, as well as my reception of it.

In a culture of forgetting, keeping the dead alive through acts of remembrance is a profoundly subversive act. In their introduction to *Loss: The Politics of Mourning*, David Eng and David Kazanjian encourage rather than pathologize a refusal to "let go" of grief. Rereading Freud through Benjamin, Eng and Kazanjian insist that melancholy, or mourning without end, can be a generative, creative, and counterhegemonic cultural practice.[72] The works under investigation in this project are an applied model of the kind of generative melancholy that Eng and Kazanjian describe: they invite history's improperly buried ghosts to surface and to linger, and invite, too, the seemingly irrational affects that accompany such melancholic performances.

Because my project presumes straight time to be an invisible instrument of state power, my scholarship also resonates with contemporary work in cultural studies that urges us to look at ordinary affects, social imaginaries, and other things not necessarily visible on the surface—even what is "not there."[73] Sociologist Avery Gordon's *Ghostly Matters: Haunting and the Sociological Imagination* has been formative, for Gordon models a cultural analysis that begins with the assumption that "power can be invisible."[74] Reminiscent of Foucault's famous assertion that "power is only tolerable on the condition that it masks a significant part of itself,"[75] Gordon's claim is that the condition of postmodernity—with all its apparent "technologies of hypervisibility"—eclipses the most seething, ghostly presences in U.S. culture, including "improperly buried bodies" and "countervailing systems of value."[76] What this means is that the unacknowledged and sometimes subtle violences of racism and classism, sexism and heterosexism, can and do surface as apparitions, ghosts, fragmented memories, acts of violence, depression, and "feelings of craziness." As the Combahee River Collective put it in their foundational essay, "A Black Feminist Statement" (1977), "Black feminists often talk about their feelings of craziness before becoming conscious of the concepts of sexual politics, patriarchal rule, and most importantly, feminism, the political analysis and practice that we women use to struggle against our oppression."[77] Craziness, grief, ghost stories—what Gordon calls "complex personhood": there is no time for such things in capitalist culture. Through U.S. colonialism and genocide, capitalism has supplanted indigenous, somatic, cyclical, and seasonal ways of being in time with the temporal mandates of the clock, the calendar, and the hourly wage.[78] There is no time to deal with "trauma" and "memory" in a heterocapitalist culture defined by rapid progress and (re)productivity. There is, however, such time in performance. Always already a place out of time, always already exceeding the present, theater, dance, and performance have the capacity to create new temporal worlds—in which queer rather than straight time is the structuring structure of the event, and where seemingly "settled knowledge"[79] can be disrupted and transformed.

My project is also in conversation with other writers who have attempted to desecularize the field of cultural studies. For instance, while the field has been heavily influenced by Benjamin's philosophies, scholars tend to situate him as a Marxist but overlook the fact that his philosophy of historical materialism is also rooted in Jewish mysticism and religious beliefs. This is significant because it is the same, dominant Western epistemologies that flatten our understanding of time that also limit what constitutes historical knowledge. Among those ways of knowing that are most readily delegitimized in the academy are those grounded in spiritual cosmologies and embodiment. Writing from a postcolonial, queer, feminist, and African diasporic cosmological framework that honors the dead, sociologist M. Jacqui Alexander models a spiritually grounded and physically embodied mode of research which she calls attending to "the sacred." For her, this includes conjuring the dead and allowing the dispossessed to write their own stories when traditional modes of archival research and writing fail, or are otherwise inadequate for recounting the stories of people who may be difficult to locate in the annals of official history. Similarly, Avery Gordon calls it "following the ghosts," which also lends itself to the title of chapter 3. Building on the work of Patricia Williams, Gordon models a radical methodology in which the scholar attunes to apparitions and other seemingly invisible and intangible things in order to write an account of history that calls forth those spirits that have been cast into its margins and footnotes. Likewise, poet Merle Feld calls it recreating "holy time." As cited in the opening epigraph to this book, Feld conjures the prophet Miriam, who recounts her experience at the foot of Mount Sinai while her brother, Moses, receives the commandments. She articulates a feminist as well as spiritual longing for the archival "record" (figured as masculine) and embodied "experience" (figured as feminine)—to be "re-membered" together. Bearing these and other models in mind, I call it falling through "the hole of history." Mine is a process by which the scholar acts as emissary. Like the angel of history, like the artists about whom I write, I attempt to slip through the cracks of time and bear witness to a past or future in need of vision and revision—while remaining grounded in the material conditions of the present. Attending to the sacred, attuning to the ghosts, remembering holy time, falling through the hole of history: this work necessitates a belief in spirit, in repair, and in queer magic, as well as the conviction that the dead and the not yet living—especially those who have or might otherwise be dispossessed by state violence—have much to say. The artists about whom I write have learned how to listen well, and how to cast a spell, and I have tried to do the same.

*Time Slips* attempts to locate and examine queer performance as a subjugated form of knowledge production. In "Society Must Be Defended," a series of lectures that philosopher Michel Foucault gave at the College of France in the mid-1970s, Foucault defines "subjugated knowledges" as ways of knowing that have been "buried" or "masked," and he advocates for their disinterment.[81] This project takes up that mantle, not only because queer and feminist ways of knowing have been delegitimized within the academy and in public culture, but because a primary premise of this book is that the artistic work about which I write is itself an embodied form of knowledge production. That is, through thick description and performance analysis of live events, visual analysis and close reading of archives of performance and visual culture, and historical contextualization, I attempt to make explicit the rich theoretical work already present in the performances I discuss. As Muñoz similarly argues in the introduction to his book, *Disidentifications*:

> The theoretical conceptualizations and figurations that flesh out this book are indebted to the theoretical/practical work of [artists]. For me there would be no theory . . . without the cultural work of [artists]. Such performances constitute the political and conceptual center of this study. I want to note that, for me, the making of theory transpires *after* the artists' performance of counterpublicity is realized for my own disidentificatory eyes.[82]

In this sense, I frame the artists under investigation in this book as scholars in their own right and the performances I discuss as doing a kind of theoretical work that precedes my analysis.

This book attempts to make visible the labor of lesbian, queer, and trans artists and the tangled histories from which we emerge. At the same time, it also aims to envision new ways of being in this world not entirely bound to past histories of harm nor to the institutions and social structures that make such harm possible and profitable in the first place. Yet institutions—both academic and cultural—play a central role in the support and development of this project: not only those colleges and universities that have employed me and/or granted me research and travel support, but also those institutions—universities, galleries, and foundations—that fund and produce much of the artistic work about which I write. As performance scholar and practitioner Paul Bonin-Rodriguez argues, institutions and funding structures that support artists and their work are themselves ideological, which affects the kind of work that gets produced in the public sphere as well as the kind of discourses that get to circulate and the kind of people that get to participate in those discourses, which in turn further shapes the cultural landscape in particular ideological directions.[83]

*Geyser Land*, for instance, produced by the Myrna Loy Center in Helena, Montana, was supported by major grants from such institutions as the Doris Duke Foundation, the Rockefeller Foundation, and the National Endowment for the Arts, as well as contributions from Montana State University and the University of Montana–Missoula. I first met Ann Carlson and Mary Ellen Strom at the University of Texas at Austin, when I was a graduate student and the Department of Theater and Dance was hosting Carlson as a guest artist. Strom's career as a video and conceptual artist has been made possible, in part, by a full-time faculty position at the School of the Museum of Fine Arts, Boston, where she has served as director of the MFA program for nearly two decades. Carlson's career as a choreographer and performance artist has been made possible, in part, by her twenty-year life partnership with Strom, which allowed her the freedom to work primarily outside academia—although her work is often produced by colleges and universities and she has held a variety of visiting faculty positions at various institutions of higher education.[84]

In a similar vein, while Peggy Shaw has notoriously made a life as a "dirt poor independent artist," it is colleges and universities that provide many of the funding structures for her work.[85] I first met Shaw when she and Lois Weaver were performing *It's a Small House and We've Lived in It Always* at a conference hosted by the Department of Theater and Dance at the University of Texas, and I became close to her when, first, I was working with Jill Dolan in editing Shaw's then-forthcoming anthology of solo work, published by the University of Michigan Press, and, later, when I hosted Shaw as a guest artist at Hampshire College, where I was teaching. When Shaw fell ill, I utilized the platform of a tribute to Shaw at Hampshire College to launch an Indiegogo campaign on her behalf, which in turn raised nearly twenty thousand dollars toward "The Peggy Shaw Pension Fund," the majority of support coming from senior scholars in the field of performance studies, many of whom have built their own careers writing about Shaw's work.[86] Furthermore, the production of *Must* that I write about in chapter 2 was produced by the University of Massachusetts–Amherst, and the original production was created under the auspices of Clod Ensemble's Performing Medicine (London), which is supported not only by the England Arts Council and other governmental agencies, but also by the School of English and Drama (where Weaver is on faculty) at Queen Mary University of London, and the London School of Medicine and Dentistry.

Similarly, the seven-year run of *floodlines* in Austin was made possible, in large part, by grants from the City of Austin, which receives trickle-down funds from the Texas Commission on the Arts and the National Endowment for the Arts. It was first produced by the University of Texas (as my master's thesis performance), and I continued to borrow tens of thousands of dollars worth of props, costumes, and media equipment from the university every year thereafter, and many of my human resources were culled from both the Theater and Dance and the Radio, Television, and Film departments at the university, including actors, stage managers, costume designers, and documentary filmmakers.

The last chapter functions as a feminist critique of the disciplining and normalizing force of the academy, detailing the challenges and limitations of queer and performance-based pedagogy in neoliberal contexts. Yet as a direct result of the prevalence of systemic violence that takes shape on college campuses, a multiplicity of countercultural spaces, organizations, ideas, political movements, and sites of art and activism erupt on those campuses. The social and political ramifications of these performatives, as I will argue, have the capacity to exceed the geographic, temporal, and affective boundaries of the academy per se, reaching back in history and forward, too, well into the future. This does not justify institutional violence in the first place, but it is important to acknowledge the ways in which the academy, for better or worse, can function as a training ground for young artist-activists.

Similarly, playwright Lisa Kron's musical adaptation of Alison Bechdel's graphic novel, *Fun Home,* which she created with composer Jeanine Tesori, and which I write about in the book's epilogue, enjoyed an eighteen-month run on Broadway at the Circle in the Square Theatre. While Kron's theatrical roots, like Shaw's, lie in the do-it-yourself, feminist, downtown theater scene (most notably, the WOW Café), and while Kron continues to maintain her ties to the queer and feminist theater communities, she is also a Broadway success story—with two plays, including *Fun Home*, ascending to this socioeconomic epicenter of institutionalized and corporatized American theater. As such, while I situate *Fun Home* as doing radical cultural work, we must not forget that it—like all of the performances in this book—also circulates in the time and space of capital. In other words, while the work under consideration in this book may have been made by lesbian, queer, and transgender artists, and while it may engage radical critiques and participate in the circulation of subaltern knowledge, the material practices that produce the conditions for the making of and writing about these works exist within multiple circuits of power.

## Colleague-Criticism

Throughout this book, I situate myself not as some distant observer to the artists' processes and performances but as a fellow public intellectual, art practitioner, feminist, queer, and cultural critic. Because I have been following the work of many of these artists for many years; because several of them I would even call friends and colleagues; because I am emotionally and intellectually invested in my ongoing relationship with them as fellow travelers and cultural workers; because I write from a place of love, respect, and admiration, the research and writing in these chapters enacts what Jill Dolan, Paul Bonin-Rodriguez, and I have called "colleague-criticism." Colleague-criticism

> is prompted in part by questions derived from our own identities and affiliations as feminist and queer artists and scholars: What does it mean to engage critically and publicly with the work of a queer artist and/or artist of color who privately is a friend, colleague, and/or collaborator? How might foregrounding one's relationship as critic to the artist produce an alternative model of critical exchange [that] redefine[s] the traditional hierarchical dynamic between critic and artist into a model of collaboration and alliance that speaks to and from the practice of queer politics . . . , mutual respect, and common cause?[87]

Colleague-criticism is aligned with performance theorist David Román's notion of "critical generosity," in which the critic foregrounds her appreciation for an artist's body of work, effectively dismissing objectivity and instead allowing the writing to come from a place of love and sustained commitment to the artist's work.[88] Colleague-criticism is akin to community-based theater scholar and practitioner Jan Cohen-Cruz's "engaged model of criticism," which invites critics to acknowledge their relationship to an artist's mission, remain mindful of notions of reciprocity and mutual aid, and write from a place of "passionate concern, prior knowledge, and ethical engagement."[89] In enacting colleague-criticism, critic and artist stand side by side, "[insisting] on their vital citizenship in a nation that betrays its artists, that queers them and exiles them to an 'immoral' fringe."[90] Colleague-criticism, then, "is an ethical practice of participatory democracy, modeled by queers, artists, critics, and public intellectuals determined to make new worlds together."[91]

Committed to the politics of colleague-criticism, I have stayed in dialogue with many of the artists throughout my process of writing about their work. They have generously opened their archives to me, sending me DVDs, VHS tapes, scripts, books, catalogues, photographs, reviews, links to private online documentation of performances, and have, in key moments, been interlocutors, collaborators, and friends. As an act of reciprocity, I invite their feedback on this writing. While I do not feel a commitment to merely praise the work, I am self-consciously aware that they will read my writing, that it will have material consequences, that I write as much for the subjects of my study as I do for any third-party reader. In this sense, I try to write as an "ethical ethnographer," drawing from the late performance theorist Dwight Conquergood's model of self-reflexive and community-engaged participant-observation.[92]

I attempt to abandon critical objectivity in favor of colleague-criticism, writing about the work of artists I know, admire, and sometimes love. I also include a chapter about my own performance practice, further complicating notions of critical distance. Because this book is a project about the collapsing of boundaries in performance—temporal, affective, national—it feels important to destabilize the hierarchical boundary between artist and critic, as well as the assumptions about power that such border policing perpetuates in contemporary arts criticism and scholarship.

## Case Studies

This book is structured as four case studies. In one respect, the format of the case study allows me to write about different approaches that performance can take to interrupt straight time in varying theatrical genres and styles and in disparate geographical and cultural contexts. As a narrative form that Freud is credited as inventing, the case-study approach is particularly salient to this study about how we conceive of time and narrate history. As Carolyn Steedman explains,

> The written case-study allows the writer to enter the present into the past, allows the dream, the wish or fantasy of the past to shape current time, and treats them as evidence in their own right. In this way, the narrative form of case-study shows what went into its writing, shows the bits and pieces from which it is made up, in the way that history refuses to do, and that fiction can't. Case study presents the ebb and flow of memory, the structure of dreams, the stories that people tell to explain themselves to others.[93]

I choose the genre of the case study to structure my analysis because, like the creative work I discuss, it refuses a linear and hierarchical understanding of time.

In chapter 1, "No Rock Straight Time Rain or Shine: Carlson/Strom Remember the Geyserlands," I examine *Geyser Land* (2003), a site-specific performance installation that was conceived and directed by Mary Ellen Strom in collaboration with Ann Carlson, members of the Crow and Northern Cheyenne Nations, and the local community. As audience members are carried by railcar between Livingston and Bozeman, Montana, out of the car's windows audiences see staged reenactments of historic photographs in the tradition of *tableau vivant* (living picture) and video projections sited in the natural landscape.[94] These *tableaux* and video projections presence the ghosts of U.S. settler colonialism, including the First Nations people who have been killed and/or displaced through Western "progress" and "development" of the land. *Geyser Land*, that is, reveals the culturally constructed nature of the master narrative that frames the colonization of the "Western frontier" as benign progress, while erasing the multiple local traumas that such a narrative eclipses. A memory project, *Geyser Land* slips between the "resolved" present and the traumatic past, offering spectators the cultural literacy to reimagine the history of the land, its colonizers, and its indigenous inhabitants. Reading documentation of the performance—including production photographs, documentary videos, exhibition catalogues, performance reviews, and the artists' expansive project website—against nineteenth-century photographic and cinematic representations of the local landscape, I examine how *Geyser Land* remembers the wound that is the West, while remaining attentive to how I remember *Geyser Land* through my analysis of these fragmented and partial performance remains.

Chapter 2, "When Elephants Are in Must: Peggy Shaw, Acts of Trans/fer, and the Present Future of Queer," examines Shaw's solo performance *Must: The Inside Story*, which she cocreated with London's Clod Ensemble (dir. Suzy Willson) and performed in Amherst, Massachusetts, in 2011, three months after Shaw nearly died from a stroke. Already a performance about mourning and loss, aging and dying, I argue that this particular production of *Must* is infused with the exigencies of the present—Shaw "must" perform *Must* in order to pass her butch legacy on to young queer and trans folk in the audience. Through a close reading of the text, the live performance, and current trends in the transgender movement, I argue that Shaw "rebecomes"[95] the butch-elder, or "trans/cestor," that many of the young genderqueers and trans men in her audience never had. Through speech acts and embodied acts of trans/fer—what Elizabeth Freeman has called "corporealized historiography"—Shaw, I argue, transmits lesbian epistemologies to a trans generation acutely in need of them. The act of witnessing her at once living and dying, I argue, is an occasion to remember her and the lesbian feminist history that she represents—binding the present "past" to the present "future" of queer through the live act of trans/ference.

In chapter 3, "Following the Ghosts: Repetition, Return, and the Disordering of America in *floodlines* (2004–2010)," I examine a multisite-specific performance installation I conceived in the aftermath of September 11, 2001, and staged in Austin once a year for seven consecutive years. In this chapter, I investigate the ways that *floodlines* uses the theatrical element of repetition to slip spectators between present, past, and future time, and between idealized and traumatized portraits of American citizenship. My notion of repetition is informed by Judith Butler's foundational essay "Performative Acts and Gender Constitution,"[96] in which Butler argues that gender is a stylized repetition of acts that only appear stable because they have been rehearsed and consolidated over time. In my analysis of *floodlines*, I widen the scope of Butler's focus on the "performative accomplishment" of gender to include a range of performative acts, including also race, religion, sexuality, class, and national belonging. If repetition is the strategy through which whiteness, heterosexuality, and other unmarked markers of normativity get reiterated over time, what kinds of social transformations become possible through "the breaking or subversive repetition" of those American "styles"?[97] Looking at production photographs, performance reviews, private archival materials, and the "psychoanalytic archive" of my memory,[98] I offer a close reading of the politics of repetition within each production of *floodlines* as well as the effects of reperforming *floodlines* over the span of seven years.[99]

Chapter 4, "Teaching Time (a *periplum*)," functions as the book's very slow fade-out to black, asking how one teaches queer time, and what the politics of pedagogy has to offer the larger discussion of trauma, temporality, and repair. To this end, I offer a thick description of a series of events and performances that took place in and around two courses I was teaching at a small liberal arts college in the 2011–2012 academic year, and I read these events against the backdrop of the Occupy Wall Street movement that was concurrently unfolding at that historical moment. Here I am interested in how the structural violence that unfolded on campus was animated by white settler desires and claims to land, and I examine how these desires and claims worked in concert with institutionalized homophobia, transphobia, and misogyny. Finally, I turn to examine a site-specific performance that two of my students, Zemora Tevah and Mateo Guadalupe, created in the wake of this violence, and I argue that it worked to "claim" injury and enact repair—without, that is, reproducing the settler logic that "reclamation" might imply. Building on Muñoz's idea of "cruising utopia," which formed the basis of the students' performance about which I write, I offer the rubric of "cruising home" as a closing gesture for describing a mode of decolonial queer politics that can emerge out of performative acts of resistance to dominant culture. By "cruising" (rather than reclaiming) home, non-Native queer and transgender artists and activists in the occupied Americas are able to dream of better futures while remembering that the foundation of this country is not natural and its future not guaranteed.[100]

The book's epilogue, "I Want to Play Airplane, or, It All Comes Back," takes us full-circle back to where this journey began: 9/11 in New York City. I write about seeing the closing production of Lisa Kron and Jeanine Tesori's hit lesbian musical, *Fun Home,* on Broadway on the eve of the fifteen-year memorial of September 11. As a closing metaphor, I argue that *Fun Home* proposes that it's possible to "fly high," to see all of space and all of time—to be, in the words of the play's protagonist, Alison, "like Superman."

In summary, this book is an investigation of the various ways in which performance can resist and transform normative concepts of time and history as linear, teleological, and progress-oriented. Instead, past and present are given permission to touch, the future can reside in the present, history can repeat with a difference, and all of time can come undone. I set this project against the backdrop of contemporary American life: a post-9/11 "homeland" security state in which such disruptions are particularly vital.

## Chapter 1

# No Rock Straight Time Rain or Shine

## Carlson/Strom Remember the Geyserlands

We mark time by events, not by the clock. We mark time by events, not by the clock. We mark time by events, not by the clock.

—Ann Carlson

Men wanted for track work cinder ballast no rock straight time rain or shine paid weekly accommodation very good. Board furnished $5 per week. It is a good job particularly for veteran gandy dancers. It's a few miles out and requires no weeks till to gets back to this borg [*sic*].

—*The Outlook*, May 1918

Actually, quite apart from anything written by Derrida, or anything reflected on by his critics, Archive Fever comes on at night, long after the archive has shut down for the day. Typically, the fever—more accurately, the precursor fever—starts in the early hours of the morning, in the bed of a cheap hotel, where the historian cannot get to sleep. You cannot get to sleep because you lie so narrowly, in an attempt to avoid contact with anything that isn't shielded by sheets and pillowcase. The first sign, then, is an excessive attention to the bed, an irresistible anxiety about the hundreds who have slept there before you, leaving their dust and debris in the fibres of the blankets, greasing the surface of the heavy, slippery counterpane. . . . This symptom—worrying about the bed—is a screen anxiety. What keeps you awake . . . is actually the archive, and its myriads of the dead, who all day long, have pressed their concerns upon you. You think: these people have left me the lot. . . . You think: I could get to hate these people;

> and then: I can never do these people justice; and finally: I shall never *get it done*.
>
> —Carolyn Steedman, *Dust: The Archive and Cultural History*

*May 17, 2009. Four a.m. I am wide awake in my bed at the Boston Youth Hostel. I've spent the past three days driving from Providence, Rhode Island, to Amherst, Massachusetts, from Amherst to Lincoln, from Lincoln to Boston—to see an exhibit of Carlson/Strom's "New Performance Video" at the DeCordova Sculpture Park and Museum in rural Lincoln, Massachusetts. I have been in unfamiliar airports and archives, museums and diners, homes and highways. (One day I drove the same route twice—the GPS in my rental car sent me three hours down the Mass Pike and three hours back again to the Enterprise lot where I had started my journey—a six-hour-long technical, temporal glitch.) I lay in the bottom bunk, listening to the coughing, the sneezing, the wheezing, the communicable diseases taking flight from the body of the European traveler on the bunk above. I have anxiety—because I need to sleep, because I have to get up in two hours to catch my flight back to Austin, because I am too old to be sleeping in a youth hostel with paper sheets. I toss. I turn. I try to sleep. I can't. I worry. I wake. I won't read Carolyn Steedman for another year, so I don't know this is all a "screen anxiety"—no, not yet. I think it has to do with shared linens, and bathrooms, and noises. Not fears of archives, of dead things, of this burden of remembering, of doing people justice, of writing things down.*

I am the feverish archivist that Steedman invokes, attempting to remember a performance that I did not see. As Steedman notes, the scholar is feverish because she is afraid of dead things—afraid, that is, of *not* doing people justice, *not* remembering properly, *not* getting it done. As I argued in the introduction to this book, the search for origins, evidence, and truth is an impossible task because histories have holes: much like the archives and memories that attempt to contain them, they are fragmented, nonlinear, and ever-changing.

A time slip, however, can function as an antidote to archive fever, acknowledging at once this pull of history, this imperative to "get back," this fear of dead things and this burden of remembering, while simultaneously disrupting the linearity and telos of time.[1] As I outlined in the introduction, time slips are moments in live performance in which normative conceptions of linear, progress-oriented time fail or fall away, and the spectator is transported into the future or past, while simultaneously remaining anchored to the present of performance. In slipping through the cracks of time, the spectator is returned to, or turned through, a moment, or hole, in history that is in need of attention and/or repair. In this chapter, I will look at the wound that is the American West, which, as I will detail, has been produced through strategic acts of U.S. American conquest and indigenous dispossession that are inextricably bound up with the histories of modernity and technology in the United States, including electrification, photography, cinema, and train travel. I examine the ways in which the performance installation, *Geyser Land*, literally transported its audiences (by train) to the belly of the beast, using the conventions of site-specific dance and video to make the interconnected violence of technology and settler colonization visible and also imaginable "otherwise."

*Geyser Land*, the performance that forms the case study of this chapter, was conceived and directed by video/conceptual artist Mary Ellen Strom, in collaboration with choreographer/performance artist Ann Carlson, members of the Crow and Northern Cheyenne Nations, and the local community. The project is framed by Strom's lifelong research and scholarship on the histories of colonialism in the Rocky Mountain West; U.S. geological surveys; and modern technology, including photography, film, and train travel—that are the subjects of this performance as well as my analysis of it. The project is also informed by Carlson's career as a postmodern dancer and choreographer, in which she and her collaborators have been blurring the distinction between performance and "real life" for decades.[2]

*Geyser Land* was performed on a remote stretch of land in rural Montana in 2003, three months prior to my meeting the artists and learning of the work. The project's title refers to the geographic area in which the performance was staged, known as the "geyserlands," which are so called because they have the most geysers, or geologic explosions, in the world. *Geyser Land* audience members were carried by train-car along a twenty-five-mile stretch of land between Livingston and Bozeman, Montana. Out of the train's windows, audiences saw theatrical reenactments of late nineteenth- and early twentieth-century historic photographs staged *in situ* (on site), on or near the original site of the photograph in the style of tableau vivant, and video projections of cinema of that era and region. *Geyser Land* literally slipped historic photographs and cinema into the contemporary landscape and, in so doing, produced a time-space collision that asked spectators to rethink the dominant, benign, "progress" narrative of nineteenth-century U.S. "development" of this land. By restaging historic photographs and moving images in situ, but *ex tempus* (out of time), the *Geyser Land* project exposed the ways in which this land—two hundred years after the beginning of the U.S. colonial expansion project westward—is still haunted by multiple, ongoing, and ostensibly past traumas, including the disappeared disappearance of First Nations people, animals, and rights to self-governance. As the project makes clear, one defining characteristic of Native American genocide is not only the strategic appropriation of indigenous land and the rape, murder, and dispossession of Native people and ways of life, but also the equally strategic disappearance of *evidence* that such acts of violence took and are taking place. By restaging historic photographs and moving images of the colonial period in the contemporary Montana landscape, *Geyser Land* re-members the geyserlands—and reminds spectators that time slips, haunts, and sticks to the very surfaces of things.

## No Rock Straight Time Rain or Shine

I opened this chapter with three disparate epigraphs, including an advertisement for "gandy dancers" that I found in the course of my research—an ad that ran in New York's *Outlook* newspaper in 1918. "Gandy Dancers," the title of a *Geyser Land* tableau vivant that I discuss later in this chapter, are also the common name for railroad section crews—composed mostly of African Americans, and also Chinese, Mexican, Irish, Italian, and Native Americans—who built and maintained the new intercontinental railroads beginning in the 1830s, under the supervision of white-owned and -operated businesses such as the National Pacific Railroad. The railroad expansion project in the United States displaced thousands of First Nations people from their land, forcibly removing them onto reservations established by the U.S. government to make way for capitalist "development," including the colonial project that would become Yellowstone National Park.

The primary task of section crews was "straightening sections of track that had been pounded out by the tremendous weight of passing trains."[3] In this 1918 ad, then, "straight time" refers to the fact that the job's hours and wage are predetermined and fixed; as such, the advertisement signals the ways in which a "good job" in the American social imaginary is framed as the straight time of wage labor—the signature invention of capitalism. Additionally, that this good job consists primarily of "straightening" railroads underscores my claim that straight time, like straight tracks, is produced through repetition and requires ongoing and often invisibilized labor to maintain its status as natural.[4] Here it is important to note, too, that the history of the railroad itself is bound up with the colonial history of time. The inception of train travel is what necessitated the creation in 1840 of what we now call "standard time," in order to standardize arrival and departure times between disparate cities. In other words, straight time is not only clock time and the time of capital but also train time, as the standardization and normativization of time is, from its inception, linked to trains, travel, and commerce.[5] In the analysis that follows, I examine how the *Geyser Land* project at once uses and subverts the technology and logic of trains and travel, while supplanting white and straight time with queer and indigenous temporalities.

The Livingston Depot, established in 1890 by the National Pacific Railroad to facilitate tourist traffic to the newly established Yellowstone National Park (1872), is the first site of this performance and a telling beginning. Here audience members buy forty-dollar tickets and board a sleek, dome-car passenger train to Bozeman, an hour-long trip that will take them through twenty-five miles of grassy plains, rolling hills, and mountainous rock, and in

*Three Women and a Porter at Livingston Depot* (ca. 1902). Photographer unknown. Courtesy of Bob Ebinger and Livingston Depot Foundation.

proximity with various live vignettes and video projections embedded in the passing landscape. While they wait for the journey to begin, audiences are free to roam about, encountering several staged performances.[6]

In the first of many tableaux vivants, choreographed by Carlson, spectators encounter a live reenactment of a 1902 photograph taken at the Livingston Depot, *Three Women and a Porter*. In the original photo—which audiences can see in their playbill—a uniformed African American baggage porter approaches three bourgeois white women who prepare to travel by train. In "Porter," the *Geyser Land* reenactment of the 1902 photograph, actors Wayne Mansaw, Ann Johnson, Megan Schneeberger, and Krista Topham-Petty stand in likeness. "The performers must be still as statues," Carlson explains to the *New York Times*, which previewed the performance in their Art/Architecture section in August 2003.[7] In inimitable style, Carlson directs the performers to "pitch their still around the world until it comes back to them." In order to heighten the verisimilitude between the archival photograph and the tableau vivant, the performers are costumed in photographic-like grayscale. The performers hold their tableau until audiences board the train.

In order to fully understand the significance of this tableau, it is necessary to situate it alongside a series of historically related events, including the construction of the transatlantic railroad and the establishment of Yellowstone

"Porter" (2003). Mary Ellen Strom. From *Geyser Land*, created by Mary Ellen Strom in collaboration with Ann Carlson. Tableau vivant conceived and choreographed by Ann Carlson, performed by Wayne Mansaw, Ann Johnson, Megan Schneeberger, and Krista Topham-Petty. Courtesy of Mary Ellen Strom and Ann Carlson.

National Park. This photograph, estimated to be taken in 1902, comes only twelve years after the 1890 completion of Livingston Depot as the gateway to Yellowstone Park. Established by the U.S. Congress and signed into law by President Ulysses S. Grant on March 1, 1872, the creation of Yellowstone was part of a larger, rapidly accelerating movement of white male-dominated explorations and violent conquests of those parts of the western United States that were considered "virgin land." In *Narratives and Spaces: Technology and the Construction of American Culture*, historian David E. Nye explains how this colonial project was enabled by technological advancements that include the railroad as well as photography, electrification, and other machines and inventions. According to Nye,

> The American West was long perceived as "virgin land," an empty region waiting to be appropriated. This peculiar sense of space is legible in the boundaries of the western states. Mountainous Wyoming and Colorado are virtually square; their boundaries have nothing to do with local topography and everything to with geometry and the compass.[8]

Here Nye cites geometry and the compass as the explanation for the illogical boundaries around "Wyoming" and "Colorado" in order to illustrate the ways in which landscapes are more than places. Landscapes are actions with political consequences: "[T]he word 'landscape' is also a verb, referring to the active process of changing the appearance of the world."[9] One technology that changed the appearance of this part of the world was the advent of photography in 1839, and its proliferation in the century that followed, including countless missions funded by the United States government and private companies to document the "unspoiled" frontier of the western states in order to justify its appropriation and development for tourism.[10] This industry directly caused the extermination and displacement of thousands of First Nations people, including the Crow, who were banned from their land in order for the U.S. government to establish Yellowstone Park in 1878, and not allowed to return until the Civil Rights Act of 1964.

The presence of the female tourists at the Livingston Depot in the original photograph as well as in its reenactment signals this larger story of conquest in the name of tourism and leisure, and specifically how white women played central roles in the conquest of Native land and people. As Americanist Amy Kaplan argues, nineteenth-century national discourses of "manifest destiny" are intricately connected to contemporaneous gendered discourses of "home" and "homemaker," and white women were seen to play a central role in the "domestication" of Native subjects as well as the rendering of settler as "native," and Native as "foreign." Writing about Catherine Beecher's *Treatise on Domestic Economy* (1841), Kaplan explains:

> Beecher's use of Tocqueville's ark metaphor suggests the rootlessness and the self-enclosed mobility necessary for the efficacy of middle-class domesticity to redefine the meaning of habitation, to make Euro-Americans feel at home in a place where *they* are initially the foreign ones. Domesticity inverts this relationship to create a home by rendering prior inhabitants alien and undomesticated and by implicitly nativizing newcomers. The empire of the mother thus embodies the anarchy at the heart of the American empire.[11]

In other words, the figure of the female tourist—one with the economic mobility to travel by train—is far from a benign image. Rather, the white, middle-class female traveler is, as Kaplan notes, at the "heart" of the logic of empire because of the pivotal roles white women played in the alienation and "domestication" of Native land and people. Because the *Geyser Land* audience is free to move around while the performers in the tableau vivant are literally frozen in time and space, *Geyser Land* casts the contemporary spectator in the role of tourist, gazing not at some sublime natural wonder like a mountain or vista but at this ostensibly ordinary past moment. In fact, many of the *Geyser Land* audiences are literally tourists, art aficionados who traveled from New York or California to see the work, or vacationing families en route to Yellowstone who learned of this unusual art event that was taking

*Park Visitors at Yellowstone National Park* (ca. 1974). Photographer unknown. John Whitman in U.S. Army blue cavalry uniform, Winchester rifle on shoulder at left, Susan Sindt in period costume (early female tourist) at center, visitors at right. Courtesy of Yellowstone National Park.

place during their leisurely "time off" from work. The grayscale costumes not only link the tableau to its photographic referent, they further highlight the temporal gap between spectator and spectacle: still versus moving, grayscale versus color. In this sense, the 2003 spectator slips and dips into the "past" narrative of this troubling social history—recast alongside the 1902 tourists caught in complicity.

The role of tourists and travelers in the colonial project is made equally evident in the next tableau vivant, "Park Visitors," which audiences also encounter at Livingston Depot. "Park Visitors" mixes three different temporalities. In the original photograph taken at Yellowstone Park in 1974, two living history guides enact an imaginary nineteenth-century scene: a uniformed solider guards the park and a civilian female tourist observes the watchman—while a group of 1974 park visitors look on. In the *Geyser Land* reenactment (see "Park Visitors," p. 49), actor Rob Story plays the role of the 1970s living history performer pretending to be a nineteenth-century U.S. soldier guarding Yellowstone Park, Holly Seitz plays the role of the nineteenth-century tourist, and Bill Koch performs as the 1970s tourists watching the living history scene. While all of the performers in *Geyser*

"Park Visitors" (2003). Mary Ellen Strom. From *Geyser Land*, created by Mary Ellen Strom in collaboration with Ann Carlson. Tableau vivant conceived and choreographed by Ann Carlson, performed by Rob Story, Holly Seitz, and Bill Koch. Courtesy of Mary Ellen Strom and Ann Carlson.

*Land*'s reenactment are costumed in grayscale, the specifics of their costumes signal the two distinct time periods that the tableau aims to represent: the soldier wears a nineteenth-century uniform replete with waist belt, rank badge, cap, and rifle; the nineteenth-century tourist wears a polka-dotted period skirt, billowing blouse, and bonnet; and the 1974 tourist wears a T-shirt and trousers, his haircut and glasses in recognizable 1970s style. If the original scene positions the 1974 tourists as contemporary and the nineteenth-century reenactment at which they gaze as past, historical time, the 2003 tableau vivant recasts the 1974 tourists as historical figures—themselves frozen in a moment of the park's history like the cavalry soldier one hundred years prior. The new present, then, is taken up by the contemporary 2003 *Geyser Land* "spect-tourist" who gazes upon them all.[12]

It is worth noting that while this tableau vivant reenacts the archival photograph, it also revises it by omitting four spectators seen in the original. While the artists' decision to revise the live image was practical, it exposes nonetheless the ways in which archives, and the histories they claim to represent, are always already partial, mediated, and malleable, serving the interests of the present as much as revealing some "truth" about past time.[13]

## Queer/Indigenous Time

Like the tableaux vivants situated at the Livingston Depot, several animated scenes also presence the Crow and Northern Cheyenne who were displaced from the site—first at the depot, and later on the train itself. While audiences wait for the railcar to take them on their performance journey, members of the Crow Nation, wearing ceremonial regalia, perform a ritual dance on the depot green. Additionally, the music group Itta'Tbachiash (Fights Alone/Crow) sing and drum in the club car; Heywood Big Day (Crow) and Bently Spang (Northern Cheyenne)—the performance artist with whom Carlson/Strom would later create *Meadowlark*—tell autobiographical stories and interact with audience members aboard the train. In including these scenes at the start of the show, *Geyser Land* draws attention to the Crow and Northern Cheyenne as the original caretakers and inhabitants of the geyserlands. In contrast to capitalist notions of land ownership, the indigenous understanding of the relationship between humans and the land is one of stewardship. According to Native studies scholar Andrea Smith (Cherokee), "Our sovereignty is based on a connection to the Earth. It is a completely different understanding of land. Land is not ownable. [We have] a relationship with and responsibility for the land. Humans are dependent on the earth, not vice versa. [When First Nations people speak of land rights], we are fighting for the right to be *responsible* for the land."[14] In staging these scenes as animated and in color rather than still and in grayscale, *Geyser Land* also highlights not just historical but contemporary Crow and Northern Cheyenne sovereignty struggles and claims to place. This counteracts the dominant tendency to figure indigenous people as a thing of the past, a mythology that elides the fact that, despite repeated attempts by the U.S. government to annihilate them, thousands of First Nations people have survived the ongoing colonization of the United States and continue to live on their land. In other words, the presence of Crow and Northern Cheyenne performers in *Geyser Land* also subverts the temporal logic of genocide, which depends on the constant production of a narrative of Native absence. As Smith argues,

> This logic holds that indigenous peoples must disappear. In fact, they must *always* be disappearing, in order to allow non-indigenous peoples rightful claim over this land. Through this logic of genocide, non-Native peoples then become the rightful inheritors of all that was indigenous—land, resources, indigenous spirituality, or culture.[15]

This logic of genocide is also palpable in a movement sequence on the passenger train. When audiences board the train for Bozeman, it is not empty but already occupied by a teenage boy, actor Judah Goes Ahead (Crow). Once audiences board the train cars, Judah Goes Ahead begins moving in stylized ways: in slow motion, he stands up; he freezes; he sits down; he freezes; he stands up again; he gestures with his hands; he repeats the sequence. His gaze is forward and direct; his tempo is metered; his movement is precise. This, of course, stands in juxtaposition to the (mostly white) passengers seated around him, who move in quotidian ways. This difference draws the audience members' attention to Judah Goes Ahead as a performer rather than a fellow spectator. In occupying the train in advance of the audience, Judah Goes Ahead also asserts his Native and sovereign status in time and space, and this framing device invites audience members to reimagine local land "development" as a story of Native displacement and to see themselves as white settler-tourists.

Carlson later explains that she felt that this movement sequence was confusing for audience members. In part, this is because they were not offered a clear framework for understanding this early scene as performance. With the other tableaux, audience members are able to see reproductions of the "original" archival photograph in their printed program against which they are able to compare the staged reenactment. In the sequence with Judah Goes Ahead, however, there is no photographic referent and, for many, arguably no referent at all. That is, the performance betrays the larger aesthetic conventions that frame dance with such recognizable features as concert stage; separation between dancer and spectator; continuous movement; music; and a clear beginning, middle, and ending. In the video documentation of the performance, for instance, we see a white teenage boy in a polo shirt—he is about the same age as Judah Goes Ahead and seated behind the actor. This boy turns around repeatedly and confusedly to watch Judah Goes Ahead: with neither historical referent nor postmodern dance literacy, he, like many other audience members, is confused by the performer's actions, unsure of how to "read" this moment.

While the artists might argue that this performance was less successful than the others because it was confusing, I would like to suggest that part of its efficacy lies in its ability to unsettle conventional understandings of performance as well as local history. At the start of the show, *Geyser Land* disrupts the aesthetic conventions of dance with the opening tableaux "Porter" and "Park Visitors" at Livingston Deport—suggesting that dance can be outdoors, ordinary, still, and durational. Then *Geyser Land* disrupts its own convention with this indoor, stylized, and animated movement sequence. In other words, *Geyser Land* is not only playing with audience members' cultural literacies of colonialism but also their various aesthetic literacies of the temporal and spatial conventions of dance. And because the multiple referents in Judah Goes Ahead's dance—political and aesthetic—are not self-evident, the scene challenges audience members to go searching for them ("Is this performance?" "What is this performance citing?") and become active collaborators in the production of cultural meaning.

*Yosemite Valley, Rock at Glacier Point* (ca. 1880). Photographer unknown. View of a photographer on Overhanging Rock on Glacier Point overlooking Yosemite Valley and Liberty Cap rock formation, Yosemite National Park, California. Courtesy of Colorado Historical Society.

Here it is important to note the disjuncture between white and indigenous understandings of time—a point of tension to which this performance on the train also gestures. As I outlined in the introduction, dominant Western understandings of time are intimately tied to the history of capitalism and the Western logics of accumulation and progress. The clock, the calendar, and the hourly wage are not natural but biopolitical systems of measurement and regulation that are used to keep individuals and populations in order and "on track." In a U.S. American context, straight time has worked as an instrument of settler colonization, literally displacing indigenous, somatic, and cyclical ways of being in time and on the land. In one of the greatest tautological moves of empire, colonial time not only replaces indigenous time as "standard," but then, not unlike Kaplan's logic of "manifest domesticity," situates itself as natural and native and casts indigenous time—and the people living in indigenous temporalities—as foreign and aberrant. Thus, when the actor Judah Goes Ahead performs his slow dance on the train as white spect-tourists look on, their confusion is also emblematic of this disjuncture between colonial and Crow, straight and queer, ways of moving in and through time.

"William Henry Jackson" (2003). Mary Ellen Strom. From *Geyser Land*, created by Mary Ellen Strom in collaboration with Ann Carlson. Tableau vivant conceived and choreographed by Ann Carlson, performed by Keith Venema, Robert Kollzar, and Justin Lubke. Courtesy of Mary Ellen Strom and Ann Carlson.

## Photography and Film and/as "Percepticide"

As the train travels to Bozeman, *Geyser Land* returns to the convention of the tableau vivant set up at the start of the performance. Here *Geyser Land* plays with the conventions of photography—stillness, grayscale, and so on—in staging the live reenactment "William Henry Jackson." This scene is unique in that it also overtly reveals the production of photographic knowledge by restaging photographer William Henry Jackson in the process of taking a photograph of the local landscape.

A close look at Jackson's career trajectory reveals the larger narrative of the role that photography played in the transformation of the landscape—and the hidden racial history of such a transformation. In 1866, at the age of twenty-three, Jackson left New England for the "West," traveling via the newly constructed Union Pacific Railroad to Omaha, Nebraska, which at the time was the end of the line. In Omaha, he started a photography business with his brother, during which time he took those portraits of First Nations people for which he would become renowned (see *Crow Northern Plains*

*Crow Northern Plains Packs The Bear and Squaw* (date unknown). William Henry Jackson. Subjects unknown. Courtesy of L. Tom Perry Special Collections, Harold B. Lee Library, Brigham Young University, Provo, Utah.

*Packs The Bear and Squaw*, p. 54). In this sense, Jackson's gaze, even before it turned to the landscape, was colonial—using the apparatus of photography to exhibit and sensationalize humans as "objects of ethnography."[16] Jackson's photographs were displayed at the storefront he co-owned with his brother in downtown Omaha, "Jackson Br.'s Photographers," as well as published for distribution. Today his work is celebrated in official national archives, including the Library of Congress, the Smithsonian, and various university collections that gather and display photographs and other relics of indigenous life for scholarly and tourist consumption.

Photographs such as *Crow Northern Plains Packs The Bear and Squaw* expose Jackson's ethnographic gaze—what Dwight Conquergood, writing about performance ethnography, labels a "curator's exhibitionism," which he defines as a "fascination with the exotic, primitive, culturally remote . . . suffused with sentimentality and romantic notions of the 'Noble Savage.' . . . Instead of bringing us into genuine contact (and risk) with the lives of strangers, performances in this mode bring back museum exhibits, mute and staring."[17] Jackson's photographs, like Conquergood's unethical ethnographer, render his subjects silent and staring, dehumanizing racialized others by appearing to bring them close, but only ever succeeding at placing them

*Crow, Black Lodge Camp, Crow Agency, Montana* (date unknown). William Henry Jackson. Subjects unknown. Courtesy of L. Tom Perry Special Collections, Harold B. Lee Library, Brigham Young University, Provo, Utah.

at a greater distance. When Jackson zooms out to include a fascination for the landscape as well as its people, he fails again, rendering his subjects not only voiceless but unrecognizable specs amid their horses, tepees, and horizon lines (see *Crow, Black Lodge Camp, Crow Agency, Montana*, p. 55)

In 1869, Jackson was hired by the Union Pacific Railroad to photograph the scenery along its routes for publicity and promotional purposes, and he was also a member of the U.S.-funded Hayden Geological Survey Team, which exhaustively photographed the local landscape on a series of "expeditions" beginning in 1869. Here Jackson's new project asked him to capture the land itself: wild, untouched, absent of inhabitants. These photographs were presented by Jackson and Ferdinand Hayden alongside representatives from the National Pacific Railroad and used as evidence before Congress—for the establishment of Yellowstone Park as a tourist destination.

If Jackson's close-up photographs of the Crow and other indigenous people cast his subjects as exotic, and his photographs of them on the land make them unintelligible, these wide zoom shots render them invisible altogether (see *Lower Falls of Yellowstone from Artist's Point*, p. 56). As such, the act of Jackson constructing the landscape as "untouched wilderness" with his medium of photography both anticipates as well as facilitates the destruction of it as indigenous land and the reconstruction of it as "free" and "virgin" land for the growing tourist industry.

*Lower Falls of Yellowstone from Artist's Point* (ca. 1902). William Henry Jackson. Courtesy of L. Tom Perry Special Collections, Harold B. Lee Library, Brigham Young University, Provo, Utah.

By representing Jackson as a character in *Geyser Land*, the project points to the tautological nature of the argument that his and other photography made in support of the railroad expansion project and the establishment of Yellowstone National Park in the late nineteenth century. Like a subject in one of his photographs, the tableau freezes and silences Jackson in time and space, inviting audiences to return the gaze and asking them to imagine the ways in which his medium was used as a form of "percepticide"—which Diana Taylor defines as "social blinding [that] kill[s] or numb[s] through the senses."[18] Because Jackson is sited in the very landscape he photographs, audiences are asked to simultaneously look at the land itself and the act of constructing that land.

*Geyser Land* intermixes live tableaux with video projections sited in the passing landscape, created by Strom. These include "Buffalo Running," video footage of packs of running buffalo, and "Muybridge," adapted from Eadweard Muybridge's stop-motion photographic studies of galloping horses. Both are projected in bright white light from the passenger car onto the mountainside, visible to audience members out the train cars' windows (see "Buffalo Running" and "Muybridge," p. 58). Additionally, westerns of the era—such as Edwin Porter's *The Great Train Robbery* (1903), about Butch Cassidy, and George Sherman's *Frontier Horizon* (1939), starring John

"Jackson Creek Barn" (2003). Mary Ellen Strom. From *Geyser Land*, created by Mary Ellen Strom in collaboration with Ann Carlson. Video projection created by Mary Ellen Strom. Courtesy of Mary Ellen Strom and Ann Carlson.

Wayne—are projected onto the side of a barn and stationary refrigerator truck, respectively (see "Jackson Creek Barn," p. 57). Porter's *Great Train Robbery* is paired with the Lumière brothers' *Arrival of the Train* (1895), touted as the first documentary film, projected onto an adjacent truck. These projections draw spectators' attention to the uncanny parallel between the colonial project and the concomitant rise in technologies such as photography, film, and train travel; the ways such technology is and has been used to construct "truth" and inform and misinform people about local and national history; and the convenient mythologies embedded in the histories of those technologies themselves.

According to Strom, the projections are meant to function as a kind of site-specific "ghosting." In "Buffalo Running," for instance, *Geyser Land* "ghosts the buffalo" that the U.S. Army systematically slaughtered between 1872 and 1893.[19] In the late nineteenth century, the U.S. government encouraged the decimation of nearly 15 million buffalo as a way to diminish the Crow and Northern Cheyenne populations, which subsided on the buffalo for food, clothing, and other necessities. As a result, only a single herd grazes the Bozeman Pass. "Buffalo Running" marks this absence by making it a ghostly presence. "Muybridge" similarly ghosts the animal, but to very different ends. Here spectators see projected animations that Strom has adapted from Muybridge's iconic animal motion studies, for which the English photographer used a series of stop-motion photography techniques to settle a

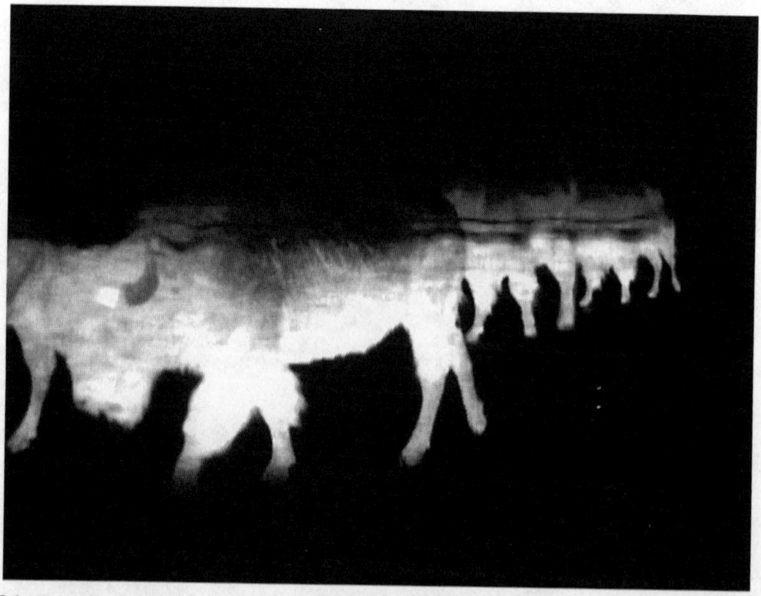

"Buffalo Running" (2003). Mary Ellen Strom. From *Geyser Land*, created by Mary Ellen Strom in collaboration with Ann Carlson. Video projection created by Mary Ellen Strom. Courtesy of Mary Ellen Strom and Ann Carlson.

"Muybridge" (2003). Mary Ellen Strom. From *Geyser Land*, created by Mary Ellen Strom in collaboration with Ann Carlson. Video projection created by Mary Ellen Strom, adapted from Eadweard Muybridge's stop-motion photography study "The Horse in Motion" (1877). Courtesy of Mary Ellen Strom and Ann Carlson.

debate as to whether all four of a horse's legs are ever airborne at the same time during a gallop. Not only did Muybridge's study prove the debate in the affirmative, but in employing a new machine called a Zoopractiscope, which successfully captured a horse in fast motion, Muybridge invented the intermediate technology on the path to documentary cinematography.

In the context of *Geyser Land*, calling forth this early history of cinematography sets the stage for audiences to begin to see the history of film—like that of photography—as a technology that is used by humans to construct arguments about the natural world (e.g., a horse "in fact" takes flight).[20] Put differently, film—particularly documentary film—easily masks its own construction and point of view, presenting the screen as truth itself, rather than constructed representations of reality from ideologically driven points of view. In citing the galloping debate that Muybridge's study sought to settle, "Muybridge" reminds spectators of film's polemic origins.

To further highlight the constructed nature of cinematography, as well as this performance itself, the *Geyser Land* project literally exposes the mechanics of production. In one car of the eight-car train that Carlson/Strom rent for the performance, the artists mount two four-hundred-pound digital projectors to custom-built turntables, which are visibly operated by *Geyser Land* crew members during the performance. Simultaneous to seeing the projected animations in the landscape, audience members see the human engineering that makes these animations possible.

Evident here is the artists' commitment to exposing artifice, to revealing the theatrical illusion and the related illusion of historical truth. Because the cinematographic illusion, the production crew, and the spectators are placed side by side, and because, as critic Catherine Lord observes, "everything and everyone [is] piled on that train: historical photographs incarnated in *tableau vivant*, projections of buffalo stampeding off a cliff, a butoh hiker inching down the aisles, Crow drummers, leathery ranchers playing poker, Ann's cranky mother, various curators, local bed and breakfast owners, stray philanthropists and uniformed ticket inspectors,"[21] alongside hundreds of audience members and dozens of crew, all without barriers between them—*Geyser Land* creates a situation in which dialogue about performance slips inside the theatrical frame, unfolding concomitantly with the performance event itself.

In the final moments of the performance journey, *Geyser Land* connects the founding myths of nation to the founding myths of film. As the train pulls into Bozeman Depot, audience members see the following triptych: the tableau vivant "Pax the Hat," framed by two films—the Lumière brothers' *Arrival of the Train* and Edwin Porter's *The Great Train Robbery*—projected onto adjacent refrigerator trucks.

Both films belong to the canon of turn-of-the-century train-inspired cinema. Like the "Porter" tableau at the start of the performance, the "Lumière Brothers" video installation asks audiences to become conscious of their mode of travel and draw connections between the black-and-white representations

Final shot, *The Great Train Robbery* (1903). Directed by Edwin S. Porter, performed by Justus D. Barnes.

of trains and their current experiences as passengers aboard the sleek Montana Rockies Rail Tour train that had carried them to this point. The films, however, do more than merely denaturalize train travel: they point to the founding myths of cinematography, which conflate film and reality and situate its early spectators as cultural dupes.

In *Arrival*, a fifty-second film depicting a train pulling into a station, the train travels from the top right hand of the frame to the bottom left, growing larger and larger as it seemingly draws closer to the audience. In *The Great Train Robbery*, actor George Barnes points his pistol directly at the camera (see Final shot, *The Great Train Robbery*, p. 60). In both *Arrival of the Train* and *The Great Train Robbery*, the diegetic action is addressed so directly to the camera that, as legend goes, early audiences who watched the films feared for their lives.

While *Arrival* is heralded as the first documentary and *The Great Train Robbery* as the first narrative film, the reception history of both films suggest that early audiences—not yet habituated to the basic convention of either genre as prerecorded—feared for their lives. The train and bullet seemed to literally head their way. In this sense, film historiography situates early audiences as spatially and temporally confused subjects, mistaking distant, prerecorded events as local and live.

In his essay "Lumiere's 'Arrival of the Train': Cinema's Founding Myth," media scholar Martin Loiperdinger evidences the falsity of this founding myth. He shows how the popular legend of the *Arrival* audience's terror over the encroaching train is little more than a convenient story that reifies the power of the medium. He also illustrates the ways in which the film was likely staged rather than documentary footage. Whether or not Loiperdinger's argument is "more true" than popular legend is beside the point. What's important here is Loiperdinger's observation that the dominant narrative of film historiography successfully frames the audience as passive victims. As such, these founding myths of film cast spectators as cultural dupes, deny them their ability to distinguish reality from representation, and absolve them of their shared responsibility in the construction of cultural meaning. That is, *Arrival* and *The Great Train Robbery* do little more than elevate the filmic genre while disempowering its spectators as discerning critics. By contrast, *Geyser Land* empowers its audiences with filmic literacy—creating moments that reveal their own theatrical construction, expose the construction of those cultural scenarios that have explicitly and tacitly shaped spectators' narratives of self and other, and illuminate the entitlement with which the settler subject experiences a false sense of belonging in place.[22]

## The Right to Live(ness)

Sited between these two video installations is the tableau vivant, "Pax the Hat," which links the founding myths of photography-as-truth to those of film—and both to those of nation. In the original photograph, "Chief Pax the Hat" (1920), Pax the Hat is seated beside a white Yellowstone tourist at the entrance to the park. Pax the Hat wears a headdress and ceremonial regalia; the tourist wears a suit and smokes a cigar. A tepee serves as their backdrop. In the reenactment, actors Randolph Big Day (Crow) and Mike Dirkers play the roles of Chief and tourist, respectively.

Read together, the archival photograph and its ghostly double make visible those strategies of cultural appropriation, denigration, and ambivalence at the core of Yellowstone's colonial history. As noted earlier in the chapter, six years after the U.S. government established Yellowstone as a national park, they legally banned all Crow from the land, forcibly removing them to nearby reservations. At the same time, white investors recognized the ways in which part of the "lure of the local" landscape was its reputation as "wild" and "untamed," personified by the figure of the Indian in late nineteenth- and early twentieth-century photography, cinematography, landscape drawings, literature, and folklore.[23] Capitalizing on this social imaginary, Yellowstone National Park employed local, indigenous people to welcome the almost exclusively non-Native tourists as they entered the park. This colonial strategy at once eclipsed the violent disappearance of thousands of indigenous

*Chief Pax the Hat. Yakima Kammit and Crow* (ca. 1920). Courtesy of Yellowstone National Park.

people while representing them as willing cultural ambassadors. In *Playing Indian*, historian Philip Deloria argues that performances of racial impersonation are animated by white ambivalence, which he summarizes as a "dialectic of simultaneous desire and repulsion" toward the Native subject, as well as white American desires to be at once both "wild" and "free," tropes that the Native represented in the dominant social imaginary. In his discussion of British novelist and essayist D. H. Lawrence's *Studies in Classic American Literature*, Deloria explains,

> Throughout the essays, Lawrence frequently turned to "the Indian," intuitively locating native people at the very heart of American ambivalence. Whereas Euro-Americans had imprisoned themselves in the logical mind and the social order, Indians represented instinct and freedom. They spoke for the "spirit of the continent." Whites desperately desired that spirit, yet they invariably failed to become aboriginal and thus "finished." Savage Indians served Americans as oppositional figures against whom one might imagine a civilized national self. Coded as freedom, however, wild Indianness proved equally attractive, setting up a "have-the-cake-and-eat-it-too" dialectic of simultaneous desire and repulsion.[24]

"Pax the Hat" (2003). Mary Ellen Strom. From *Geyser Land*, created by Mary Ellen Strom in collaboration with Ann Carlson. Tableau vivant conceived and choreographed by Ann Carlson, performed by Randolph Big Day (Crow) and Mike Dirkers. Courtesy of Mary Ellen Strom and Ann Carlson.

The redface spectacle of "Chief Pax the Hat" playing the role of happy ambassador to the park takes place around the same historical moment as its blackface counterpart. In his foundational account of blackface minstrelsy in U.S. culture, historian Eric Lott uses the terms "love and theft" to similarly describe this phenomena of concomitant white desire and repulsion, identification and objectification, attraction and ambivalence, at the heart of the logics of racial impersonation. Lott writes, "'Black' figures were there *to be looked at*, shaped to the demands of desire; they were screens on which audience fantasies could rest, securing white spectators' position as superior, controlling, not to say owning, figures."[25] By representing the encounter between "tourist" and "Chief" as history rather than fantasy, the photograph reproduces the nation's foundational myth of thanksgiving while eliding the economic and racial motivations—the "dollars and desire," as Lott puts it—behind such an act. What's more, in figuring the relationship between colonizer and colonized as one of peaceful cultural exchange, the former is using his power over the latter to stage and document a performance that will later slip into the history record as evidence for the official story of early contact as one of equanimity. The Chief is made into a colonized subject—in Homi Bhabha's sense of the term—one who must, as a survival strategy, masquerade under duress as friendly ambassador. The violence of colonial contact is replaced by an illusion of racial harmony, concealing the larger story of white expropriation of and control over the local landscape and its people. By their very ontology, master narratives necessitate the destruction of subaltern experiences of lived history. History, Walter Benjamin reminds us, is written by the victor.[26] History, Roland Barthes adds, is hysterical. "It is constituted only if we consider it, only if we look at it—and in order to look at it, we must be excluded from it."[27] Excluded from the process of representation, the Chief is only ever allowed to live as a dead photographic remnant, a relic, a thing of the past. A dead subject, the Chief's right to self-expression and self-determination is both destroyed and contained by the enforced reservation that is the photographic frame.[28]

In the staged reenactment, actor Randolph Big Day (Crow) performs the role of Pax the Hat. The bold red, white, and blues of Pax the Hat's regalia are not whitewashed by the photographic apparatus. *Geyser Land*'s Chief wears bright colors, while the tourist remains in black-and-white. Nowhere else in *Geyser Land* is this illusion of photographic verisimilitude disrupted. Costumed in color rather than grayscale, Big Day, like Judah Goes Ahead, recharges himself with the right to live(ness) that the colonial history and its photographic record deaden and deny. In wearing differing color palettes, Big Day and Dirkers are also placed in different temporalities, flipping the social script: the tourist exists in past time; the Chief lives in the present. The Chief sits still, but his stillness reads like a performative act, as if he could break free of this theatrical convention at any moment, animate, get up, and go, leaving the tourist and tepee and all that they signify in this counterfeit scenario of brotherly peace.

A close comparison of the archival photograph and its reenactment also reveals that unlike Yellowstone, Carlson/Strom cast a young, light-skinned actor to play the role of Pax the Hat (compare *Chief Pax the Hat*, p. 62, and "Pax the Hat," p. 63). It comes as little surprise that, in 1920, Yellowstone National Park would want to hire a "Chief" who is older and dark-skinned: by definition, a racial stereotype transmits knowledge through a performance of excess. Staging the stereotype of the Native lent Yellowstone's original scenario its authenticity. *Geyser Land*, however, interrupts this stereotype when Big Day slips himself into the archive, recasting and revising historical memory. The casting of this young Crow man to impersonate an older Crow man who himself impersonates an imaginary Chief-as-willing-ambassador exposes this Chief as a "fictive ethnicity"—a sham, a performance of identity with no original referent, only racial simulacra and simulation.[30]

## The Gandy Dance

Before disembarking from the train, *Geyser Land* spect-tourists encounter "Gandy Dancers," referenced in the opening of this chapter. In the 1946

*Gandy Dancers* (1945). Warren McGee. Bozeman Tunnel Operation, July 1945. Subjects unknown. Courtesy of Gallatin History Museum, Bozeman, Montana.

"Gandy Dancers" (2003). Mary Ellen Strom. From *Geyser Land*, created by Mary Ellen Strom in collaboration with Ann Carlson. Tableau vivant conceived and choreographed by Ann Carlson, performed by Graver Johnson, Emily Brodsky, Daniel Johnson, Jack Dyer, Alex Scaff, Bruce Johnson, John Hedges, Gary Fish, Rob Raney, Dave Gehrke, Anthony Eisenstein, Sten Hertseus, and Jake Whittenberg. Courtesy of Mary Ellen Strom and Ann Carlson.

archival photograph, we see a large section crew at work on the tracks as well as the rolling hills, trees, and brush that comprise the surrounding landscape. Surrounded by darkness, the section crew works to straighten the tracks—knees bent, backs arched, tools engaged: their repetitive movement sequence is synchronized to an inaudible beat. To their left, a man also wearing work clothes—a foreman perhaps—looks on. To their right, a large man in a suit and tie stands at rest.

Perhaps more than any other scene in the performance, "Gandy Dancers" enacts a queer slip of time as the 2003 audience witnesses a 1946 section crew working on the very same tracks that have carried them to their present-time destination. To witness a 1946 section crew straightening a 2003 track connects what Strom calls the "conceptual tourist attraction" known as *Geyser Land* to the ongoing one known as Yellowstone.[31] And it is not, of course, the tremendous weight of the *Geyser Land* train that has forced the tracks out of joint but 113 years of tourist trains ripping through the Bozeman Pass. Because they are captured in the midst of extreme physical exertion; because they are black and brown; because their white supervisor hovers menacingly nearby; because they labor in what appears to be the middle of the night (while the next day's imagined tourist slumbers peacefully somewhere nearby), this gandy dance is exposed to *Geyser Land* audiences as the performance of empire itself. And the seemingly seamless flow of bodies and capital across this haunted landscape is also exposed as a "performative act"—with their synchronized, quite literal "stylized repetition of acts" keeping things intact.[32] The sublime wilderness, the harmless tourist, the happy Native, the invisible ghosts: *Geyser Land* reveals the myths behind these myths, and shines its floodlight on the many gandy dances that keep the trains, and the time, running straight.

# Chapter 2

## When Elephants Are in Must

### Peggy Shaw, Acts of Trans/fer, and the Present Future of Queer

> "I love that part, when Frankenstein splits his stitches and he dies, fertilizing the earth where that little girl grows tomatoes."[1] . . . Though he seems to inseminate the little girl (for his body fluids will indirectly enter the orifice of her mouth when she eats the tomatoes), he transcends both the supposedly natural pain of childbirth and the cyclical time of reproduction. Like Walt Whitman, he disseminates himself. Together, his body and the act he performs with it suggest a historiographical practice wherein the past takes the form of something already fragmented, "split," and decaying, and the present and future appear equally porous. Indeed, they seem to answer Roland Barthes's call . . . for a model of dispersed but insistently carnal continuity, which I call binding. In this sense, the monster's body is not a "body" at all but a figure for relations between bodies past and present, for the insistent return of a corporealized historiography and future making of the sort to which queers might lay claim.
>
> —Elizabeth Freeman, "Time Binds, or, Erotohistoriography"

> I've been waiting for you / and now you're here.
>
> —Peggy Shaw, *Must: The Inside Story*

It is early April in Amherst, Massachusetts, which means that the air is wet and crisp, and the dogwood trees are just about to burst with pink. It is almost eight P.M. The house is packed. Butches, dykes, femmes, faggots, dandies, tranzies, queens, queers.[2] And that is just my row. We've come to the Bartlett Hall Auditorium at the University of Massachusetts to see Peggy Shaw and Clod Ensemble's production of *Must: The Inside Story*, directed by Suzy Willson, which had been touring for three years prior to this 2011 production.[3]

The majority of spectators are college students[4]—including a large number of queer, genderqueer,[5] and transmasculine-identified people, all newly steeped in those theories and practices of "feminism" and "queer" out of which Shaw's life and work is wrought.[6] A number of the students in the audience are already familiar with Peggy Shaw as performer, teacher, and butch icon. While her collaborative work with the Hot Peaches, Spiderwoman, and the original Split Britches preceded them by decades, the young queers in Shaw's audience know her work because she has recently visited the Five College area to teach and perform, as she had been doing with regularity for three decades. It was Hampshire College that commissioned Shaw's first solo show, *You're Just Like My Father* (1994),[7] for their Friends and Family Weekend, and Shaw has been a frequent artist-in-residence in the college's Theatre Program since the 1980s.[8] In this regard, Peggy Shaw has been trans/mitting lesbian feminist cultural history through live "acts of [trans/fer]" to young, local queers for quite some time.[9] Embodied forms of pedagogy—what Freeman calls "corporealized historiography"—are vital in a United States where "straight" history is archived in public institutions of memory (museums, libraries, film, popular media), but the marginalized lives of queer and trans people slip from history because there are few institutions devoted to collecting, protecting, and transmitting their history and collective memory.[10] Acts of trans/fer are particularly crucial at this historical moment in queer politics, when emergent trans identities are in want of a queer past and clear future to which they might lay claim. In this sense, Shaw emerges as living/dying history, opening the archive that is her aging, butch body for her young audiences to research.

In the previous chapter on the site-specific performance, *Geyser Land*, I argued that time slips allowed the past to be superimposed onto the present, exposing the violence of settler colonialism in the United States and its continuing effect on First Nations people and land. These time slips, I argued, illuminated the cultural and material violence foundational to the establishment of this nation-state, while calling into question how history is written and which (and whose) narratives come to be included in or omitted from the official record. In a somewhat similar vein, this chapter examines butch lesbian icon Peggy Shaw's performance *Must* as a case study in which time slips do the work of transforming "official" narratives of how history gets transmitted over time—focusing on the ways in which narratives of butch and transgender masculinities get reified, while attempting to chart another way of telling this story that allows our fractured histories to bleed and mend.

In light of this, it is important to highlight the fact that the focus of this chapter is the relationship between butch and trans masculinities, specifically.[11] My focus on transmasculinity is animated by Shaw's status as butch icon and the tangled history between butch lesbian and transmasculine identities, which I will detail in the pages that follow. But this focus is also reflective of a disproportionately high percentage of trans men in the audience, which itself reflects not only the trans male boom in queer culture, but also simultaneously mirrors the parallel exclusion of trans women from various spaces and discourses—including women's colleges, two of which are located in the Five College area in and around Amherst, and whose students comprise much of the audience of *Must*. Institutions of higher education in general, and women's colleges in particular, have, in the last decade, increasingly become a battleground over transgender politics in the United States—a point to which I will return in the book's final chapter. While most women's colleges have official or unofficial policies that guarantee that trans men, transmasculine, and gender-nonconforming female-assigned students be considered for admission regardless of gender identity or expression, very few will admit women who are trans, perpetuating the misogynist and cissexist belief that trans people in general, and trans women in particular, are not "really" the gender that they say they are. In this regard, the underrepresentation of transfemininities in this chapter reflects not only the perhaps more obvious link between butch and transmasculine histories and identities but also the broader trends of exclusion of trans women from various institutions, educational and otherwise, including and sometimes especially those with ostensibly feminist missions.[12]

In the pages that follow, I situate the aging, fragile, virtuosic, self-proclaimed "grand-butch-mother"[13] Peggy Shaw as the kind of skin-splitting, seed-spreading Frankenstein that Elizabeth Freeman describes in the opening epigraph. Like the monster that splits his body open to fertilize the earth and inseminate the little girl who eats the tomatoes that grow in its fertile soil, Shaw, I argue, ever so queerly slips inside her young, "porous," and desirous audience, fertilizing the "present future" of queer with historiographical knowledge.[14] Already a performance about temporality and loss, this particular production of *Must*, I argue, is infused with the exigencies of the present—Shaw "must" perform *Must* in order to pass her butch legacy onto the young genderqueers and trans men in the audience. In this regard, this chapter argues that Shaw "reproduces" queerly—defying the simple logic of biological reproduction in transmitting queer cultural knowledge through theater and across generations. Bound together, Shaw and her heirs, I argue, resist straight timelines and normative metrics of "reproduction" while also claiming their shared history of vulnerability and medicalization, psychic and material violence, and resistance to and transformation of a rigid gender binary that enacts trauma and violence in subtle and insidious ways. In this regard, I am arguing that the process through which Shaw, an icon of butch lesbianism, "seeds" a generation of transmasculine spectators and fans is inherently a queer one. I am interested, too, in what can be gained from reading this act of trans/fer as one of intergenerational pedagogy and touch. As Ann Daly writes, "From a distance, the critic is poised, porous and, as Deb Margolin correctly suspects, wanting to touch and be touched, like Pollock's excursive stroke, the one that touches without making contact."[15] In touching (us) without even touching us, Shaw transmits her butch past onto the next generation of queer, genderqueer, and trans spectators and fans. Like Frankenstein, Shaw disseminates herself, "dying" so that she and we may live in perpetuity.

Here I would like to return for a moment to an argument I made in the introduction to this book—namely, the idea that institutions such as colleges and universities have been central sites in which Shaw's labor is produced. In light of this fact, this chapter considers the intergenerational impact of Shaw's performance work within the college/university structure, a site that inherently facilitates intergenerational contact (such as between faculty and students) that can, particularly in the case of queer and performance studies, result in the formation of meaningful, nonfamilial, queer kinship structures organized around the circulation of subaltern knowledge—a point to which I will return in this book's final chapter.[16] Bearing in mind this inherently intergenerational exchange between elders and youth that the academy makes possible, this chapter attempts a thick description of a particular moment of queer "insemination" made possible by Shaw's iconicity, virtuosity, and vulnerability, as well as the students' desires to be bound across time.

## Acts of Trans/fer

Diana Taylor writes, "Performances function as vital acts of transfer, transmitting social knowledge, memory, and a sense of identity through reiterated, or what Richard Schechner has called 'twice-behaved behavior.' "[17] To touch, transmit, and inseminate without making contact is not only ontologically performative, as Taylor asserts, it is quintessentially queer. As nonbiological reproduction, it subverts the heterocapitalist mandate that situates the production of surplus capital and nuclear families as *the* nationalist project. Contrary to dominant culture, Shaw uses performance as a technology for producing affect rather than capital, and queer kinship ties, rather than bio-"logical" family.

For instance, when Shaw refers to herself as a "grand-butch-mother," she is at once invoking her literal role as a butch grandmother to her grandson, Ian—a relationship bond that forms the core narrative in *To My Chagrin* (2001)—but also her symbolic role as the "grand" butch elder to and for many butches, genderqueers, and trans men. As Dolan explains in her editor's introduction to Shaw's recent performance anthology,

> In a generation in which lesbians and trans men take pleasure in stretching the envelope of conventional masculinity, and queer communities engage politically in transgender identity and style, Shaw's performances of a complex combination of femininity and masculinity preceded contemporary transgender political activism and theorizing, making her in some ways the "butch hero" who came to model, for many trans folk, the potential of refusing biological gender assignments.[18]

Shaw is esteemed by transmasculine, genderqueer, and gender-nonconforming youth even though she unequivocally maintains her status as "butch," "lesbian," and "woman"—labels that are sometimes pitted against, rather than seen as part of, the trans liberation movement. Shaw's status as "butch hero" to transmasculine youth can be traced in part to those various practices such as breast binding and suit wearing that she performs in *You're Just Like My Father* (1994) and *Menopausal Gentleman* (1998) and that today are associated with transmasculinity as much as (if not more than) lesbianism per se.[19]

The transmasculine boom that characterizes the last decade of queer culture has been made possible, in part, by increased access to various legal and medical technologies that support gender confirmation. It has also been made possible by a more general move within LGBTQ politics to finally reckon with the category of "man"—like it did with the category of "woman" sixty-five years prior[20]—and to reimagine it as a viably feminist identity position—even though certain feminisms have historically critiqued the appropriation of seemingly "male" aesthetics and desires.[21] As (butch) writer Cherríe Moraga explains to (femme) writer Amber Hollibaugh:

> Remember how I told you growing up what turned me on sexually, at a very early age, had to do with the fantasy of capture, taking a woman, and my identification was with the man, taking? Well, something like that would be so frightening to bring up in a feminist context—fearing people would put it in some sicko sexual box. . . . [It] became this really repressive movement, where you didn't talk dirty and you didn't want dirty.[22]

Or, as Shaw herself succinctly puts it, "Feminists made me hate dolphins, I mean dildos."[23]

While a "paranoid reading" of transmasculinity might lament the "disappearance of butches," a "reparative reading"—one that I prefer to rehearse—acknowledges the ways in which all trans identities effectively "mutilate" the notion of gender altogether (to borrow legal theorist Dean Spade's evocative phrasing).[24] In this sense, transmasculine is akin, rather than opposed, to butch lesbian gender identity and expression. Both butch and trans masculinities undo the neatly binary sex/gender system of dominant culture, while continuing to provoke in many people—lesbians and feminists among them—extreme feelings of fear, loathing, and moral panic.

For the current generation of gender outlaws that sit in Shaw's audience, she "re-becomes" the queer ancestor that we never knew we had (or that we never had at all).[25] As performance theorist Richard Schechner explains, "Restored behavior offers to individuals and to groups the chance to rebecome what they once were—or even, and most often, to rebecome what they never were or wish to have been or wish to become."[26] Shaw was never trans, but through our desire her body becomes that of a *trans/cestor*—something that this particular community desires and hasn't had, because so many of our trans/cestors have been disappeared from history.[27]

By no means is everyone in Shaw's audience transmasculine, genderqueer, or even queer, for that matter. But because many of my friends, colleagues, and the students with whom I watch and later discuss the performance are, and because I, too, identify as queer, genderqueer, and transgender in addition but not opposed to lesbian, butch, and woman as identities and practices, my reception and analysis also reflect *my* desires to make whole the ideological gap that separates lesbian from trans, and past from present and future. Simply put, this desire is for butch and trans histories to touch, and to become alive, livable, grievable, and bound.

Bound breasts. Revised childhoods. New names. When it comes to temporality, trans is about as queer as you can get. One of my friends, for instance, refers to having become a "*Bar Mitzvah*"—even though he identified as a girl at the time. Another is embroiled in a legal battle for a birth certificate that retrospectively evidences her new legal name and sex. And another is starting puberty at the age of thirty-six: voice cracking, jaw widening, hair growing, ratios between muscle and fat redistributing all over their body. As Jack Halberstam notes, transgender bodies are always already in a "queer time and place" because their very ontology invites a rejection of historical truth, a reconstruction of bodily and material archives, and a radical reimagining of future possibilities.[28]

While the current historical moment is, on the one hand, marked by gender liberation, mutilation, and new terrains in gender expression and determination, it is also a period of heightened gender repression, surveillance, and violence. As I've been arguing throughout this book, the "homeland" security state in which we now live is defined by increasingly tightened borders: it is the temporal logics of capitalism, colonialism, and compulsory heterosexuality that support, sustain, and sponsor such a police state. It comes as little surprise that the border between male and female, too, would be increasingly policed, its migrants deported, detained, or denied their trans/national crossings. As the introduction to this book made evident, those supposedly "gay" male teens who recently killed themselves, for instance—one after the next—were citing not only each other (and, for those who chose to hang from closets, and shower stalls, and old-growth trees, citing, too, the haunted racial history of this nation-state) but also refusing the restrictions put on their expressions and transgressions of gender.[29] Like Peter Pan, these sissy boys refused the logic that mandates the only way to grow is "up."

While, on the one hand, some trans individuals have increased access to hormone replacement therapies and gender confirmation surgeries, trans people are often forced to produce "alteritist histories that abject the past in favor of the renascent."[30] In order to gain access to vital medical care, many transgender and gender nonconforming people are forced to narrate themselves according to linear, successive, and teleological mandates. Building on Foucault's model of power and governance, Spade elaborates:

> A Foucauldian critique of the diagnosis and treatment of transsexualism exposes how the invention of this "disorder" and its purported therapy do, indeed, function to regulate gender performance. Containing gender distress within "transsexualism" functions to naturalize and make "healthy" dichotomized, birth-assigned gender performance. It casts the critical eye on the gender performance of those transgressing gender boundaries, and produces a norm that need not be criticized. Similarly, this model establishes a structure for addressing violations of gender rules that individualizes, privatizes and depoliticizes the meaning of those transgressions. It is "in the minds of the ill" that gender problems exist, not in the construction of what is "healthy." Similarly, the disciplinary power exercised by the gatekeepers (doctors, surgeons, psychiatrists, therapists) of [gender confirmation surgery] requires the repetitive, norm producing exercises to which Foucault refers. The "successful" daily performance of normative gender is a requirement for receiving authorization for body alteration. Similarly, the successful recitation of the transsexual narrative in meeting after meeting with medical professionals, and in session after session with counselors and psychiatrists, is essential to obtaining such authorization.[31]

In other words, it is because the trans subject must often be professionally diagnosed as having a gender identity or gender dysphoria *disorder* that needs medical *correction* in order to gain needed access to various medical services, the trans subject is sometimes forced, under duress, to self-pathologize ("there's something 'wrong' with me"); produce essentializing narratives about the past ("I was always this way"); as well as the future ("I promise to perform my 'new' gender legibly, consistently, and normatively").[32] In this regard, the gender nonconforming subject is made into a disabled one—capable of rehabilitating into a gender-conforming, time-abiding citizen: their disorder is reordered in alignment with not only their (sometimes) coercively articulated preferred gender, but with a straight and narrow sense of time. Granted, for some trans people such linear narratives are in alignment with their lived experience of their gender identity and history; however, for others this is not the case. What's important here is the very fact that the trans subject is forced to construct such alteritist histories about the past—"true" or not—illustrating the myriad ways in which dominant culture continues to use temporal mechanisms to manage subaltern subjects.

Here it's important, too, to note that the "transgender" moniker is by no means defined by body modification and that such an equation elides the class-based privileges that make such medical interventions possible.

Additionally, many trans-identified people choose not to take hormones (sometimes called "no-ho's," short for "no hormones"); not to undergo surgeries, or bind; and not to change their names and/or pronouns. There are a variety of economic, political, and personal reasons for not medically and/or socially transitioning while maintaining a trans identity, including a feminist and queer investment in not passing as either normatively male or female. In either case, the trans subject defies the logic of normative and binaried gender expectations and, in so doing, the related logic of linear (read: straight) gender development. I am going to great lengths to describe the current terrain of trans politics because the identities of those queer and trans people among Shaw's *Must* audience—as well as among her contemporary fan base writ large—were central, I argue, to the kinds of acts of trans/fer that can and "must" take place.

## When Elephants Are in Must

The Amherst production of *Must* came on the heels of a stroke that nearly killed Shaw only three months prior. Already a performance about memory and loss, mourning and dying, Shaw's palpable frailty the night of this performance filled me with this eerie feeling that this could be the last time I would watch her perform.

I had seen Shaw only a few days before the stroke, in New York City, where she lives. She and Split Britches collaborator Lois Weaver were performing their equally elegiac *Lost Lounge* at Dixon Place.[33] When I received the publicity photo for *Lost Lounge* in my inbox a few weeks before their performance, I was alerted to the ways in which time had slipped without my knowing it. Shaw's face looks older than I remembered it: wrinkles around her eyes, forehead, and mouth; gray sideburns; a tiny lump below her left eye. Weaver, too, seems aged: her blond hair bleached platinum and black; her skin heavy with foundation. Weaver's face refracted outward and onto Shaw (and vice versa); *the* butch and femme after which the aesthetic was named—at least in our field—had, quite simply, grown old.[34] And while Shaw insists that "a woman passing as a man looks like a younger man,"[35] to me Shaw read less like a young gentleman and, for the first time, more like an aging woman.

This is not how I remembered Shaw, nor Weaver, for that matter. In my memory, Shaw's hair is full, and brown, falling in a curl above her Roman nose. Her skin is smooth—like Weaver's—whose blond curls gather at her bare shoulder, the place that Shaw would clutch when they would kiss. *And they would kiss*. They have not only grown old, it seems they have also grown apart.[36]

In the weeks leading up to Shaw's previously scheduled *Must* performance—scheduled prior to her stroke—it was not even clear whether she would be able to perform. Her London tour was cancelled. She was no longer living

*Lost Lounge* (2010). Lori E. Seid. Publicity poster for *Lost Lounge*, Dixon Place, New York City. Created and performed by Peggy Shaw and Lois Weaver, produced by the Joseph Papp Public Theatre "Under the Radar" Festival. Courtesy of Lori E. Seid.

with her "grand-companion-son," Ian, in her rent-controlled East Village apartment but down the road with her former lover and current collaborator Weaver, who was serving as round-the-clock caretaker.[37] Emails circulated, dates changed, auxiliary events like classroom visits and house parties—typical for Shaw's visits to western Massachusetts—were suspended. She would perform *Must* and give one artist talk. No more. Shaw's stroke and its aftermath made me aware that Shaw and the history she carries through performance wouldn't be around forever. And so: I knew I must see *Must* and, more to the point, that I must bring my students.

## The Inside Story

A solo performance, *Must* examines how traumatic histories live in the body, on the body, and between bodies, and how, too, "when something is real, it leaves a trace."[38] Shaw makes a very Benjaminian move with *Must*, attempting to re-member—"make whole"—multiple things that have "been smashed." These include her broken heart, broken bones, the broken plates

*The Kiss* (ca. 1995). Eva Weiss. Photograph of Peggy Shaw and Lois Weaver. Courtesy of Eva Weiss.

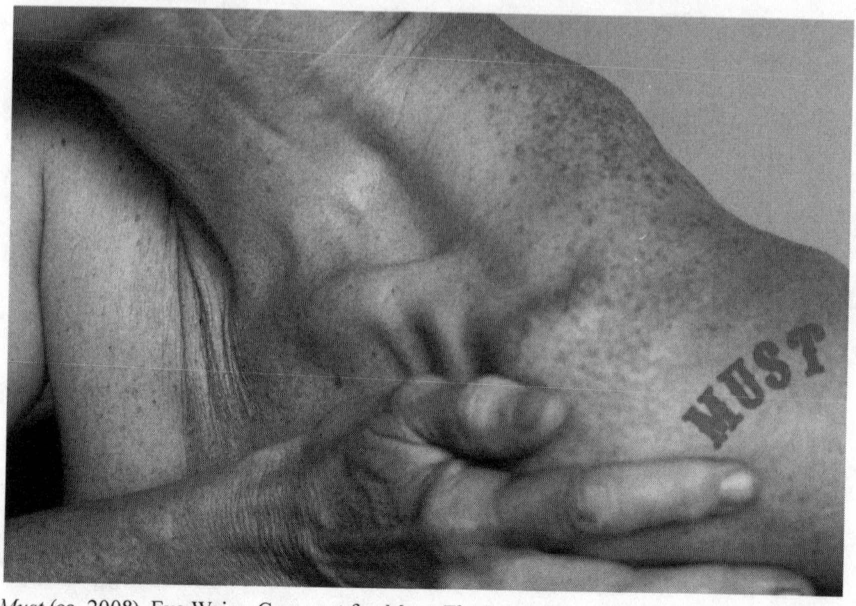


*Must* (ca. 2008). Eva Weiss. Cover art for *Must: The Inside Story* (book). Created by Peggy Shaw and Clod Ensemble, written by Peggy Shaw and Suzy Willson, directed by Suzy Willson, performed by Peggy Shaw. Courtesy of Eva Weiss.

her mother hurled against the wall, as well as the metaphorical splitting open of her skin with eleven "stories" about her "inside[s]."

The performance uses second-person address: the "you" to whom Shaw speaks is both the spectator whom she asks to serve as witness, as well as the "you" that was the loved one who left her and ostensibly catalyzed this need—this *must*—to speak.[39] "When elephants are in must," Shaw explains toward the end of *Must*, "tears flow freely from their eyes. I'm crying for you. . . . Stuff is leaking out, draining from my eyes, dripping from my holes everywhere, tipping my head over like a tea pot, emptying my brain, pouring all the residue out onto the floor in a pile."[40] Shaw, like the elephant she cites, is in must. "Must" (or musth) is a periodic condition experienced by male elephants indicated by increased levels of testosterone, aggressive behavior, and, most notably, the swelling of the temporal glands on the side of the head, which causes the discharge of a thick, tar-like secretion from the elephants' temporal ducts.[41] As Shaw notes, this secretion creates the impression that when elephants are in must, they weep—"tears flow[ing] freely from their eyes." In this sense, Shaw is in must because her love has left: "The tips of my fingers trace you on a foggy window," she laments:

> They trace your outline and they make a heart with an arrow through it. Such a simple map showing the pain of an arrow through the heart, explaining that feeling when you have something outside yourself that draws you to it—like a crash at the front of the bus, or a commotion outside the square, like blood cells rushing to an injured place where they desert the rest of your body and leave you exhausted.[42]

Shaw is in must not only because her love has left her but also because the other "you" to whom she speaks, the audience, has *not*. We are her new femme, receptive to her butch need to touch gently, penetrate deeply, and inseminate (us) with words. This desire to speak, to split, to seed, draws her "like blood cells rushing to an injured place" close to her audience—leaving her exhausted, and us full.

Shaw begins, "I've been waiting for you / and now you're here."[43] In signature style, Shaw emerges from the audience toward the stage: making eye contact, saying hello, touching a shoulder, shaking or kissing a hand. As always, this conceit feels genuine coming from Shaw, not theatrical per se, as if the gesture is as much for her as it is for us. "By pressing the flesh, [Shaw] humanizes herself down to size, and refuses the awe her own charisma inspires."[44] Watching, I am reminded of community-based choreographer Liz Lerman's ritual of shaking hands and making eye contact with each person in the room before teaching a workshop. It feels good to be on the receiving end of Lerman's touch, too: she makes her participants feel welcome and hailed, or interpellated, in Althusser's sense of the term.[45] But Lerman claims that this practice is not about her participants; it is for her. She says that she makes contact so that she might feel more at ease in a roomful of wanting strangers who have gathered with very high expectations of the life-affirming work they hope will follow.[46] Perhaps it was not in spite but because of her grand(-butch-mother) reputation that Shaw similarly lingers with us before the show. In touching us, she humanizes herself as well as us—literally and symbolically inviting us into the process of "corporealized historiography" by which she will become not only "'a body' but a figure for relations between bodies past and present,"[47] and by which we, to her, will bind.

The fact that she has "been waiting for [us]" and "now [we] are here" immediately establishes her as our "elder," signaling her prior existence in time and space, as well as her desire that we join her, which we've fulfilled. Because Shaw is already in the house, more or less, from the moment we arrive; because she is wearing the same suit, more or less, that we've seen her wear countless times before; because we are, more or less, young enough to be her grandchildren; because students and professors and local queers have been revolving in and out of these same seats, more or less, in this same town, for three decades to watch her perform, it is as if Shaw has been waiting, and wading through, all of time for the "you" that is "us" to arrive. In this sense, the *Must* stage is what theater semiotician Marvin Carlson would call a "haunted" one, and *Must* a "memory machine." Shaw continues, "And now you're here." She could finally say whatever it was that she had waited all this while to say. We are not passersby, random spectators, accidental or incidental audiences. She chose us as the witnesses she has been waiting—*longing*—for.

Shaw moves slowly from the house to the proscenium stage to begin her "inside story." This forty-minute performance is less physical than many of Shaw's prior shows. It is delivered as a monologue: poetical, fragmented, and stream-of-consciousness spoken text broken into eleven parts with only one musical number.[48] Shaw only occasionally moves—descending and ascending the stairs between the apron of the proscenium stage and the pit. In this sense, *Must* feels less like a play or performance art and more like an elegy. But perhaps because, as Shaw herself once put it, "Every word you speak is forever in the air, it will never go away,"[49] I am perfectly content to simply listen to her words. At one point, I even close my eyes; I want to hear her voice *inside* my head.

Inside herself, Shaw is broken. The lost love she mourns, for instance, seems to have spurred this melancholic tale, and her desire to split herself open is a search for answers, an attempt to make sense of this great loss: "I count the hours since you left, / but the numbers never add up. I have to admit / they never add up."[50] And instead of finding the "truth" about this past loss inside her body, what Shaw finds are more lost and broken things: broken bones, sunken slave ships, Ziploc bags, dead pigeons, garbage, MacBooks, melting icebergs, drowning polar bears, oil spills, New York City—all swirling within her inner ecosystem. She calls these things "the future" and pulls them out to show and tell:

> I keep finding the future inside of me. I can hear it really loud, coming from a field of windmills, or a hive of bees. / I know, I know, I know. / I am digging. Deep past the topsoil. There's no cutting involved. Just turning over the soil. I am afraid of finding something I didn't know about—like a bear shitting in my woods, or a field of Irish potatoes in my uterus, or a huge, garbage-swirling, plastic toxic mass in my pituitary gland that is close to the size of Texas. Fish and turtles and things are growing in it and eating it and fossils are traveling on it to foreign dangerous places where they are not meant to be.[51]

While perhaps Shaw is initially "digging" through her personal past, she seems to have dug so deep—"deep past the topsoil"—that she has found the global future of this planet. Like *Geyser Land*, *Must* presents time not as linear but as a thick, deep palimpsest—a serializing swirl of public culture. "The plastic toxic mass . . . the size of Texas," for instance, refers to the Great Pacific Garbage Patch—layers upon layers of accumulated, discarded plastic from the second half of the twentieth century to the present, which swirls and stagnates in the middle of the Pacific Ocean. Plastic, the new parchment, is growing thick—deep in the ocean and other places where consumers don't have to see it. Shaw's invocation connects her private loss of love to ecological disaster. "My desire is melting my icebergs so fast, they're drifting further and further apart and polar bears are dying from exhaustion. . . . Underneath my thighs is where all the oil is being stolen from, leaving empty pockets inside."[52] Through her desire, her loss, and her longing, Shaw becomes Gaia herself.[53]

In framing herself as old as the planet, Shaw also reinforces her role as primordial trans/cestor and casts us as her contemporary heirs. At the same time, in making herself the world, Shaw represents an otherwise marginal identity—butch, lesbian, working-class, Irish, grandmother—as literally, *universally* human. As Dolan has similarly argued, with such a rhetorical move "Shaw's body comes to stand in for all bodies, revising what lesbian theorist Monique Wittig once called 'the axis of categorization' by putting a butch lesbian body at the center of an illustration of life."[54] What's more, because her *Must* spectators occupy similarly marginal identity positions, *our* bodies are also, uncharacteristically, placed at the center of the univers(al).

Throughout the performance, various parts of Shaw's body are illuminated by large, colorful, photo projections of elemental details of the human body: cells of the upper respiratory tract, a striated muscle, a hair cell of the inner ear, a newly fertilized human egg, a sectional image of the human tongue (see "Section through the fovea," p. 81, "Section of human cerebellum," p. 82, and "Newly fertilized human egg," p. 85). These scientific, archival images expose the inner—usually invisible—workings of the human body as neither gross nor grotesque but as beautiful mythomorphic landscapes, spectacular action paintings. Projected onto Shaw's body, this theatrical device at once acknowledges and subverts the stereotype of the butch as "exterior"—that

*Must* (2011). Manuel Vason. Publicity image for *Must: The Inside Story*. Created by Peggy Shaw and Clod Ensemble, written by Peggy Shaw and Suzy Willson, directed by Suzy Willson, performed by Peggy Shaw. Courtesy of Clod Ensemble.

is, the notion that butch bodies are merely surfaces: contained, composed, impenetrable. Though the images rest on the surface of her skin, they suggest an enfleshed interiority that we otherwise cannot see.

Shaw continues, "There are different ways of seeing inside me: / You could guess what's in here. / You could x-ray me. / You could touch me. / Or you could believe what I tell you."[55] Because we want—we've come—to see inside of her and, in so doing, see inside ourselves, we choose to believe what she tells us:

> I have been thirteen bodies in my life.
> This is only one of them.
>
> I cracked my pelvis. I broke my heels. I smashed my knuckles on my right hand. I smashed my knees in the woods. I fell off the porch and got a stick in my eye. The wind was knocked out of me when I smashed into a tree. I cut open my hand when my grandma died. I was on crutches for six months when I jumped off a fence. I had fourteen spinal taps curled in a ball like a fetus. I was born with

Section through the fovea (center of the retina). Chris Guerin. Transparent image. From *Must: The Inside Story*. Created by Peggy Shaw and Clod Ensemble. Courtesy of Wellcome Library, London.

> broken clavicles. I got pneumococcal meningitis when I slept with a woman for the first time. I died for three minutes. I was in a coma for two weeks. I had mononucleosis and couldn't kiss a boy for a year. I had cancer on my face and got twenty-eight stitches. I had a lump removed from my breast. I have lumps on my forearms and the front of my thighs where I store my original thoughts. I smashed my two front teeth on the ice fighting over a girl. I had a baby.[56]

Like the transparent images projected onto her body, this litany of cuts and incursions reveals an inside—and a vulnerability—to her ostensibly inviolate, butch flesh. The fact, for instance, that she has had a baby exposes the penetrability of her butch body, which we only otherwise suspect, but cannot see.

During the performance, she keeps track of this litany by "counting" each traumatic event on her fingers. It doesn't seem like she is pretending to remember the past as much as actually trying to remember her lines. Shaw speaks slowly and deliberately, occasionally looking up and to the left as some people do when they are fishing for a word or a memory just beyond their grasp. I listen intently to her list, wanting/waiting to see if she will include her stroke in this first performance of *Must* in its wake. Perhaps I want to hear her stroke named because it reflects my reception experience, as I am acutely aware throughout that Shaw subtly but palpably struggles to

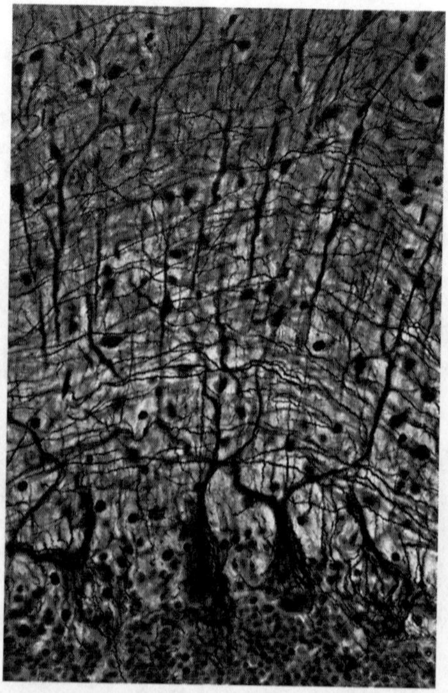

Section of human cerebellum. Spike Walker. LM, silver-stained transparent image. From *Must: The Inside Story*, created by Peggy Shaw and Clod Ensemble. Courtesy of Wellcome Library, London.

speak and remember the performance while she's executing it. Perhaps I want to hear it because I feel protective of Shaw—I want the youngest of the young people in the audience, who may be seeing her perform for the first of what they imagine will be many times, to know that Shaw doesn't usually fumble for lines, or seem weak, or fragile, or exhausted.

Here I am reminded of other iconic artists in the field—Joseph Chaikin, Robbie McCauley, and Deb Margolin, to name a few prominent examples—who have similarly had to navigate the impact of illness, aging, and/or debility on their work. Unlike Shaw's *Must*, however, Joseph Chaikin's *Struck Dumb*—a solo performance about the relationship between speech and mind—was created only *after* the artist's own poststroke aphasia. Similarly created after the artists' onset of illness are Deb Margolin's *3 Seconds in the Key* (2001), a solo performance about Hodgkin's disease, motherhood, and basketball; and Robbie McCauley's *Sugar* (2012), about diabetes, health inequities, and the transatlantic slave trade.[57] While Shaw's solo show, *Ruff* (2011, dir. Lois Weaver),[58] was conceived in the aftermath of Shaw's stroke (and for it Shaw/Weaver would brilliantly incorporate video monitors as script prompts, reminiscent of the hanging text, rope and pulley systems, and TV monitors that Chaikin similarly relied on in *Struck Dumb*), *Must* was written three years prior to Shaw's stroke. As such, Shaw's physical and mental frailty the night of the 2011 Amherst production of *Must* is neither rehearsed nor theatricalized. Rather, it is laid entirely bare—functioning as an unintentional yet uncanny overlay onto a performance originally created for medical students and health care practitioners—people who, that is, devote their lives to thinking through questions of illness and loss.[59]

Because Shaw is not only a woman but a butch lesbian, the particular ways in which her vulnerability is exposed in this production work to complicate essentialized notions of (butch and trans) masculinities. Perhaps the fact that Shaw is particularly vulnerable the night of this performance provides a necessary role modeling for butch and transmasculine people in the audience—myself included—who don't always know how to navigate feelings of fragility and powerlessness.[60] As poet Bonnie Barringer explains, "When butches cry / they weep, they wail / they gnash their teeth / and moan / Strong women's pain / it's just the same / except it's mostly done / alone."[61] It's "mostly done alone" because to be witnessed in a state of vulnerability exposes what Moraga has called the pink "underside" of the butch turtle shell. Shaw's palpable frailty shows us how even (or perhaps especially) "butch heroes" experience so-called failures of memory, masculinity, and strength.

While this particular performance may reveal her body as vulnerable in new ways, her large, commanding presence—and the erotic longings that this presence notoriously incites in her audiences—is palpable nonetheless. Writing about Shaw's 2000 production of *Menopausal Gentleman* in Austin, Dolan writes, "Her presence moved through the house like a current; she electrified us, bound her to us, and brought us close to the complexities of her longing and our own."[62] With *Must*, the complexities of her longing and our own include the desire to be bound across generations, to feel the erotics of intergenerational, trans/temporal touch.

For instance, making eye contact with a young queer person in her audience during *Must*, Shaw asks, "Would you like to see my body?" We vicariously understand the generosity of such an offer, and it draws us close. She continues, "I'm sixty-four and I'm lucky: I have both my breasts still, / safe, inside my suit."[63] Shaw's words penetrate *our* suits, which may or may not still have both breasts, safe inside. "I can't lie down to be examined," Shaw confesses. "It makes me feel like I will die. It scares me to expose the front of my chest without my arms covering it. I am feeling foolish in your room—like in the ladies room—a bull in a china shop."[64] The medical gaze has violated her butch body. Being on an examination table, like being in a ladies room, has made her feel "foolish," "scared," and even like she "will die." "How do I know you haven't got a gun in your pocket, or a *stethoscope*?"[65] While the medical gaze may be violent, our gaze is not, and she knows it. We pull her close, like a lover, allowing her to expose her butch beauty and flaws alike:

> My upper arms are big, 'cause my dad said life is hard, so he made us lift weights every day before we went to school. My wing on the right side is lower than the one on the left; you will notice that right away. It kinda droops. I have been told that my clavicles are the sexiest part of my body. There's a photo of them recorded on a cell phone somewhere.[66]

Shaw unbuttons the top of her shirt and carefully lets her big arms, droopy wing, and sexy clavicles hang out (while covering her chest with her elbows and forearms).

*Must* models more than butch heroism. Her mother, for instance, refused the normative demands of femininity, needing "eleven shock treatments to get her to wash the dishes."[67] Her friend Migdalia Garcia—a "sexy" femme who liked to "suck the calcium outta the inside of chicken bones"[68]—saved her life. When Shaw fell off a fifteen-foot fence and broke her pelvis and heels, it was Garcia who looked after her body.

> I wouldn't let anyone bring me to the hospital, 'cause I wanted to die at home. Migdalia carried my body up five flights of stairs and slept all night on my floor. The next day, when I wasn't dead, she carried me to the emergency room. While the doctors were telling me I could have died from internal bleeding, she stole all the bandages out of the cabinets and stuffed them in her jacket pockets, to give to her girlfriend to strap down her breasts, so she could pass as a man on the streets of Brooklyn.[69]

Garcia emerges as femme hero not only because she saved Shaw from dying but also because she saved her own lover from being attacked on the streets for being butch, and queer, and not quite passing—by repurposing medical technologies for queer survival. "Migdalia Garcia. That's her name," Shaw repeats. "Don't forget it." We are asked to remember Garcia not merely because she saved Shaw but because like Shaw, her body serves as a sliding signifier for a multiplicity of lives from their generation of aging, working-class gender outlaws that modeled how to live and love, how to fight for one another, and how to remember for one another.

In the final moments of the performance, Shaw removes her shirt completely and stands—topless—near the projection screen with her back facing the audience. Her shirt gathered loosely around her waist, she allows a flood of images to be superimposed—one after the next—onto the soft, bare skin of her back. For some of us, this filmic dance across her back is reminiscent of that moment in *To My Chagrin* when Shaw bares her breasts so that images of her "grand-companion-son," Ian, could be projected onto her chest. "She replaces cultural presumption [about racial difference] with what she truly carries in heart," says Dolan of *Chagrin*.[70] In *Must*, it was

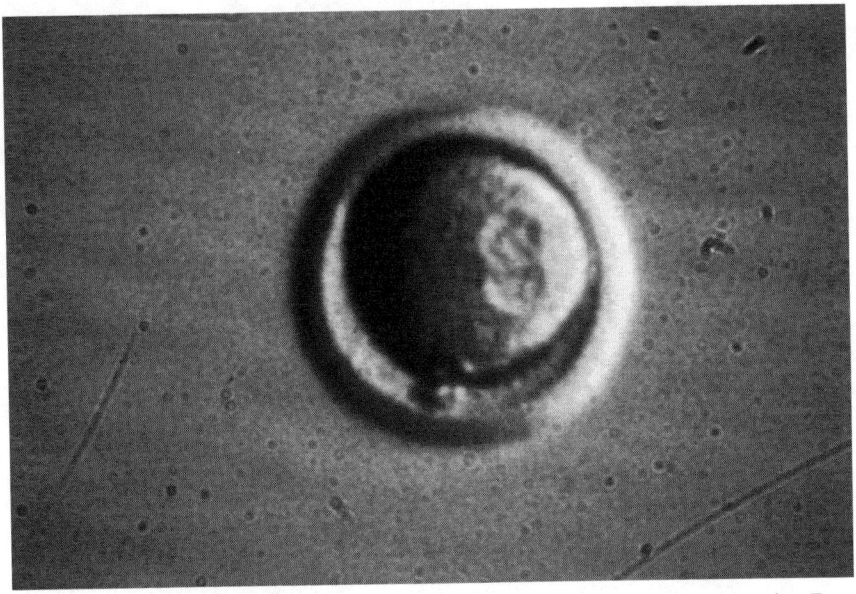

Newly fertilized human egg. Joyce Harper. Transparent image using Nomarski optics. From *Must: The Inside Story*, created by Peggy Shaw and Clod Ensemble. Courtesy of Wellcome Library, London.

not her mixed-race "blood" grandchild she reveals as carrying in her heart, though, but us—her mixed-gendered grand-butch-children. Shaw explains, "Elephants teach their young to slide their trunks over dead bones. They hold their baby elephants' trunks in theirs, listening as they smooth out the memories." At once the living grand-butch elephant and the elephants' bones, Peggy Shaw held our baby butch trunks in hers—and taught us, brought us, in and out.

## Conclusion, or, "The Next Generation"

The next night, we gather again at the University of Massachusetts. We are across campus this time, watching *Sister Spit: "The Next Generation."* Organized by author Michelle Tea, *Sister Spit: "The Next Generation"* is a revival of the original San Francisco–based, lesbian-feminist spoken word and performance art collective that toured between 1994 and 1996, performing regularly at colleges, the Michigan Womyn's Music Festival, and Pride events around the country. Beginning in 1997, Tea relaunched the tour, inviting gay men, straight men, straight women, trans women, and trans men to join cis lesbians on the tour, reflecting the changing demographic of the feminist and queer movements.

Like Shaw's performance the night before, it is an evening full of queer time slips. In "Squirtle," poet Myriam Gurba ironically says:

> I feel connected to all my male ancestors. I visualize ball sack after ball sack after ball sack, each of us living in one another's testes. . . . I see the scrotums of ancient Slavs, Visigoths, and East Siberian tribesmen, those who trekked the Bering land bridge and became the first Americans. I dwelled long ago in these balls.[71]

While Gurba imagines a past of deep time—with the many balls of her past tucked one inside the next like Russian dolls—poet Andrea Lawlor imagines a slow future, where people communicate by leaving intricate, handmade messages in trees, rather than by cell phone or email:

> In my new country, we will have various and more efficient systems of communication, including trees. . . . From saplings' delicate limbs we will dangle our friend requests, and around the magnolia gnarls we will tie with ribbons the notices of our name-changes and new pronouns.[72]

Photographer Amos Mac chronicles the many ways that trans people rewrite their pasts and futures with new bodies, names, and kinship structures: Mac shares his photographic portraits from *Original Plumbing: Trans Male Quarterly*, the premier print magazine dedicated to the culture and lifestyle of transgender men; as well as the then-forthcoming *Translady Fanzine*—cocreated with artist Zachary Drucker—trans culture's newest fine art magazine, featuring the then-twenty-seven-year-old Drucker standing on the snow-covered lawn of her high school football field—lips pink, chest exposed, eyes piercing. An amber stole warms her neck and a golden fur hat crowns her head. Behind her, the blank scoreboard reads "HOME" and "GUEST": her ever-changing trans present literally touching down on her frozen past.[73]

And then there is Dori Midnight, queer witch and healer, who asks us to close our eyes and visualize a forest with a trail, and on that trail to see our "queer grandmothers, grandfathers, and grandtrannies"—as well as our "queer grandchildren"—to whom we are bound, Midnight claims, not by blood but imagination. When I close my eyes, I see the outline of Shaw's body seared on my retina[74]—and, as I hold my eyes closed a little longer, I see my students'. And then I open them. And decide I might—I *must*—write this down.[75]

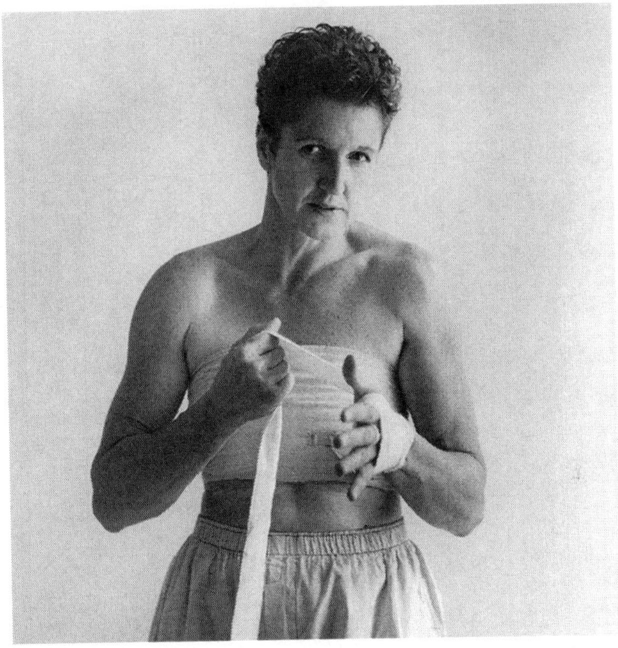

Peggy Shaw in *You're Just Like My Father* (1994). Eva Weiss. Courtesy of Eva Weiss.

## Chapter 3

✦

# Following the Ghosts

## Repetition, Return, and the Disordering of America in *floodlines* (2004–2010)

We return to the same place over and over until we don't need to anymore. We turn it over until we cease to need to turn it over.

—M. Jacqui Alexander, "Sites of Memory: The Atlantic and Other Crossings"

We were not spectators. The spectators were the Hyde Park neighbors and the shopkeepers who stood outside their doors to watch the procession of Volvos go by. . . . We, the ones who rose from our seats, were witnesses and accomplices, selected and compelled by a ghost who needed to accomplish the ritual that would allow her (did I say her?) to leave us.

—Alyssa Harad, "Following the Ghosts"

Repetition: something is changed.

—Gilles Deleuze, *Difference and Repetition*

*The* floodlines *project began at a storefront in Soho. Strolling my then-neighborhood streets of Lower Manhattan one weekday afternoon—shortly after September 11, 2001—I happened upon a photography exhibit,* Here Is New York: A Democracy of Photographs.[1] *I walked around the crowded, white-walled room, gazing at the photographs of the industrial and human wreckage that filled that tiny gallery space. An abandoned bicycle, caked with dust; a pair of work gloves, stuck to a brick wall; a crying boy on a curb, wearing a firefighter cap. Because "what is lost is known only by what remains of it," these photographs at once made present the missing (the bicyclist, the worker, the fireman), while also confirming the materiality of their absences.*[2] *I was mesmerized by these thanatographies, these studies in death and dying.*[3] *One series, in particular, captured my attention—I found myself continually looping back to photographs of people jumping out of buildings. One woman hung from a window pane: her delicate, black pumps pointing downward like two cardinal signs in the direction of gravity's pull. Others were captured midflight: hands gripping leather purses and attaché cases like parachute brakes, specks of white shirt and blouse and paper dotting the crystal-blue sky—the thin membrane between life and death forever frozen in time and space. I stayed in that gallery all day. I never wanted to look away.*

*Two years later, I attended the Association for Theatre in Higher Education Conference in New York City. In a packed seminar room of the Marriott Marquis Hotel, Peggy Phelan showed slides of Mark Rothko's signature work—two ethereal rectangles floating on a canvas—while she talked about the aesthetics of 9/11 and illustrated how, in its design, execution, and representation, 9/11 embodied one of the simplest and most basic theatrical elements: repetition.*[4] *The second airplane going into the second building exactly eighteen minutes after the first; the dual nature of the event as both real and representation, immediate and mediated, with endless loops of video footage circulating moments after that second attack, such that the distinction between the "original" and the "copy" became, for many (myself included), blurred—like the fuzzy line between two colors of a Rothko painting.*[5]

*Because 9/11 was orchestrated as a repetition, it brilliantly and eerily anticipated the traumatic repetitions it would catalyze in its wake. Not only the endless video loops of airplanes crashing into buildings, but the missing persons photos tessellated one after the other on sidewalks, hospital walls, and chain-link fences throughout the city; Twin Towers "memorabilia" at every bodega, dollar store, and vendor stand; the red, white, and blue votive candles on stoop after stoop, in shrine after shrine; the* Virgenes de Guadalupe; *the obituaries; the American flags; the recycled sound bites spoken on the news and on the street: "victim," "hero," and "now, more than ever"; "homeland security," "mission accomplished," and "getting back to normal." To commemorate his father's invasion of the Middle East a decade prior, Bush Jr. repeats the act. We are a nation "at war with terror": we hear it again and again. For the first time in history, war has been declared on an emotion.*[6] *I learn to scan for signs of difference.*

A multisite-specific and serial performance installation, *floodlines* was conceived in the aftermath of 9/11, and it was staged in Austin on the streets, lawns, sidewalks, and alleyways of a quiet residential neighborhood adjacent to the University of Texas campus. The performance premiered in 2004 (as my master's thesis project), and it was reperformed every spring for seven consecutive years, completing its run in 2010. In this chapter, I investigate the ways in which *floodlines* produced time slips by using the theatrical element of repetition to queer the affective texture of American life.

In the introduction to this book, I argued that dominant culture abjects subaltern subjects through the construction of time as linear, teleological, and progress-oriented and the idealized citizen as similarly straight, productive, and amnesic. I argued that straight time is inextricably bound to individual and collective experiences of trauma, both in the way in which it creates the psychic and material conditions under which bodies out of sync with dominant cultural beats are disciplined and punished by the state, and also in the way in which capitalist time forecloses necessary processes of reparation. In other words, this book asks how performance can function as a site of repair by investigating how the act of stopping, rewinding, replaying, and perhaps even fast-forwarding past an unresolved traumatic event—individual and collective, ordinary and cataclysmic, historical and ongoing—can help to transform sites of violence, injury, and/or harm into something else. "Repetition: something is changed."[7]

In the last chapter, we saw how the performance *Must* enacted a time slip by binding butch, trans, and queer identities and histories across the seemingly fixed boundaries of time and biology. Shaw's performance encouraged spectators to celebrate a multitude of possibilities for deviant and defiant gender and sexual expression by modeling a refusal to submit to the linear logic of gender normativity. At the same time, the performance also replaced straight notions of biological reproduction with queer cultural transmission, forging kinship ties between young, transmasculine spectators and this icon of butch lesbianism, making their shared affects and traumatic histories visible and palpable at a moment in LGBTQ politics and theater history when such repair and connection was vital. In this chapter, I extend this line of inquiry, asking what happens when a performance repeats the normalizing logics that structure dominant culture, but infuses, as Judith Butler urges us to do, the repetitions *with a difference*—marking the serializing logics of ideal citizenship while simultaneously scrambling time and dis-ordering America.

This chapter looks at repetition in three ways. First, I analyze salient moments of repetition that were staged within each ninety-minute performance of *floodlines*—moments in which text, images, and motifs repeated in the course of the performance. Throughout this chapter, I also interrupt my performance analysis with personal anecdotes—stories that situate *floodlines* as a durational project and aim to highlight the impact of repeating the production every year for seven years. What does the ritual of repeating *the performance itself* do? Here I acknowledge the fact that all performance, to varying degrees, repeats itself: the long-running Broadway play, the revival, the festival, the sequel. As American theater director Anne Bogart reminds us, "The French word for rehearsal is *repetition*. Certainly it can be argued that the art of theatre is the art of repetition."[8] But because it was performed annually, and exactly seven times, and in the same sites, the performance became for many participants—especially actors and neighborhood residents—a kind of community-based ritual. As these narratives intend to reveal, the annual repeating of the performance—like the repetitions within the performance—allowed another kind of keeping time to take place.

In the spaces between my writing and the production photographs included in this chapter, I slip family photographs that bear uncanny verisimilitude to the production images. Their striking resemblance is formal but also thematic: they similarly document performances of ("not quite") whiteness.[9] In these family photos, the social actors are rehearsing that tenuous claim to whiteness known as Jewish assimilation—by doing quintessentially bourgeois "American" things such as biking, sunbathing, and playing ball.[10] Unlike *Geyser Land*, the scenes in the *floodlines* production are not based on the archival photographs; rather, I found these photographs in a dusty drawer of my parents' suburban home in 2009, only after having staged the performance for six years. I do not remember seeing these photographs before then, but perhaps I had come across them in my childhood and produced retrospective memories as a result.[11] Or perhaps I had never seen them—the mirror images that I created for *floodlines* the result of stories that I had heard or lives that I had imagined, but never known. In any case, the production images do not repeat the photographs. Rather, the photographs—though they precede the performance by decades in straight time—repeat the performance. In slipping these private family photographs into and after photographs of the public performance images that they resemble, it is my hope that they will toss my readers backward in time as they move forward through the chapter. Like the performance itself, I keep two beats here: the seemingly straight processional of my present argument, and performative flashes of history that interrupt the flow of time.[12]

My notion of subversive repetition, or repetition with a difference, is informed by Judith Butler's foundational essay "Performative Acts and Gender Constitution," in which Butler argues that gender is a stylized repetition of acts that only appear stable because they have been rehearsed and consolidated over time. Butler writes,

> Gender . . . is an identity tenuously constituted in time—an identity instituted through a stylized repetition of acts. . . . If the ground of gender identity is the stylized repetition of acts through time, and not a seemingly seamless identity, then the possibilities of gender transformation are to be found in the arbitrary relation between such acts, in the possibility of a different sort of repeating, in the breaking or subversive repetition of that style.[13]

In my analysis of the *floodlines* project, I widen the scope of Butler's focus on gender to include a range of "performative accomplishments," including race, religion, sexuality, class, and national belonging. If repetition is the strategy by which whiteness, heterosexuality, middle-classness, and other unmarked markers of normativity get reproduced over time, what kinds of social transformations become possible through "the breaking or subversive repetition" of these American "styles"?[14]

## Staging the Stereotype

The audience members, who have purchased their tickets in advance of the performance, are instructed to meet at Eastwoods Park, a public commons situated a few blocks from the university campus.[15] Audience members are asked to find their way to the start of the performance, which is not clearly marked amid the cement picnic tables, drained swimming pool, open field, and old-growth trees. Tucked at the far end of the park, two rows of white folding chairs face a cracking tennis court. Audience members find seats, chat among themselves, and watch two actors play a casual game of tennis. Some spectators come alone; most arrive in couples and other typical theatrical arrangements. The players—a white man and woman in tennis whites—mirror the vast majority of the spectators and their shared enjoyment of a leisurely Sunday in Austin in April.

Twenty or so minutes after the advertised start-time of the performance, a small Jewish man in a soaking wet black suit, white shirt, yarmulke, and *tzitzit* (played by me) runs across the tennis court and greets the audience with an urgent, blank stare (see "Wandering Jew," p. 97). American writer and literary critic Alyssa Harad, who saw the performance in 2006 and again in 2010, describes the moment like this:

> Without announcement, a slight dark figure appears on the far side of the park. He (she?) moves quickly and silently toward us across the green grass, passing through knots of picnicking families and flirting teenagers. When he reaches the tennis court, the players drift apart without protest to let him pass. He wears a shapeless, rusty black suit; a white collared shirt, too big; good black shoes—polished, the way your grandfather kept them—and thick glasses. His *yarmulke* (skullcap) with long *payoth* (sideburns) straggling from beneath and white *tzitzit* threads hanging below his half-tucked shirt mark him an Orthodox Jew. He seems to have come from a long way off—New York maybe, a different century, or some piece of buried history—and to have walked the whole way here, to this broken tennis court, where he stands beckoning to us silently.[16]

The interruption of this white, bourgeois game by this "dark figure," a strange and "straggly" Jew, attempts to prepare spectators for a performance that, while set amid the backdrop of a picturesque neighborhood, will twist and turn familiar conventions of this town and country. As with *Geyser Land*, the copresence of the contemporary spectator with this Jewish specter from "a long way off" also attempts to produce a time-space collision between the theatrical present and the historical past—and a racialized encounter between the conceptual tourists and the cultural spectacle they have come to witness.

Here it is important to highlight how this opening encounter between the audience and the Jew is a theatrical scene but also a performative scenario, or a "meaning making [paradigm] that [structures] social environments, behaviors, and potential outcomes."[17] Building on Richard Schechner's theory of "twice-behaved behavior" cited in the previous chapter as well as Roland Barthes's notion of "mythical speech," performance theorist Diana Taylor defines "scenario" like this:

> Scenario, "a sketch or outline of the plot of a play, giving particulars of the scenes, situations etc.," like performance, means never for the first time. Like Barthes' mythical speech, it consists of "material which has already been worked on" (*Mythologies*, 110). Its portable framework bears the weight of accumulative repeats. The scenario makes visible, yet again, what is already there: the ghosts, the images, the stereotypes. The discoverer, conqueror, "savage," and native princess, for example, might be staple characters in many Western scenarios. Sometimes they are written down as scripts, but the scenario predates the script and allows for many possible "endings." At times people may actually undertake adventures to live the glorious fantasy of possession. Others may tune in regularly to television shows along the lines of *Survivor* or *Fantasy Island*. The scenario structures our understanding. It also haunts our present, a form of hauntology . . . that resuscitates and reactivates old dramas. We've seen it all before.[18]

In other words, both theater and everyday life are framed by scenarios, those cultural scripts which "conjure up past situations, at times so profoundly internalized by society that no one remembers the precedence."[19] Conquest narratives, heteronormativity, white ascendancy: these scenarios are so familiar, so ubiquitous, as to render themselves, at times, invisible. And as Taylor reminds us, theatrical performances of these cultural scripts cite their occurrence in everyday life, not only conjuring up past and present situations but also making visible the normative conventions, cultural stereotypes, and violent histories that precede them.

In this regard, the couple who opens the show with their game of tennis—a couple in real life as well as in the fiction of the performance—can be read as both a theatrical scene as well as a performative scenario, and so, too, the wandering Jew who interrupts their game with his surprise entrance. Put differently, it could be argued that this spectacle of tennis cites every prior game of tennis that has taken place on this court, or on any court for that matter; every prior Sunday afternoon in this park, or any park for that matter; every prior heterosexual couple who has enjoyed the privilege and pleasure of being "out" in public. The fact that the actors are also actually married—simultaneously performing as both real and fictional husband-wife team—repeats the familiar, cultural script of the heterosexual couple as the basic building block for family and family as synecdoche for nation.[20] "We've seen it all before."

The audience, too, are social actors—repeating an "act that has been going on before one arrived on the scene."[21] The practice of gathering and dispersing for theater, as Victor Turner, Richard Schechner, and Jill Dolan have all argued, is a ritual act and, as such, repeats with each iteration an infinite number of prior actions: buying, traveling, arriving, gathering, witnessing, dispersing.[22] The spectators who sit and watch this opening scene cite all the prior times that they, or any audiences for that matter, have gathered to witness performance in Austin, or any city for that matter, as well as those *floodlines* audiences in years prior who have found their way to these same white rental chairs overlooking a cracking concrete court. In other words, the performance, in general, and this scene, in particular intends to stage the stereotype—through casting, costume, and blocking choices, among other things—which sets the tone for the performance as a whole. Staging stereotype, like breaking it, is one way to make its serializing logic visible and its subversion possible.

At the same time, because the performance begins in a public park, certain conventions of performance are called into question from the start: "Where do I park?" "Where should I go?" "Am I in the right place?" "When will it start?" Each year, I received calls on my cell phone at the start of the performance from confused, lost, and panicking friends trying to navigate this unusual theatrical start. Once audience members found their seats, they relaxed, though some reported afterward that they still carried reception anxiety, unsure whether the tennis game was part of the performance. Because the players are not particularly skilled; because the court is not particularly well kept; because there is no curtain speech, house lights down, and stage lights up; because there is nothing other than the forty seats facing the court that frames the game as "performance," many spectators are left not knowing exactly how to watch. Even Jill Dolan, *the* feminist spectator and critic, who saw the performance in 2004 and again in 2005, was destabilized by the performance's beginning.[23] Comparing her experience as ticket-holding spectator to that of various passersby, Dolan writes, "It takes a moment to realize we're in the presence of performance. And some people, along the way, never realized."[24] As Dolan's response suggests, the performance is not clearly recognizable as such because it is not clearly circumscribed in either time nor space: it is not clear, that is, when exactly it begins, or where; who is in the performance and who is merely in the sightline of the performance—who, that is, are actors and who are neighborhood residents. Granted, site-specific performance is, at this historical juncture, as conventional within experimental theater practices as the black box or proscenium stage. And Austin audiences are well primed to be able to read the avant-garde. After all, this is the city that gave birth to the Rude Mechs—whose genre-bending performances have been dazzling local and national audiences since the mid-1990s—as well as world-renowned postmodern choreographer Deborah Hay, aerial dance company Blue Lapis Light (Sally Jacques), Forklift Danceworks (Allison Orr), performance artist Linda Montano, Frontera @ Hyde Park Theater's "Mi Casa es Su Teatro" festival of site-specific work, and Refraction Arts critically acclaimed Fusebox Festival, to name just a few local artists and ensembles working within as well as redefining the postmodern conventions of site-specificity and performance art in the twentieth and twenty-first centuries.[25]

What is not common either in the Austin experimental theater scene or in local public culture, however, is the specter of the Hasidic Jew, whose presence in this context is at once extremely recognizable and completely foreign. The black suit, white shirt, yarmulke, *payot,* tzitzit, "thick glasses," and "sensible shoes": on one hand, his image calls forth prior, fictive performances of Jewish masculinity on the diasporic stage, from Shylock to Yentl.[26] Because, as theater historian Harley Erdman reminds us, Jewish impersonation is "grounded in exteriority," the visual details of this character's costume form "a discursive system based not on hidden meanings but on outward signs."[27] The fact that most of the audience members know that the actor playing the Jew is also a Jew in real life further validates the authenticity of this racial impersonation—producing what Erdman has called "a vividly true Jew."[28] In this regard, while the figure of the Hasidic Jew may be recognizable—that is, the character may be familiar as a trope or a stereotype—this fails to account for the ways in which the sudden presence of a Hasid (in drag, no less) in a public park on a Sunday afternoon in Austin, Texas, is an uncanny scene. Each year, on the morning of the performance, after getting into costume, I would run errands around town: getting a haircut, picking up sandwiches for the production team, pumping gas. Not surprisingly, people would stare, wide-eyed and watching my every move—"Is that a real Jew?" "Is that a real man?"—as I stood waiting to place my order at the deli counter at Whole Foods. In other words, this figure is totally out of time and out of place in Austin, Texas, in the twenty-first century. And so when the Jew approaches the audience at the start of the show—soaking wet, breathing heavily, staring blankly, beckoning silently to the audience to follow him (where?)—it is as if he has literally slipped out of history ("New York maybe, a different century, or some piece of buried history") and landed here, on this cracking court, in this American South, on this Sunday afternoon in April.

From the tennis courts, the Jew leads the audience to a dead-end street behind the park, which is lined with Volvos and chauffeurs (see "Volvos," p. 98). A funeral sticker with a Star of David hangs from each car's windshield. Audience members find new seats in one of each of these cars, which will carry them through the show. Because many feel the urgency of the performance's beginning—the Jew rapidly circling around the parked cars, hazards blinking, waiting for them to settle in—and because there are only exactly as many seats as people scrambling to find them (and sometimes not

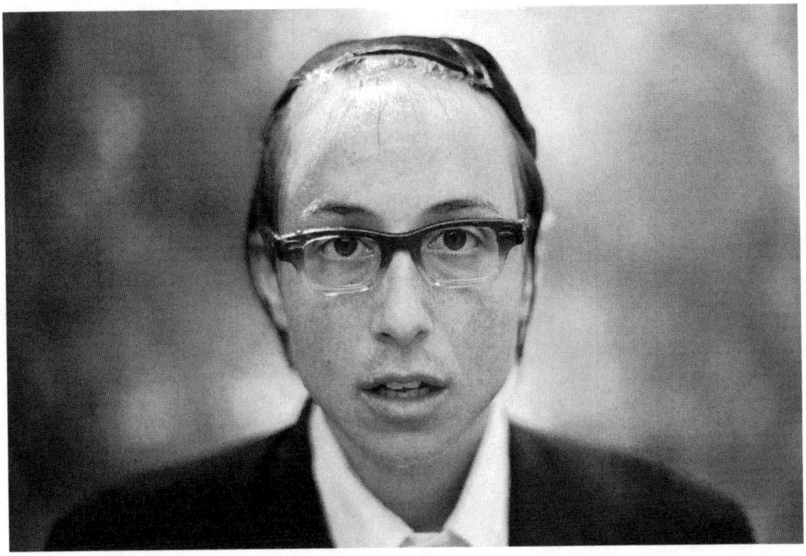

"Wandering Jew" (2009). Blake Gordon. From *floodlines*, conceived and directed by Jaclyn Pryor, performed by Jaclyn Pryor. Courtesy of Blake Gordon.

quite enough), many spectators get separated from their partners, children, and friends. Dolan describes her opening impressions:

> It's been a while since I've been in a funeral cortege, and those horrible moments have always been in Pittsburgh or Baltimore, with family. There was something about the transposition of that historical experience into the present moment that moved me. Here I am with these people whom I consider my adult family, who reconstitute, for me, a sense of caring and belonging. And they'd all been resignified as Jewish, which would only resonate in that very particular way to me and to the perhaps one or two other Jews along for the ride. I was very conscious of my friends and colleagues being asked to wear, for that moment, in that car, the public sign of my own identity.[29]

Here Dolan is attesting to the ways in which the funeral processional—the framing conceit of the performance—transposed history and memory with present experience, calling forth her personal, past experiences with family funerals amid the public, present performance. Because each car is marked with a funeral sticker and a Jewish star, the performance event is signified as a specifically Jewish funeral and the spectators as Jewish family and friends of one another, connected by their shared loss. As Dolan's description also makes clear, this make-believe funeral not only reactivates memories of actual experiences of mourning; it also asks them to "wear the public sign" of an

"Volvos" (2008). Blake Gordon. From *floodlines*, conceived and directed by Jaclyn Pryor, performed by Jack Steiner, Madeline Marabella, Tony Kotecki, Sandi Bender, Kay Bryant, Genevieve Frisch, Derek Young, and Arlen Johnson. Courtesy of Blake Gordon.

identity that may or may not be their own, to slip into role themselves: to become, that is, temporarily Jew-*ish*.

From here, the processional careens through a residential neighborhood. The passengers are tightly packed (and often hot, in old Volvos with broken air-conditioners). The drivers are instructed to keep close to one another: windows up, hazards on, running red lights, if necessary—in order to keep the cortege in tact. The running Jew leads the way on foot; his slow and steady jog sets the processional pace. His back is turned to the audience as he runs, turning his head right and left to view the staged scenes on the side of the road; occasionally he turns to gaze at the cars behind him, beckoning that they follow. In staging this, I thought of my character as Benjamin's "*Angelus Novus*"—blown forward, gaze backward, piles of wreckage hurled in front of his feet.

## Spare Parts

*Bubbles, my 1991 black Volvo 240 wagon, has made six appearances in* floodlines. *She's also been featured on the cover of L Style/G Style magazine, her owner squatting queerly on the hood. I first saw her in the Whole Foods parking lot with a "for sale" sign taped to the windshield. This was the summer after the premiere of* floodlines: *Julia's wagon, which led the way the year prior, had since died, and I was aching for one to call my own. I met the owner in a parking lot outside a pool hall called Slick Willie's. At the time, the irony was lost on me.*

*Bubbles has had her problems. Her odometer, I soon discover, is busted: she is forever frozen in time at that unremarkable moment she happened to reach 219,727 miles, and then, like any old woman might, decided to stop keeping track of time. Her front passenger seat cushion is always stuck on "heat." The volume button on her stereo is missing: she's always silently playing that same CD that's trapped inside—like her own secret mantra she'll repeat in her head until the day she dies.*

*It's Saturday morning, and I am on my way to the dress rehearsal. I've woken early to give myself enough time to stretch, dress, and drive all the way to Hyde Park from a cabin in Westlake Hills where my new girlfriend and I are playing house for the semester. As I am backing Bubbles out of the driveway, I crash into a tree. Her lights are smashed. Her bumper is hanging. For months, I will continue to find little bits of orange and red plastic littering the carport. For some reason, I think it'll look better if I remove the whole rear unit. For a year, I drive around like that—with the disfigured, gaping hole exposed, and tangled wires and empty bulb sockets peeking out. Before the second-to-last production of* floodlines, *I decide to move through the world with more dignity, and fewer traffic tickets: I go to the junkyard in search of spare parts.*

*I take a seat beside a young man in a golf cart, who takes me where I want to go: past the Mazdas, the Toyotas, and the Mercedes Benzes. These are not cars, though—they are cadavers, remains, evidence. Shattered windshields. Totaled hoods. Doors hanging off of hinges.*

*"It's like a graveyard back here," I say to the driver, as we pass the VWs. "Yeah," he chuckles, "I guess it is." "All the accidents, all the dead people," I say. "Yup," he replies.*

*We pull up to the Volvos, and he asks me what I want. "A rear unit," I say.*

*"Driver's side or passenger's?" he asks. "Driver's," I reply, as he pulls out a wrench.*

*I start to see other things I want: a hubcap, a door handle, a stereo that works. He gives me what I want (except the stereo: this will have to wait). I feel greedy, and a little perverse, scavenging like this off the already dead. On the ride back to the office, I hold the light, hubcap, and handle on my lap. The sun is setting. The junkyard is closing. I am the last customer of the day. I close my eyes as he drives, and I silently recite a prayer—like my own secret mantra I'll repeat in my head until the day I die.*

## Repetition and Revision

As the cortege careens through the neighborhood, the Jew jogging in front, *floodlines* begins to cite itself—repeating and revising images, objects, and motifs from prior moments in the show.[30] The opening tennis scene, for instance, repeats twenty minutes later in the performance. In the first scene, two adult actors played a game of tennis. In the second, two children play "boxball" in front of a residential home, their open palms volley a tennis ball back and forth on the sidewalk. In other words, the second scene repeats the first, with a change in scale: the tennis court is replaced by concrete sidewalk squares, the net by a groove in the pavement, the adults by children, and the racket by the players' hands. Because the adult actors are replaced by children, the scene enacts a slip in time as well as scale—as if the window to the adult players' childhoods has cracked open.

Because of the iconicity of many of the images, including, as Dolan notes, the conceit of the funeral processional—but also scenes of familiar sports and leisure—the spectator's memories, sensations of, and associations with these activities are being called forth during the performance. When the scenes begin to repeat, so, too, do the spectators' memories, not only of their individual pasts, but of the performance's past. In other words, *floodlines* attempts not only to activate spectators' real memories of the past, but to produce new, fictional ones during the course of the performance. As Meredith Monk explains of her site-specific performance *Juice*, which similarly plays with the materiality of time: "Memory became part of the present tense experience. We played with scale, taking motifs and then changing scale, blowing out time and space, and trying to do something else with it."[31] The repetition and revision of scenes within performance can have a powerful psychoanalytic effect: spectators connect the repeating images, characters, and motifs to prior ones within the performance and, in so doing, assimilate the fictional memories into their own memory bank. As such, the distinction between memories that are fictive and those that are real, memories that are one's own and those that are part of a collective past, begin to blur and blend. Like Eng's description of Rea Tajiri's film *History and Memory*, a passage I discussed in this book's introduction, it is as if my personal memories and fantasies which have inspired the scenes in this performance have slipped out of my mind and into public space—becoming a kind of "postmemory" for the audience to psychically incorporate.

This technique is employed throughout the performance. In another scene, "Chaise Lounge," two adults lie in white canvas chairs, sunbathing in front of a stately mansion. They wear swimwear and tanning goggles. The woman reads, the man sleeps—a towel wrapped around his waist, one hand resting on his bare chest, the other dangling limply on the grass. Another couple cruise by on a tandem bike—the man in front, the woman behind—turning their gaze and ringing a bell as they pass the chaise lounge scene. Johann

"Boxball" (2010). Blake Gordon. From *floodlines*, conceived and directed by Jaclyn Pryor, performed by Jesse Woolley-MacMath and Nate Carlson. Courtesy of Blake Gordon.

"Boxball" (ca. 1985). Harry Poholsky. My cousin Robert Jaffe and I play boxball outside my grandparents' house in Skokie, Illinois. Courtesy of the author.

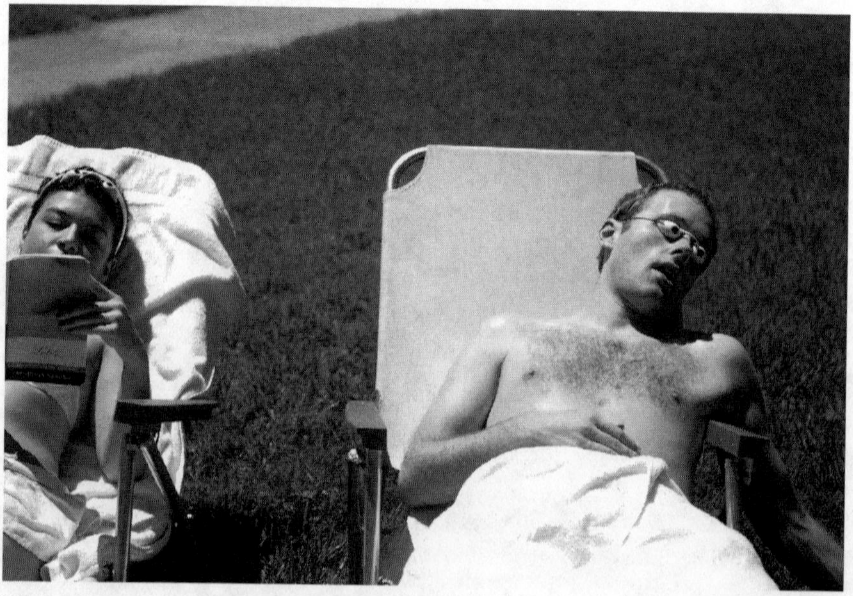

"Chaise Lounge" (2009). Blake Gordon. From *floodlines*, conceived and directed by Jaclyn Pryor, performed by Stacey Garza and Benjamin Summers. Courtesy of Blake Gordon.

Pachelbel's *Canon in D* plays in the spectators' cars, connecting this present moment of coupledom to the prior (fictive) wedding that produced it, as well as to every other (real) couple—heterosexual or otherwise—that have married to the sound of this march.

These scenes are scrambled later in the performance. In the second set of scenes, two men—one black, one white (the same actor who appeared in the earlier chaise lounge duet)—sunbathe on a different lawn. The second tableau is identical to the first—chairs, towels, book, goggles, sleep—with the exception that the woman has been replaced by a man: he reaches across to touch the other man's wrist. The scenario of normative heterosexuality has been revised into one of interracial gay male desire. When the cyclists ride past them (this time heading straight toward the running Jew who leads the processional), it suddenly becomes clear that they ride not one but two separate bikes—the woman following closely behind the man and creating the illusion of a tandem bike. Just before they hit the Jew, they part, passing the cars on the left and right. It is as if their bicycle built for two—the quintessential technology of leisurely coupledom—has literally broken apart. For the audience member who looks closely as the cyclists flit by, it becomes apparent, too, that blue surgical masks cover their noses and mouths.

To invoke an America forever caught between the ordinary and the cataclysmic, the private and the public, regimes of normal and regimes of normalization, I juxtaposed scenes of leisure with catastrophe throughout. The interplay between prosaic and violent images of American life functioned as a kind of "surface tension" throughout the performance. "[America] vibrates with surface tensions spied or sensed. . . . Unwanted intensities simmer up at the least provocation. . . . Things happen. . . . Power snaps into place. . . . The everyday is a process of going on until something happens, and then back to the going on."[32] As anthropologist Kathleen Stewart—who saw the final production of *floodlines* in 2010—reminds us, contemporary U.S. culture is always surging with "surface tensions"—low-level intensities of trauma, shock, pleasure, and danger—which occasionally erupt in localized violence, and then quickly revert back to "normal." That is, *floodlines* does not attempt to represent the United States as it is but rather to capture the affective texture of the contemporary cultural landscape that we've come to call America. In other words, *floodlines* not only repeats and revises how America looks but also how it feels. In the wake not only of 9/11, but also, as poet and performance scholar Deborah Paredez reminds us, "the anti-immigration legislation of the 1990s, the horrors of . . . the levees in New Orleans, the unsolved murders of young Latinas at the U.S.-Mexico border, [and] the disproportionate recruitment and deaths of black and Latina/o soldiers in Iraq," the "official national affect" toward nonnormative citizens and noncitizens in the contemporary United States is increasingly one of suspicion and surveillance.[33]

In staging these scenes year after year, I was increasingly aware of what it meant to place actors—of diverse identities—in roles that required them to be standing, sitting, or lying in public for hours on end (actors were asked to be in places two hours in advance of the show). The three actors who perform the "Chaise Lounge" scenes are half-naked and engaged in domestic acts like reading and sleeping—even though they are in public—placing them, to varying degrees, in precarious positions vis-à-vis the "gift of normative citizenship." That is, their "right to privacy" is determined by their perceived proximity to dominant markers of American citizenship. As Jasbir Puar explains:

> A claim to the right to privacy is not even on the radar screen for many sectors of society, unfathomable for whom being surveilled is a way of life. . . . [T]he welfare administration demands that a client open her life to them in the form of income verification, computer matches and other tactics in what can only be called a full-scale surveillance assault. . . . We see that LGBT youth constitute 25 to 40 percent of the total homeless youth population, an indictment of private liberty at home if ever there was one. The private is, therefore, offered as a gift of recognition to those invested in certain normative renditions of domesticity. . . . The private is a racialized and nationalized construct, insofar as it is granted not only to heterosexuals but to certain citizens and withheld from many others and from noncitizens. . . . The precious haven of the private [is] always a relative, tenuous, and often impossible affair for people of color and immigrants.[34]

"Chaise Lounge" (1972). Harry Poholsky. My grandmother, Esther Poholsky, in the side yard of her suburban home in Skokie, Illinois. Courtesy of the author.

As I will detail, certain performers were less able to safely perform their privacy in public because of their perceived proximity to racial and sexual dissidence.[35] As the introduction to this book claims, a livable, grievable life is not only given by birthright, it must be maintained through normative displays of doing one's citizenship correctly, repeatedly, and without difference.

Here, it is important to recall that Butler's notion of gender as a performative rests on J. L. Austin's claim that it is the linguistic utterance "I do" that produces a bridegroom and bride. This utterance has material consequences because it is nonoriginal: it cites every prior "I do" utterance, and in this repeating it gains its "performative" power. The *floodlines* project engages most directly with Butler's thesis in the staging of the scene "Brides." While most vignettes in the show repeat once—slowly appearing, quickly receding as the cars roll by, and then recurring again with some kind of visual shift, "Brides" repeats, twists, and transforms itself five times over the course of the performance.

The first time a single bride appears, she is sitting on a swing adjacent to a white house. She wears a white dress and veil and holds a bouquet of daisies in her hand. Her blank stare evokes something peculiar and a bit melancholic. When she reappears later in the performance, she is among a

"Brides" (2009). Blake Gordon. From *floodlines*, conceived and directed by Jaclyn Pryor, performed by Dustin Wills. Courtesy of Blake Gordon.

dozen who are gathered in pairs on the front lawn of a church. On the one hand, this church could be any church in America: the steps, the steeple, the double doors. However, unlike at a typical wedding, there are twelve brides (and no grooms): six lesbian couples stand on the grassy knoll, fingers interlaced—a bouquet of daisies between them—whispering their vows. Looking closely, it also becomes apparent that several of the brides are played by cisgender men—with unshaven faces visible beneath veils; large bodies spilling out of tight gowns; and flat hairy chests peeking out at the neckline.

The sight of men in wedding dresses sparked alarm in the local community. On more than one occasion, I had to meet with church leaders to reassure them that this was "theater," not "real" (gay) life. It also produced racial and sexual anxieties for some of the cast members. One Asian American male actor whom I cast in the role of a bride dropped out of the show, explaining that the idea of performing publicly in a dress made him uncomfortable. This actor was aware of the privileges and dangers of "sex in public," and aware, perhaps, too, of the orientalist stereotype that his performance might evoke—of the Asian or Asian American man as emasculated, and therefore always already queer.[36]

"Buggy" (2010). Blake Gordon. From *floodlines,* conceived and directed by Jaclyn Pryor, performed by Charmaine Nichols. Courtesy of Blake Gordon.

When the cortege reaches the church, the brides are directed to flood into the street, discarding their bouquets on the grass. They run alongside the processional like competitors in a race. After several blocks, they encounter another scene—a bucket brigade that chants "go, go" as they pass one-gallon jugs of water down the line. Each bride is handed a jug, and she dumps it on her head. Now wet like the Jew who runs alongside them, the brides turn a corner and disappear from view, and then reemerge at the climax of the performance wearing swim caps and goggles. As they race toward the processional of cars, they perform a synchronized, militarized dance—sharply turning their heads back and forth in unison, stomping their feet, and chanting a sequence of guttural sounds. The Benjaminian dreamworld that "Brides" evokes—the flood into the streets, the bucket brigade, the synchronized swim turned military march—attempts to place the American wedding against the backdrop of the "'state of emergency' in which we [now] live"[37] in this unraveling post-9/11 "homeland" security state.

In this America, it is the working class and working poor who labor on behalf of the state. As *Geyser Land*'s "Gandy Dancers" illustrated, it is often the invisibilized labor of people of color that keep the trains, and keep the time, running straight. This racialization of capital is cited in two scenes that

"Violins" (2010). Blake Gordon. From *floodlines*, conceived and directed by Jaclyn Pryor, performed by Ricardo Cruz and Robby Gonzalez. Courtesy of Blake Gordon.

audience members encounter during the processional. In "Buggy," a black woman pushes a pram across the street—citing the history of care work that women of color perform for mostly white families. When she reappears later in the performance, she is pushing a white man (who was previously seen sorting mail outside his home) in a wheelchair.

In "Violins," two men in matching white tuxedos stand side by side on a concrete traffic median. In one hand, they each hold a rusty metal frying pan that they rest under their chin like violins; in the other, they hold a long-handled ladle and spoon, respectively. Their movements are synchronized as they slowly extend and release their "bows." Their gaze is focused outward, into the distance (see "Violins," p. 107).

Like "Buggy," this scene locates people (of color) at work rather than at play. The "work" is both the playing of imaginary music and the playing of the real performance, *floodlines*. At the moment the processional encounters this scene, Aimee Mann's "Nothing Is Good Enough" begins to play in each car—the duets' live, air violin brushes up against the prerecorded string instrumentals on the track, producing the illusion that it is the men (rather than Mann) generating the sounds. Because this is the first scene audiences encounter in the processional route, the violinists are meant to be signified not only as the producers of this particular song but as *the* musicians for the show—as if through some slip of time and space and queer magic they will continue to create the twelve tracks of music that will play from each car's stereo for the next ninety minutes.

"Buggy" (1947). Photographer unknown. My grandfather, Harry Poholsky, in Chicago, Illinois. Courtesy of the author.

This performance also reveals the performers' actual labor. Standing in their candy-white tuxedos in the middle of the road, these actors display their theatrical virtuosity by moving precisely and gracefully in spite of the blazing heat, the beeping and whizzing traffic, and the often drunk (mostly white male) college students that heckle them from the pub across the street. Five out of the seven years of staging this scene, I cast Latino actors in these roles, and all of these men were also queer. Because the two mirrored one another in costume and movement, they not only cited each other but also called forth a familiar and precarious structure of feeling other, what José Muñoz calls "feeling brown." Building on the observations of cultural critic Raymond Williams and feminist theorist Norma Alarcón, Muñoz argues that feeling brown is a subversive performance modality that negotiates *latinidad* with and against the "official national affect(s)" of white America. Here *latinidad* signifies less a coalitional pan-Latino identity and more a structure of feeling other(ed) in/by a dominant U.S. culture that exploits the labor of Latina/o immigrants and migrants. "What unites and consolidates opposition groups is not simply the fact of identity but the way in which they perform affect, especially in relation to an official 'national affect' that is aligned with a hegemonic class."[38] Both the fictive musicians and the real actors labor for an overwhelmingly white, heterosexual audience—including the official passengers (those who have bought thirty-dollar tickets) and the accidental audiences who encounter the scene by chance. The men at the nearby pub who hoot and holler and stare do so, in part, because they recognize that this pair is out of time and place—two brown dandies in white tuxedos with frying pans on an otherwise "normal" Sunday afternoon in April.

Like the bride who dropped out of the show, these actors' right to privacy in public was tenuous because the performance placed them in proximity with "real" people who had no framework for making sense of the performance, and in proximity to the everyday racism and homophobia of the university campus, which serves as backdrop for the scene.[39] Later, when the processional travels past "real" black and Latino construction workers laboring in the streets of this predominantly white neighborhood, it becomes unclear which performance is staged and which is not.

## Watching and Waiting

*I am asleep in my East Village apartment. Karen and I have spent the day running from the Bowery to Midtown and back again—searching for food, water, cover, and information—so, as any newly terrorized civilian might, I've fallen into a strange, lucid, nightmarish sleep, which will continue for several years.*

*The dream itself will go something like this: we are sitting at a long, white banquet table on the street. I am wearing a wedding dress. Karen is wearing a wedding dress. Our guests are toasting, clinking, and smiling for the camera. I look up—an airplane is crashing down on us. I can see its nose. We scream. It strikes. We fly: queers in outer space.*

*Time will pass. On April 3, 2004, I'll stage the very first scene: a wedding. Two brides will stare up at the sky, frozen in alarm. The next year, I'll add eight more brides: they'll stand two by two by two by two on the church lawn, exchanging vows. When the processional approaches, they'll flood the streets.*

*Keeping art true to life, Karen will play a bride. She will swing on a swing and stare in the distance—as if watching, and waiting—before reappearing in the wedding at the church. I'll give her the best dress—a long, beaded gown we'll borrow from a local production of Chuck Mee's play, appropriately titled* Big Love.

*Time will pass. On May 3, 2007, two weeks after the fourth production of* floodlines, *Karen and I will split. I'll move out. I'll move a lot. I'll get an apartment, and then another, and then another. After some months, she'll ask me to get my shit out of the garage. She'll say, "since you're obviously not coming back," but inside I'll know she is bluffing. For years, she'll keep a picture of me on the back porch, next to the rusty tin of "thyme" I had cleverly gifted her when we first met in 2000—when, that is, the whole millennium was still possible. I'll pack as many banquet tables and Styrofoam cups as will fit in the trunk of my Volvo. I don't know it yet, but I will be—and for many years to come, I will continue to be—rootless, and in motion.*

*The* floodlines *project will remain the constant. Production meetings. Benefit parties. Running through the streets, a wandering Jew. (Life has caught up with art.) New bodies will fill old roles. The six-year-old boy in the kiddie pool will turn thirteen, mustache fuzz above his lip—his little brother will step in. Another actor will die from a rare cancer at the age of twenty-six. She, too, will be replaced. People will move away, or change their emails: new casts will emerge. Over the years, and much to my surprise,* floodlines *will develop a following—neighborhood residents, many of them seniors, will want in on the action. I'll dress them in nightgowns and give them walkers and shopping carts to push down the road—replacing my twenty-something friends who originated the roles. Sometimes they'll cast themselves in the show—setting up chairs and picnics and tripod cameras all along Avenue B, like it's some kind of parade. Or they'll just show up out of the blue in the middle of the show, wearing white trousers, or swimming goggles, or riding a bike.*

*Time will pass. I'll invite Karen to continue to perform in* floodlines*; she'll decline. I'll consider leaving the role uncast, the swing empty, but decide again and again that the show must go on: a redhead, a South Asian woman, a lesbian with tattoos. For the next three years, I'll run past these women, and always see double: the person on the swing at that present moment, and Karen—watching and waiting.*

## Future (Anterior) Citizens

In creating scenes with young people, *floodlines* engages the dominant social imaginary that frames children as idealized, future citizens of the state. These scenes "work" in part because spectators have been primed to see children as representations of the national future. In "Lemonade," a young girl in a white dress stands behind a handmade lemonade stand, pouring pink lemonade into a clear plastic cup for an imagined customer. Beside her, a Mason jar collects her earnings. She chants "Lemonade, lemonade, get your lemonade," but her singsong is muffled by the rolled-up car windows and by the soundtrack that plays in each car—a scratchy, hypnotic drone of steel guitar, reminiscent of a flickering film reel, or an oncoming train.[40]

The lemonade girl is ubiquitous, perhaps because she brings multiple imaginaries together at once: the innocence of childhood, in general, and white girlhood in particular; female domesticity; and nascent capital production.[41] That is, this scene captures children rehearsing grown-up, normative, civic life. The lemonade ritual serves as role-play, and so it goes: one day this little girl will have a kitchen, a family, and a job of her own. But there is something "off"

"Lemonade" (2009). Blake Gordon. From *floodlines*, conceived and directed by Jaclyn Pryor, performed by Maya Lawrence. Courtesy of Blake Gordon.

about this particular lemonade girl. Her long blond hair is unkempt: it blows wildly in the wind. Her gaze is trancelike: eyes cast downward, focused, and intense. Her "lemonade" refrain is repeated in a monotonous, affectless tone.

Interpreted differently, perhaps this little girl is not off at all. Perhaps this lemonade girl's flat affect could be read as a refusal to participate in the construction of normativity. Or perhaps her numbness to the intensities that swirl around her should be read as a symptom of "nerve weakness"—a uniquely postmodern condition that American writer and literary critic Tom Lutz characterizes by disturbances in the nervous system, such as "brain collapse." Building on Lutz as well as novelist and literary critic Raymond Williams, Stewart describes how this "unsteady and fraught structure of feeling" was produced by "large-scale modernist social transformations" that, "like stress now, was a weird sign of difference turned on the body."[42] In this sense, the lemonade girl's flat affect can also be read as evidence of the low-grade trauma of contemporary culture turned inward.[43]

Similarly, in the scene "Teen Dance," a boy and girl sit on a concrete slab in a dirty alley. They wear formal attire, the corsage around her wrist matches the boutonniere pinned to his lapel, marking them as teens attending some kind of ritualized date—homecoming or prom, perhaps, or maybe a turnabout dance. This scene, that is, evokes those formal dances that many teens attend in middle and high school, which are rehearsals for heterosexual courtship and adulthood.

However, sitting in an alley rather than a grade school auditorium, this girl and boy seem out of place. Her corsage is dismantled; his shirt and tie are unbuttoned; a cigarette hangs from his lips: while their intention may have been to attend a dance, the plan seems to have somehow gone awry. Perhaps they never made it there; perhaps they left early. In either case, the idealized portrait of nascent and normative sexuality that is the teenage dance has, like the boy's bowtie and the girl's corsage, begun to come undone.

Later in the performance, the young couple appears again, this time standing on a manicured green lawn and posing, as the boy's mother in real life as well as in *floodlines* takes pictures. Like "Boxball," this scene suggests a slip backward in time—to the moment just a few hours prior, when the couple prepared to depart for the dance. The fact that the boy's mother takes photos underscores the picturesque nature of this prior moment. The time before the dance, that is, mirrors the broader social imaginary of adolescent sexuality—a period marked by hope. Like Dan Savage's message to his imagined community of suicidal queer teens, the grade school dance aims to discipline its participants into believing that the future pulsates with promise.

"Teen Dance," however, reverses that promise. As the first (future) scene reveals, these kids' lives get dirtier, lonelier, and more undone. By placing the future before the past, the production also asks its audience members to participate in the construction of this scene's meaning: "Why are they dressed up, sitting in an alley?" "Where are they coming from?" "Where are they going?" The next scene completes the story, restoring the teens to a prior moment of respectability—but for the audience member who remembers the scene in the alley, the happy scene on the lawn is overlaid with melancholy and loss. Because, too, the boy's mother is shown in the process of documenting the event, the scene also gestures to an unseen future moment when this present moment would be remembered in print. Rosalyn Deutsche, citing Lacan, calls this the "future anterior." She explains:

> The future anterior is used to describe an action that has not yet happened but that will have taken place before another stated occurrence or reference point in the future. . . . The future anterior is an order of time that lacks closure because in it the meaning of a past event is conditional on an inconclusive future. The past isn't simply there to be recovered; past events and action are what will have happened as history mutates. As Jacques Lacan puts it, theorizing the future anterior as the time of *personal* history, "What is realized in my history is not the past definite of what *was*, since it is no more, or even the present perfect of what has been in what I am, but the future anterior of what I *shall have been* for what I am in the process of becoming.[44]

This Kodak moment on the lawn encapsulates not only the future moment in the alley but also that future moment of the not-yet-developed photograph when this present *shall have been* the past. As detailed in my discussion of *Geyser Land*, the act of taking a photograph is the quintessential performative of the American Dream: like Freud's feverish archivist, the American with the camera attempts to locate, secure, and fix an imaginary, idealized (future) past. What's more, this scene, while banal in isolation, is surrounded by a flurry of mounting chaos. A militarized brigade rations water on the adjacent street corner; terrorized brides in wet gowns and half-naked men in suits run past the scene; two bicyclists split and flit by, surgical masks covering their noses and mouths. While the boy, girl, and mother perhaps do not yet sense the pull of imminent danger, the *floodlines* audience, who have been given a literal window through which to see the larger picture of this unraveling America, do.

This scene also mirrors and anticipates the project of documenting the performance event itself. Surrounding the woman with the camera are dozens of other people with cameras: neighborhood residents who have come ready to point and shoot; curious passersby catching and capturing a flicker of their queer afternoon; and the *floodlines* production team, whom I have hired to create the "official" record of the event. Year after year, with little sense of irony, we spent thousands of dollars trying to "save" the performance with digital photography and video, as well as 35 mm and 16 mm film: to know that it happened, and to suggest that it meant something. And while we did create a record—I have the hard drives and shoeboxes full of tapes and reels and discs and prints to prove it—there are lots of missing DV tapes and misplaced memory sticks, missing scenes and missing things. One year, we even had a camera rolling without film. In other words, the archive, like trauma, is and is not what is seems.

## The Accretion of History

Due to the serial nature of the performance, a significant amount of real time passed and real events transpired between the first and last run of the show. To reflect this, each year I slipped in a new scene or two, or recast roles; I changed details of costume or gesture, site or sound. In other words, I repeated and revised not only within the structure of the performance but also the performance itself to stay true to the passage of time and the accretion of history.

For the final production of *floodlines,* I created the scene "Runners." Four men run down the street: their jogging whites, bright sneakers, and the yellow numbers safety-pinned onto their shorts mark them as competitors in a race. If this scene is one of labor—marked by their quick pace, intent focus, and rhythmic, heavy breathing—it is the kind of privileged labor one chooses to

"Runners" (2010). Blake Gordon. From *floodlines*, conceived and directed by Jaclyn Pryor, performed by Steve Goldman. Courtesy of the author.

endure out of sport. The actors playing the runners range in size and ethnicity, but they are united by their shared desire to flex their physical and mental endurance through competitive athletics, a quintessential performance of normative masculinity. When the runners reappear later in the performance, they are wearing business suits, and they are covered in white dust (see "Runners," p. 114). If "Boxball" reverses time, "Runners" accelerates it, the second image fast-forwarding the men and the audience from a moment of leisure to crisis.

The scene is meant to evoke the time of capital derailed, progress disordered, and masculinity disarrayed. In each of their hands, the runners cling to familiar objects of late capitalism: a disposable cup; an attaché case; a stack of paperwork and cell phone; a MacBook: business as usual. Their pants have gone missing, evoking a dream or a nightmare alongside reality and exposing the fragility of their masculinity—literally stripping them down to the flesh.

I had thought of this image when first creating the piece in 2004, but at the time it felt too literal, and too tied to the visual spectacle of 9/11 in New York City. By 2010, however, it felt to me like the passing decade had repositioned the event as more iconic than particular, more emblematic than exceptional:

an American Dream gone awry, again and again and again. Arts critic Mike Agresta writes,

> A tone of grief pervades *floodlines*, from the funeral procession tags on the Volvo windshields, to the wailing Sigur Ros on the car stereos, to the textual clues playing on words "missing" and "falling." Of course, September 11 comes to mind—and Pryor cites her experience in New York in 2001 as a catalyst for the piece. However, the show does not feel so much tied to history as alive to it. More recent references like Hurricane Katrina and imminent ecological disaster resound just as powerfully.[45]

Thus, while the project began in response to the events of September 11, 2001, the events in the decade that followed—personal and collective, ordinary and cataclysmic—continued to inform the making, remaking, and reception of the work: a dead grandmother, a dead grandfather, a hurricane in the Gulf. A lost lover, a lost home, a lost job. A dead cat, another lover almost lost, another mind almost lost, a tsunami in the Pacific, an earthquake in the Caribbean. For me, *floodlines* functioned as container for and retainer of the accretion of losses over time. Grief accretes and accretes, repeats and repeats—such is the nature of grief.

Two other actors, Julia M. Smith and Nate Zivin, also performed in *floodlines* for all seven years—their personal histories overlaid onto the official production history like a kind of memory graft. The span of Nate's childhood is marked by his participation in *floodlines,* as he began when he was six years old and continued until he was fourteen (when, for the final production in 2010, he composed, recorded, and performed live piano for the show). His mother performed in the show for six of those years, his little brother for four, and his father for one. To adapt to the changing age and size of Nate and his brother, Jacob (who was in diapers when the seven-year run began), we restaged their scenes from year to year, changing their costumes, activities, and roles to reflect the ways their lives were changing outside the framework of the performance. "Kiddie Pool" however, was central to the narrative arc of the show, and it remained in place for the entire seven-year run.

Like "Runners," "Kiddie Pool" was directly inspired by the events of 9/11 and their aftermath. In creating this scene, I was recalling my experience having dinner with my then-girlfriend at Tavern on the Green in New York City a few days after September 11, 2001. As I detailed in the introduction to this book, New Yorkers were urged, again and again, to shop, eat out, and get back to normal. We had taken ourselves out for an expensive meal because we thought it would make us feel better. But we ate silently and felt overdressed, surrounded by other New Yorkers who appeared equally out of time and out of place and out of sorts. A man and his young son were seated at a small table beside us; they were also silent and sadly overdressed—the father slowly cutting and gently moving pieces of food from his plate onto the boy's. To my girlfriend, I remarked that it reminded me of that moment in *Titanic* when the violinist, with little other choice, begins to play the hymn "Nearer My God to Thee" as the ship slowly slips beneath the sea.

When the Zivin family arrived for their first rehearsal three years later, I tried to stage this feeling. Because it happened to be Passover, and because the Zivin family is Jewish, they had brought matzo sandwiches and a container of salt to rehearsal. During that two-hour rehearsal, we played with these props and a variety of staging possibilities until we set the scene: two people sit at a table, inside of a kiddie pool, which is inflated on a cement sidewalk adjacent to a neighborhood church. One person—most years played by the boys' mother—holds a container of Morton salt, which she pours in a steady stream into her son's cupped hands. Adjacent to this scene is "Violins," who have reappeared wearing orange life vests. Read together, these two scenes are meant to suggest that the titanic that we call family and nation is slowly, gently, going down. And what is more quintessentially American than two brown queers left to man the hull?

One year, Nate's father stepped into the role that his wife had originated. The real-life parents were now separated, and, as is often the case with young children and divorce, the father was now "taking his turn." The next year, the father moved back to Chicago, and the mother stepped back into her role. And in the final year of the performance, the eldest brother had become a towering teen—too big to read as a little boy—he stepped into the parent's role and his little brother into his own.

In the final version of the scene, the two boys sit alone in the pool. Like the Jew and brides before them, they are soaking wet. Their stares are blank. The eldest pours a steady stream of salt into his little brother's hands. There is something eerie and foreboding about this scene: "What are they doing?" "Why are they alone?" "What has happened to their parents?" Like Lot's wife, it is as if their mother has turned into the very salt they pour between them—and the boys have turned to stone. Deborah Paredez—who saw the performance in 2005—said that the scene reminded her of the story of Lot's wife, which she herself had written about extensively in her collection *Lot's Wife Series*. She writes:

> When the forsaken city starts to burn,
> after the men and children have fled,
> stand still, silent as prey, and slowly turn
> back. Behold the curse. Stay and mourn
> the collapsing doorways, the unbroken bread
> in the forsaken city starting to burn.
> Don't flinch. Don't join in.
> Resist the righteous scurry and instead

stand still, silent as prey. Slowly turn
your thoughts away from escape: the iron
gates unlatched, the responsibilities shed.
When the forsaken city starts to burn,
surrender to your calling, show concern
for those who remain. Come to a dead
standstill. Silent as prey, slowly turn
into something essential. Learn
the names of the fallen. Refuse to run ahead
when the forsaken city starts to burn.
Stand still and silent. Pray. Return.[46]

Like Lot's wife—who dares to look back in defiance as the city is devoured by fire and brimstone—perhaps this mother is not so much punished as praised by her God, for "showing concern" for those who remain. In turning back to look, in turning back to salt, the disappeared mother reminds us, perhaps, that remembrance is more "essential" than obedience.

A small black letter board—the kind that usually announces worship times and pancake breakfasts—hangs on the brick facade outside the church that frames this scene. This letter board always says the same thing, as it did for seven years:

WITH THE
HELP OF GOD
I SHALL BECOME
MYSELF

GRACE

There are a number of signs and text embedded throughout the performance: a chain-link fence with the phrase "i swam across the atlantic ocean through detritus and survived" spelled out with Styrofoam cups; eighteen missing signs staked on the grass—"missing children," "missing my flight," "missing my period," "missing you." Because of this, many audience members later report that they presumed that the text in the kiosk had also been staged; but it was just a "sign." For the Zivin family, who performed in the show for seven years—returning to this same spot each April in spite of, or because of, the changing shape and size of their family—this sign, we joked, was the floodline of *floodlines*.[47] It was the fixed mark on the landscape by which they, and I, observed and measured the change all around and within ourselves. As Nate grew from boy to man, and Jacob from infant to boy, the former assumed his parents' role, the latter his older brother's. And as their mother went from wife to single mom, her husband moved—not unlike in real life—first in, then out, of her place.

## Digging Rites

*"That yard is co-rrect!" says Daniel Alexander Jones, before adding that I should consider giving them a pie. That yard is correct—I know it—so if it has to come to pie, I will do it.*

*In its first two years,* floodlines *held its final scene in the side yard of a stately Hyde Park mansion on Avenue D: a three-story colonial, corner lot, with meticulously manicured grass. It was tropical, too: coral paint, jade trim, giant magnolias, agaves, and palms. The entire estate was gated by a three-foot-tall wrought iron fence, which swung open in one secret spot. It was the contrast of the quintessentially American—and specifically southern colonial—look of the site, with the odd Jewish ritual that it hosted, that made it, in Daniel's words, so "correct."*

*I discovered this gem because my then-friend, colleague, and sometime dramaturg was renting a room in its attic. When I would visit, I knew to remove my shoes before ascending the spiral stairs; to not gather in numbers greater than five, or after the hour of nine; to enter through the side and not the front. These were not her rules, but house rules, handed down by the lords of the land.*

*"Remember, they're Republicans," my friend warns me, as I prepare to knock on their door. "Right," I say, understanding "Republican" as shorthand for "traditional," "methodical," and "quick to call the police." My plan is to be calm, kempt, and most of all factual—but because I am essentially asking permission to invite a few dozen strangers to watch me dig a hole in their yard, I also know to go easy on the details.*

*By some grace of God, they say yes. And so for two years, I lead the cortege to this magical spot, where I place one tiny American flag, two locks of my freshly cut hair, and a cupful each of salt and water into a glass vial—burying them as far down into their earth as my fingers will take me.*

*By the third year, I don't even think to ask. I already have two vials buried under their sycamore—somehow, I reason, this gives me digging rights. I am wrong.*

*"I don't think it's a good idea," she says. "Not this year." It's a beautiful Sunday afternoon in April. We are rehearsing; she and her husband are sitting on their wraparound porch, drinking juice and reading* The Statesman.

*"The show is next week!" . . . "One more year, please?" . . . "But I am leading them here, to this place, specifically—the whole performance is structured around it." I'm clearly desperate. I'm losing my ground. I implore. I persist. I perpetuate stereotypes about pushy Jews.*

*"I don't know." She glances toward the porch. She fingers the top button of her blouse. Her husband, we notice, has disappeared inside; this conversation is over, his folded paper seems to say. I shift tactics.*

*"I totally understand. It's a lot to ask. You don't need to say for sure right now. You can think about it, and let me know." She pauses. She squints. She says, "Okay. I'll think about it."*

*As I drive away, I run into Daniel, walking to campus. I tell him my tale. "Here is what you do," he says, with conviction and flair. He is bent over, his head peeking in through my Volvo window. He is speaking to me, but he is also performing for Chrissy, who is filming from my passenger seat.*

*"Give them a pie." Something fresh, he says. Cherry, blueberry, peach. "You'll be golden," Daniel adds, as he winks and walks away.*

*I go to Quack's down the road. I buy a cherry tart and leave it on their stoop with a note and my email address. I report back to Daniel. He is upset.*

*"A tart? You gave them a tart? Oh, no! Not a tart! Not a pastry! 'A pie,' I said—'an American pie'!" His objection is dramaturgical, and impassioned. "Can you swap it out?"*

*I do a drive-by, but it is already gone. I go home. I tell Karen about the tart. She thinks I'm nuts.*

*"They're not going to eat your tart, Jaclyn. They're going to think you're a total meshugenah." Karen has started speaking in Yiddish.*

*What was I thinking? I go online to send them a note, to explain, reframe, contextualize. I have a new message in my inbox:*

> *Dear Jaclyn Pryor:*
>
> *After much consideration, we have decided to decline your offer to use our yard for your performance. Our sycamore—where you dug—is dying. We think you killed our tree.*
>
> *Best of luck with your event.*
>
> *Sincerely yours . . .*
>
> *p.s.: Thank you for the tart.*

*Hastily, I find another yard, down the street. It has less of a southern than a suburban feel, but it will do. The mediocrity of the new site is outweighed by the congeniality of the Houstons, its owners. The Houstons prepare: mowing the lawn, hanging a flag, picking up poo from the grass. They're curious, committed, and participatory: they even come to see the performance from beginning to end, to see what all this digging is about. They like it; they love it; they invite us back for five more years.*

*While burying vial number 6 during the penultimate performance, I hit something hard. I figure it's rock, or a root, or some caliche soil. Looking down at my hands, I see glass, and cork, and a matted clump of my hair, floating inside. I place vial number 6 beside it—it being either vial number 3, 4, or 5—and cover them with fresh dirt. I disrobe. I disappear. As I race back to the park, I imagine my underground collection of tubes—first one, then two, now six, soon seven—as rootstock, or rhizome, growing and spreading ever so secretly beneath our feet.*

## The Return

At the climax of the performance, the running Jew makes his final turn down a quiet, residential street. An American flag hangs from every house on the block, their repeating pattern suggestive of the kinds of sobering national disasters that call people—including those whose sense of patriotism lies dormant—to mournfully hang the symbol of nation for all the world to see.

The ultimate repetition in *floodlines* takes place immediately after the processional turns this bend. Running toward the Jew is another dressed in likeness, played by Smith. This second Jew has been haunting the performance throughout—conspicuously jogging behind the runners, watching the train of Volvos and brides and men caked with dust careen by from his perch on a nearby swing. Like his doppel that leads the way, this Jew's movements are slow and steady—until now—as the two race toward one another in the center of the flag-lined street. It is as if they have been running toward each other this whole time, or perhaps their whole lives. When they reach one another, they collide and embrace. They hold one another tightly for some time, quieting their breathing as the passengers emerge from the recently parked cars and gather around them to witness. The men walk in step to a young sycamore, where they pray.

The two Jews—repetitions of one another—simultaneously wrap their arms with vinyl tape measures; read from tiny, black paper books; sway; and chant a long litany of things fallen: "Falling down. Falling apart. Falling for it. Falling in love. Falling out of love. Falling star. Falling property values. Falling sperm counts. Falling empire. Falling in. Falling through. Falling through the cracks. Falling snow. Falling rain. Rainfall . . ."[48] One Jew, the runner who has led the audience to this point, gestures for them to follow him behind the house. There he cuts his *payoth* and buries them with a cupful each of salt and water and a tiny American flag that he peels from his tongue. He unwraps the tape measure from around his arm and reads text that is inscribed inside. He discards his suit, yarmulke, tzitzit, and glasses, revealing a black dress underneath. He (now she) walks away, leaving the audience behind. A small boy—the one who moments earlier had caught the stream of salt in his hands—stands alone by the tree in an oversized suit. It is as if the adult doppel, who stayed back at the tree while the rest of the audience followed their leader, had himself slipped back, or forward, or elsewhere, in time.

In the end, *floodlines* repeats itself. After the funeral ritual, the passengers return to their cars, the chauffeurs tracing the processional route in reverse.[49] The actors are gone, but the detritus of their worlds remain: kiddie pool,

“Funeral” (2009). Blake Gordon. From *floodlines*, conceived and directed by Jaclyn Pryor, performed by Jaclyn Pryor and Julia M. Smith. Courtesy of Blake Gordon.

“Tefillin” (2010). Blake Gordon. From *floodlines*, conceived and directed by Jaclyn Pryor, performed by Jacob Zivin. Courtesy of Blake Gordon.

lemonade stand, water jugs, daisies, chaise lounges, wheelchair, walkers, pram, shopping carts, and Styrofoam cups litter the streets. As Peggy Phelan writes,

> I am investigating the possibility that something substantial could be made from the outline left after the body has disappeared. My hunch is that the affective outline of what we've lost might bring us closer to the bodies we still want to touch than the restored illustration can. Or at least the hollow of the outline might allow us to understand more deeply why we long to hold bodies that are gone.[50]

Like the bicycle, the work gloves, and the firefighter cap with which I began this chapter, the "outline left" makes visible not the leftovers but the missing—drawing our attention to our individual and collective desires to "hold bodies that are gone."

In reflecting on the performance's seven-year (and ninety-minute) run, I often wondered what compelled audience members to follow me—to get in those cars and say yes to the ride. Sure, they had purchased tickets. Some had read the reviews and knew it was going to be "a good show." But I was struck, time and time again, by those passengers who submitted themselves to uncomfortable seats in hot cars on an otherwise beautiful Sunday afternoon when they could be anywhere; who put their lives in the hands of a silent stranger at the wheel—one who ran red lights, kept windows up, music loud, blinkers on, no holds barred. As previously noted, in the later years of the performance's run, the production's following grew: neighborhood residents set up folding chairs, cameras, and sometimes scenes of their own, lining the streets to watch, record, and participate. Some years, bicycles joined the processional. In 2010, the final year of the performance, there were what felt like hundreds of cyclists tagging along behind the cortege. One chauffeur, who had driven her Volvo in *floodlines* for several years, remarked to me after the final show, "We would have followed you anywhere."[51] While I cannot claim to know exactly what she meant, it is my sense that she meant that she *trusted* me, and perhaps, too, that she believed that wherever it was that I was leading her was somewhere she wanted to go. Jill Dolan similarly explains,

> The first moment I think I realized what the performance would mean to me was when we turned on to San Jacinto. . . . I turned back to look behind me, and saw my colleagues and friends in the following cars, and felt my throat close with a kind of love and wonder, that here we all were, following you, Jaclyn, in these strangers' cars, as you ran. We took a leap of faith with you: we got into cars with strangers driving, we didn't know what would happen to us, or where you would take us, but we trusted you enough to put our bodies in those cars and continue on.[52]

"Tefillin" (date unknown). Photographer unknown. My grandfather, Jerry Pryor, at the Western Wall in Jerusalem, Israel/Palestine. Courtesy of the author.

It is my sense, then, that this performance; this ghost following; this being asked to see things, and then see them again, but differently—trusting and taking "a leap of faith" in deciding to come along for the ride—was something that audiences not only wanted but perhaps, like me, somehow needed to do. Critic Barbara Chisholm, who saw the performance in 2007, writes:

> [I am] a resident of Our Fair City for more than 20 years . . . so the eerie feeling of being lost in Hyde Park induced by the performance *floodlines* was unsettling to say the least. It wasn't that it had us careening through the neighborhood . . . with landmarks whizzing by too quickly to be clearly perceived; we were creeping along at a speed joggers could keep pace with. But it was precisely this deliberate pace that induced a dreamlike stupor, and more than once, I had the disarming feeling of being completely lost. . . . The landscape isn't physically altered, but the meditative pace and hypnotic effect of the unexpected inserted into the familiar creates the sense of a dream, the kind you start to describe by saying, "I was in Hyde Park, but it wasn't really Hyde Park." At one point, I thought, "If I were let out of the car now, I would have no idea where I am or how to get out."

> Which was ridiculous; these were streets in a neighborhood I've traveled countless times.[53]

In one sense, Chisholm's narrative suggests that it is the slow pace of the journey, coupled with the "hypnotic effect of the unexpected inserted into the familiar," that disorients the spectator during the performance. I would argue that perhaps this "eerie feeling" of being lost stems also from a desire—or perhaps need?—to be led, to be "induced [into] a dreamlike stupor," to get lost somewhere familiar, to not know how to get out, all the while knowing that you can, and will, and must. Critic Robert Fairies, who saw the performance in 2006, adds, "The work, which I experienced last spring, has the feel of a waking dream, making the familiar unfamiliar, drenching the known in mystery and opening one to wonder and change."[54] In this sense, the performance perhaps offers its participants a kind of caretaking, or stewardship, for the mysteries and wonders of grief. As Harad puts it, "*floodlines* is, most of all, a gift to all of us who have been afraid to venture into the salt ocean of our familial, historical grief, for fear we would drown. Pryor swims for us, and throws a line from the other side."[55] Getting lost somewhere familiar, getting lost somewhere familial: "We return to the same place over and over until we don't need to anymore. We turn it over until we cease to need to turn it over." I needed to swim for seven "straight" years, and then, one day, I stopped. Repetition: something is changed.

# Chapter 4

# Teaching Time

## (a *periplum*)

While things seem to be going smoothly for power, while things seem to be moving along, out of sight, and hidden away, people are elaborating responses to the kind of insults that they—we—are all required to take daily. And there comes a moment, and nobody knows when or how, when those hidden transcripts of resistance—all those classes you've taken, all the projects you've done, that seem so idealistic, so utopian—they have their moment, they burst forth, and they spread like a fever.

—Margaret Cerullo, Occupy Rally

We had lost our professor. She didn't die, but *something* did. Perhaps the *spaces* she created in her classrooms; perhaps the way those spaces allowed us to feel melancholy and rage and to feel okay about those things. Perhaps the way she allowed us to touch our histories and study them academically, in order to better understand our locations under systems of oppression, and to better empower ourselves.

—Riko Fluchel, "Behoming [*sic*] the Impossible: Queer World-Making in the Filipin@ Diaspora"

Those familiar with [Ezra] Pound's *Cantos* will be aware of Pound's use of the *periplum*—those early texts, from before the advent of universal latitude and longitude, that allowed the navigation of the Mediterranean. . . . Pereploi were detailed descriptions of the coastlines of the mainland and the various islands, which, when coupled with a bit of common sense about directions and travel times, allowed early navigators to ascertain where, after a storm, they might have ended up, once the coast came into view.

—Samuel Delany, *Times Square Red, Times Square Blue*

*May 2012. I am sitting in the backseat of my friends Onni and Uditi's baby blue Hyundai Matrix, my gaze fixed on the side of the road as it flits by. Tracy Chapman's "Fast Car" fills our car and narrates my life, for the moment. When she gets to the refrain, that part about having a feeling, about belonging, about being someone, I break—tears rolling down my face. It feels good to cry, for the moment, so much has been held together for so long: my terror, my rage, the students' grief . . . . This is perhaps what my friend Zemora and her friend Arianna mean when they call crying "drowning the patriarchy"—because to let ourselves feel any less is to be complicit in those aspects of our oppression that take shape as silence.*

*By all other accounts, it is a glorious May day. We have shared a lovely week of reading, cooking, eating, writing, swimming, politicking—me, Ellie, Onni, Uditi, and Margaret—at Margaret and Marla's Cape house in Truro, Massachusetts. We are the queer and feminist faculty at a small liberal arts college in New England, and this is the end-of-semester ritual for Margaret and company, as it has been for many years. This, however, is the end of a very long year.*

*I finished my dissertation. I fell in love. I broke my foot. I loved my job. I lost my job. I crashed my car. I got a new job. I was about to move clear across the country, where I knew no one, and no one knew me. I was about to get very sick, with an illness that no one knew how to diagnose, let alone treat. I was about to hit my head. I was about to lose my memory. I was about to lose my love, lose my mind, quit my new job, crash my new car, buy a used car, drive clear across the country again, and again, and again, until I would find my way back to this same spot, here, right here, by the sea, where I write, by myself, two years later, gazing out the window at the black locust trees on Hughes Road, in Truro, Massachusetts.*

## Teaching Queer Time

How does one teach queer time? What specific pedagogical practices lend themselves to the teaching of (the politics of) time in and through performance? And what particular obstacles—incommensurable or otherwise—do these practices present, particularly when considered in the context of the disciplinary and normalizing force of the academy and the culture of surveillance and criminalization inherent to a "homeland" security state in which the academy is situated?

As this book nears its close, I want to both zoom in and out for a long moment, in order to relate the theories and practices I have been detailing in this book to the politics of pedagogy, as a place and time where the rubber hits the road. Throughout this book, I have been arguing that performance has the capacity to rewind time; bind people and places across disparate geographies, identities, and temporalities; repeat the serializing logics of normativity, with a queer difference; and, ultimately, revise and repair trauma through a performative "claiming" of experience. In the previous chapter, I wrote about *floodlines*, a seven-year-long serial performance that used time slips to illuminate the ways in which normative notions of citizenship become solidified over time through a Butlerian "stylized repetition of acts." I argued that *floodlines* enacted "repetitions with a difference" that exposed and transformed the serializing logics of belonging in place. In this final chapter, I will build on those claims, asking how queer time can be taught and felt, while highlighting the difficulties of using performance to teach queer time within institutional contexts that are inherently invested in the serializing logics of whiteness, colonialism, heterosexuality, and gender normativity—invested, that is, in time *not* slipping.

Beginning in 2010, as I was in the final year of writing my dissertation, I began teaching at a small liberal arts college in New England—first as an adjunct and later as a visiting assistant professor. My appointment allowed me to teach at the interstices of queer studies and theater/performance practice, an intersection that had become the focus of my scholarship and pedagogy. As a professor, I was, and continue to be, particularly interested in performance not only as an object of analysis but also as a research methodology. How is knowledge about culture stored in the body and in the places our bodies inhabit? How can performance function as a mode of historical excavation? Like many scholars trained as theater practitioners, I often split class time between discussing a given text around a seminar table and having students do work "up on their feet." I facilitate games and exercises culled from various applied theater techniques, including many drawn from Augusto Boal's Theater of the Oppressed arsenal; I have students stage scenes from plays and performance art; and I train students in a variety of physical and experimental theater techniques, including movement improvisation, devising, and site-specific performance. These teaching tactics provide avenues through which students can begin to play with the materiality of time and of knowledge production alike.

Another thread that connects our seminar discussions with our studio work is a constant interplay between theory and practice. I ask students to regard theoretical texts as frameworks through which to interpret culture writ large, but also as raw performance material. To this end, students are required to adapt the weekly readings—performance theory, feminist theory, queer theory, critical race theory, crip theory—into short performances, which we then use to catalyze, anchor, and concretize our class discussions. In my experience, the practice of adapting a theoretical text into an embodied performance allows young scholars and artists to break down a particularly complicated text or theory into its parts while simultaneously binding this knowledge to their individual lives, to their collective experience in the classroom, and to the present that is both teaching and performance. This is what Jill Dolan describes as "using performance in the classroom to embody knowledge."[1] At the top of my syllabus, I often quote feminist theater scholar Elin Diamond—"How does theater make 'culture discussable'?"—and explain to my students that the aim of the course will be to learn how to do close readings with their bodies as well as their minds. Because the texts and theories with which we are engaging present a culture of trauma and violence, this style of teaching insists on the very high stakes at play in the act of performance insofar as it self-consciously positions performance as a methodology through which to engage—and possibly repair—harm.

After completing my dissertation on the topic, I decided to teach a course on queer time. The politics of temporality had been a thread in several of my prior classes, students were interested in the topic, and I was excited to teach from my research archive. We read queer and feminist theory that takes up questions of temporality, archives, history, and memory (many of the authors whose words and ideas form the backbone of this book): Jasbir Puar, José Muñoz, Elizabeth Freeman, Jack Halberstam, David Eng, Judith Butler, Walter Benjamin—as well as scholars and writers like Gloria Anzaldúa, Gayatri Gopinath, Saidiya Hartman, Douglas Crimp, and Samuel Delany. We also looked at film, video, theater, dance, and performance art that played with the materiality of time in subversive, queer ways. As a teacher and scholar, I was and am interested in time theoretically and culturally, of course, but also pedagogically. Like this project as a whole, this course asked, how does *performance* (and other time-based media) teach time? But it also asked (or at least I asked myself), how does *one* teach time?

For me, teaching time, and teaching time queerly, has necessitated the use of counterhegemonic teaching tactics, including performance-based pedagogy. This, in ways I will detail, can stir up deeply entrenched values and systems of the academy that are squarely at odds with many of the fundamental tenets of both queer theory and queer performance—not to mention the "unproductive" ontology of theater and performance practice—especially at a moment in which the neoliberal university upholds academic conventions of disciplinarity, canonization, and capital and progress-oriented preprofessionalism. In his book on the "queer art of failure," which we read in the course, Halberstam elaborates:

> Disciplinarity, as defined by Foucault (1995), is a technique of modern power: it depends upon and deploys normalization, routines, convention, tradition, and regularity, and it produces experts and administrative forms of governance. The university structure that houses the disciplines and jealously guards their boundaries now stands at a crossroads, not of disciplinarity and interdisciplinarity, past and future, national and transnational; the crossroads at which the rapidly disintegrating bandwagon of disciplines, subfields, and interdisciplines [that] has arrived offer a choice between the university as corporation and investment opportunity and the university as a new kind of public sphere with a different investment in knowledge, in ideas, and in thought and politics.[2]

As Halberstam convincingly argues, academic conventions—including disciplinarity, canonization, and corporatized preprofessionalism—are techniques of modern power and administrative forms of violence. Such conventions are rooted in academia's hidden investments in straight time as produced through routines, traditions, and regularity. *We've always done it this way*. What's more, the straight line of academic "success" is governed by yet another time-based instrument of power (and sometimes violence): the tenure clock. Put differently, academic time is the time of capital: the system of discipline, punish, and reward within academic institutions is akin to that within modern corporations (and, not surprisingly, modern prisons and clinics as well, on which many of Foucault's theories of biopolitics are based). As such, departures from the kind of academic traditions that disciplinarity, canonization, and corporatized preprofessionalism uphold are surveilled and recorded, the results of which can and do produce recourse for academic "failure" in the form of nonrenewal, nonpromotion, nontenure, and/or dismissal.

We met once a week in the evening in a packed seminar room with flickering fluorescents and two dry-erase boards. Many of the students had taken multiple classes with me, several were my thesis advisees past and present, nearly all were queer, half were trans. I was stoked from the start. Of course, I did not know this would be the last course I would teach at this institution, nor the beginning of my education in the challenges of queer pedagogy in neoliberal times.[3]

In the pages that follow, I will detail a series of ruptures that unfolded over the course of what became my final year of teaching at a specific institution of higher education. While the circumstances and events that I outline here were specific to this college and to a particular moment in time and history, this case study is not meant to serve as the exception. Rather, I could imagine a similar series of events unfolding on another college campus and, no doubt, they probably have. In this sense, my story is and is not my own, and it is not meant to indict any specific group nor individual but rather serve as testament to a broader culture of violence within higher education, while upholding the belief—as I have been doing throughout this book—in performance as a site where transformation becomes possible. To this end, I will outline these ruptures as I observed and felt them on a particular campus—events which, I argue, exposed the fragility of colonial whiteness, heterosexuality, cissexuality, and patriarchy—the building blocks of straight temporality—in ways that necessitated a violent backlash to restore and protect the power culture of the college-as-institution and the institution-as-state/nation.[4]

I begin my analysis with a discussion of the Occupy movement, which was unfolding concurrently to the events on campus that I describe. In some ways, Occupy can be read as an important antecedent to the Black Lives Matter movement with which I began this book—insofar as it made clear how social media and direct action can effectively mobilize a vast, global network of millions of young people toward a radical social good. While my analysis includes a Native studies critique of Occupy, I remain interested in what this and other social movements teach us about the temporality of social transformation and/as performance. What we now consider critical turning points in social history, of course, were often, in their time, mere ruptures in business as usual. The queers and queens and trans women at the Stonewall Inn, for instance, were merely "bashing back" during a typical police raid on a hot summer night in Greenwich Village in 1969, not plotting a social movement. In this sense, social movements are always already in a queer time and place insofar as they cannot anticipate, in advance, the kind of future impact they may make. They betray a linear teleologic of simple cause and effect. They are often quotidian, as José Muñoz reminds us,[5] ordinary moments turned extraordinary when they "flash up" in a moment of danger, as Benjamin might put it. In this sense, the flashpoints, or ruptures, that I describe here, as well as the social movements that were concomitantly unfolding in their midst, are *time slips*—tiny portals through which I and my fellow travelers caught a glimpse and a glimmer of another world.

## Rewind: #Occupy/Decolonize (Bathroom)

*November 17, 2011. Campus Occupy rally. I catch the last five minutes of my friend and colleague Margaret's speech. She talks about the Occupy movement and the politics of naming. She insists on calling the encampment site "Liberty Plaza" and not "Zuccotti Park." She doesn't cite 9/11, nor the corporate-funded makeover of the park after it was buried in debris and dust of the World Trade Center, but some of us know that history notwithstanding—the direct line between the now of November 2011 and the then of September 2001, and back again.*

*She talks about "mike checks" and how they incite terror in the hearts of the powerful. She talks about the brilliance of its reappropriation of technology for the literal voice of the people. She talks about the temporality of political insurrection, what she calls "hidden transcripts of resistance." "Revolution is slow," she reminds us, but it is also fast, something that bursts forth, like a fever.*

*And she talks about police brutality. About "stop and frisk" in New York and hygiene crackdowns in Liberty Plaza, where police have confiscated the books of the People's Library after claiming to have found needles hidden between the pages. She likens this sanitization project to the Disneyfication of Forty-Second Street, and I am reminded of Samuel Delany's image of the "periplum," which he, echoing Ezra Pound before him, describes as a detailed description of the coastline which allowed sailors to ascertain where, after a storm, they might have ended up, once a coast came into view.*

*I have heard none of this. Because I wasn't there; no, not yet. I wasn't there, but I know what she said, because I just watched the YouTube video, scanning to see if I could find myself in the crowd, even though I know I wasn't there, even though I remember showing up at the end. I scan to see if I can find my students in the crowd, because I want to go back to the beginning, even though I know this isn't possible, even though I am writing a book about the problems of origin myths, even though it won't change the outcome of the story—at least not materially so. But that psychic impulse to repeat, to get back, to sort it out so we can just remember properly, is strong. Not to mention, I am arguing that repair is possible, so why not go there, to that moment, right before something burst forth, like a fever, or a storm?*

On the same day as the Occupy rally and walkout on campus and across the nation, I was teaching my fall course, "Performing Identity," which combined seminar discussion with studio practice, focusing on how identity is produced through the act of performance. Alongside studies of race, class, gender, sexuality, and disability in performance, students were asked to consider the role of history and memory in the construction and experience of identitarian ways of knowing. One unit, for instance, was called "Space/Place/Race/Trace." Students read Carmelita Tropicana's *Milk of Amnesia* alongside essays about cultural memory. One weekend, we took a field trip to a nearby festival to see site-specific video installations by artists working in the Afro-Futurist tradition, including the Afro British Otolith Group's *Hydra Decapita*, a fabulist film about the Middle Passage, and Brooklyn-based artist kara lynch's *invisible—the archivist's vault*, part walking tour, part site-specific video/sound installation, about racialized ghosts, particularly those Native ones that haunt the very site of the festival.

The students who were enrolled in "Performing Identity" that semester were bright, curious risk takers who loved the class and each other. It was one of those classes that just ignite with alchemy. All but a few students were queer and/or transgender, half were students of color. They ranged from first-years to seniors, performance concentrators to novices.

On the day of the Occupy rally on campus, students were currently working on developing their performance ethnography projects, which involved them transforming transcriptions from fieldwork interviews into monologues for performance, and then, in small groups, transforming those individual monologues into collaborative, site-specific performances for a live audience. A few students were absent on account of the rally and walkout, but most students decided to attend class, the walkout notwithstanding, urged in part by an email from the course TA the day prior who had encouraged them to "walk in." So, in we went.

I placed them in small groups and asked them to choose a location in which they wanted to site their performances, giving them a list of "ingredients," or rules for devising, in the tradition of performance composition that I had learned from American theater director Anne Bogart. One group went to a music practice room, another to the student lounge, yet another to an empty hallway, and the last to the bathroom. Here it is important to note that bathrooms, as would become increasingly clear to me in the weeks and months that followed, were a vexed site on this campus. The signage was inconsistent, with some bathrooms being designated based on the gender of its user ("women," "men") and some its architecture and plumbing ("bathroom equipped with urinals," "bathroom equipped with sanitary bins"). The latter set of designations was a result of student protest to sex-segregated bathrooms and the ways they reinforce a gender binary and produces a system in which transgender, genderqueer, and gender-nonconforming students, faculty, and staff do not have a safe, accessible, clear, and/or viable place to go to the bathroom. The contentions over bathroom politics played out in a variety of ways, the most obvious and persistent of which was the tearing down of sex-segregated bathroom signage (ostensibly by students), and the reposting of sex-segregated bathroom signage (ostensibly by faculty and staff). This often resulted, over time, in bathroom signs being hand-scrawled in black Sharpie and the like, with some bathrooms occasionally having no signs at all, everyone presumably too tired from fighting about it so damn much.

As detailed previously, the policing of the socially constructed line between male and female is part of a larger regime of what activist Harsha Walia calls "border imperialism" in a culture of increased securitization of national borders, checkpoints, airports, schools, sites of commerce, places of domesticity, and the virtual world.[6] Here I am not arguing that the policing of gendered sites, as in the case of bathrooms, works analogously with the logic of race/racialization but, rather, that the two systems interlock. For instance, as Roderick Ferguson argues in the introduction to *Aberrations in Black*, the apartheid American South—one of the clearest examples of "border" policing and surveillance in U.S. history—was not only a regime of racialized segregation—articulated through Jim Crow laws that segregated, among other things, public bathrooms into categories of "white" and "colored"—but also and equally a regime of gender and sexual segregation. As Ferguson illustrates through his deft reading of archival photographs of the era, the racial laws separating whites from blacks specifically functioned to "protect" the so-called purity of white *women* from the so-called danger of black *men*—or, more to the point, to protect pure white womanhood from black male sexuality.[7] When, for instance, Chicago teen Emmett Till was murdered in Money, Mississippi, in 1955 by an extralegal posse of whites, this hate crime was read through and against the dominant narrative, true or not, that he had "whistled" at a young, southern, white woman. In this regard, we can see how the color line is always also a gender and sexuality line, too—that is, how race, gender, and sexuality are coeval (as well as disability—Till had a speech impediment, and evidence suggests that his so-called wolf whistle was actually a habitual whistling sound he made when trying not to stutter). And as previously argued, this kind of spatialized border policing is a response to a crisis in temporality. As performance theorist Harvey Young reminds us in his extraordinary essay about lynching performatives, U.S. lynching culture emerges precisely at a time when African Americans were gaining advances in civil and economic freedom. Lynching—"extralegal" or otherwise—like all forms of disciplinary violence, functions as a method through which dominant culture attempts to curtail the liberation of subjugated populations: it is a form of violence that attempts to *halt* time.[8]

*About thirty minutes into class, a white, queer, transgender student comes running to find me. He tells me that a music professor came in to the bathroom and yelled at his group, saying things like "This is my building" and "This is my bathroom," and "This is a men's room," and "There should not be girls in the men's room." He asks me what to do. I find the professor and introduce myself. Seems like a good idea. He tells me he doesn't know who I am. He tells me that he doesn't care who I am. He tells me that he "works" here. That he is a professor of "music." He reiterates that this is his building. That this is his bathroom. That this is a men's room. That girls do not belong. I explain that the student is not a girl. I explain that the bathroom is not a men's room. I explain that the group had my permission to use the bathroom to rehearse their performance. I explain that there is another bathroom next to it, and another down the hall. I am polite. I am afraid. I extend my hand when I say my name. He is tall, and white; we're both wearing ties. He refuses to shake my hand. He walks away. I do not know what to do. So I tell the students to put a sign on the entrance to the bathroom, and to be mindful.*

*Ten minutes later, another student—a black queer woman who has been rehearsing with her group in the lounge—comes running down the hall. The professor has returned to the bathroom. The professor has flipped his lid. The professor has knocked her over, books spilling everywhere. The professor is calling the police: she heard him on the phone saying things about girls and bathrooms. I assemble all the students back in the classroom. I go to find my colleague in the dance department—the one who oversees the space—to ask for her help. I let the class go home early, so I could make it to a meeting with my colleagues in the theater program, which runs concurrently to my course. My colleagues are sympathetic, but the timing is awkward, as I am a finalist for a position in the department and they are all committee members. "My hands are tied," says one senior colleague, who is chairing the search. My campus visit had been last week.*

*My department chair calls me that night on the phone, telling me that I "put the students in harm's way"; when she and I speak in person the next week, in a small room full of big deans and students and other faculty and me—everyone, that is, except the professor who had called the campus police—she grabs my wrist as she is heading out the door, her fingers curling tightly around my bones. I call my girlfriend in Lebanon. She writes a letter to Margaret. Margaret calls the dean. The dean calls me on my cell phone, a number that I do not have listed with the college. I am in Chicago at the moment, an unexpected trip. I explain that I am not available to talk, that I am sitting shivah for my grandmother (my father's mother, the one who made me promise to "forget." She died of colorectal cancer, and my acupuncturist later explains that the colon and rectum are the seats of accumulated anger and grief, unexpressed). It's not a good time, I tell him, again and again and again. My cousin advises me to disengage, as she is driving me back to O'Hare. My colleague in the dance department sends me an email, apologizing that she couldn't be of more help. The subject heading is "a perfect storm."*

Before detailing the rest of the story, I want to pause and ask how these events resonate with and against those of Occupy that serve as its backdrop, those Native critiques of the Occupy movement that also emerged in its wake, and the broader themes of trauma and time with which they both engage and which, of course, also have been the focus of this book. As Margaret's speech that same November afternoon makes clear, the Occupy movement captured the hearts of many liberals and radicals alike, fed up with corporate greed, the violence of capitalism and imperialism, police brutality, and feelings of disenfranchisement. "We are the 99%" and "We are unstoppable, another world is possible" became the rallying cries of the movement and the moment. Rooted in an ethics of cooperation, direct democracy (in the form of the general assembly), and mutual aid, Occupy was an outgrowth of the ongoing work of a range of radical social movements to date, including anarchy, reproductive justice, climate justice, migrant justice, prison abolition, debt resistance, and radical queer politics, to name but a few. With a handful of notable exceptions—including Unoccupy Albuquerque and Decolonize Oakland—the movement failed to acknowledge one glaring linguistic and ideological oversight: the relationship between the current violence of capitalism and imperialism and the historical and contemporary violence of settler colonization. Liberty/Zuccotti Park, for instance, like all of New York City, is U.S.-occupied Native American (Lenape and Algonquin) land. And Wall Street, prior to being the site of the New York Stock Exchange, was the Slave Market where Africans were bought and sold as human stock—those who would be forced to build this nation-state, from the ground up. Similarly, this particular college campus is also occupied Native (Norwottuck and Pocumtuck) land—the town itself made famous in history when its namesake, then commander-in-chief of the British army, ordered troops to "gift" blankets infected with the smallpox virus to the Natives, the first known act of biological warfare in history. In other words, the Occupy movement enacted an occupation of an always already occupied site while failing to acknowledge such a foundational connection. The movement also failed to acknowledge the profoundly interwoven narratives of capitalism and empire—which Occupy attempted to critique—and the logic of U.S. settler colonialism. As anthropologist J. Kēhaulani Kauanui argued in her 2015 keynote address, "Nothing Common about 'the Commons': Settler Colonialism and Indigenous Difference," this critique is not mere semantic irony, but deeply "epistemological" and therefore "ontological." She states:

> #OWS was a powerful movement that centered on a radical reclaiming of the commons in demanding the return of that which was stolen through "the corrosive power of major banks and multinational corporations over the democratic process." And while many of the on-the-ground practices at various #OWS locales relied on non-binding consensus-based collective decisions and direct actions, the rallying cry to "occupy" and "reclaim" with little to no recognition of the history of settler colonial land expropriation that gave rise to the corporate plutocracy of the 1%. But what about the *other* 1%, that is, American Indians? . . . Wall Street itself is built on indigenous dispossession. As Lenape activist-scholar Joanne Barker delineated . . . , the wall that used to stand erect on the actual street called "Wall Street" was built by the Dutch to keep out not only the English but also the Lenape Indians from their own territory. This is not an abstract claim. . . . As Cheryl Harris argues, the very origins of property rights in the United States are rooted in racial domination based on the expropriation of indigenous land and African labor.[9]

As J. Kēhaulani Kauanui makes clear, while the intentions of Occupy may indeed have been anti-empire in its theoretical and on-the-ground critique of corporate and multinational power, its failure to connect the history of this particular empire with Native dispossession and African enslavement prevents the movement from being capable of dismantling the state apparatus. Settler colonization is what activist Angela Davis, speaking in another context, has called the foundational error of this country—a country that was "founded on an exclusion."[10] In this regard, any social movement that intends to dismantle capitalism and imperialism must not only address settler colonization but also work in collaboration with indigenous sovereignty and reclamation movements as part and parcel of the project of human freedom.

I am going to great lengths to outline the connections between settler colonization and the Occupy movement in order to frame my analysis of what became known on campus, first, as the "bathroom incident," later as "Decolonize Bathroom," and, finally as "The Queer Does Not End Here." Like J. Kēhaulani Kauanui, my critique and analysis is not merely semantic. Rather, the "bathroom incident" and the student activism and performance that it catalyzed in its wake can only be fully grasped when placed not only in the perhaps more obvious contexts of systemic homophobia, transphobia, misogyny, and cissexism, but also the coterminous context of New England neoliberalism which, I argue, bears a direct line to the history of settler colonization of the land and the larger culture of male entitlement, white privilege, and settler claims to land and space that gave and give it shape. What, for instance, prompts a professor to claim a building, or a bathroom, as his own? Granted, his whiteness, masculinity, heterosexuality, and tenured status situated him in a position of power, particularly in contrast to the students' blackness and brownness, their queer femininity and transmasculinity, their age, and their dissident sexualities. The same, too, can be said of me, his various identity positions literally towering over me and the "femaleness" with which he regards my counterfeit masculinity—my tie and buttondown an offensive power grab, as it were, which merely highlight, perhaps, my lack of both gender and institutional gravitas, the queer and contingent faculty member that I am ("I don't know who you are. I don't care who you are. I *work* here.") Our presence in the bathroom and in the building was an unwelcome challenge to his perceived authority.

Here it is worth noting that to turn a bathroom into a performance space is to acknowledge that it already is one—a site in which "scenarios" of race, class, gender, disability, and sexuality—to borrow again from Taylor—unfold on the regular. For instance, is it mere coincidence that Blanche spends the majority of Tennessee Williams's Pulitzer Prize–winning play, *A Streetcar Named Desire*, in the bathroom? Or that in her final (rape) scene with Stanley, he emerges from the bathroom in his red silk pajamas, before "getting the colored lights going"? Or that it is while crying and pissing, respectively, in the men's room of the New York offices of the Federal Court of Appeals that soon-to-be gay lovers Louis and Joe first meet in Tony Kushner's *Angels in America* (which won the same American prize exactly forty-five years later)? To turn a bathroom into a performance space is to acknowledge that it already is one; it is also to insist on the value of theater—what Framji Minwalla and Alisa Solomon have rightfully called "the queerest art" (rife with centuries of cross-dressing and gender bending)—in a culture that readily dismisses it, alongside the nonnormative gender and sexualities of many of its players, as mere folly.[11] In this regard, "this is my building," when spoken by a renowned professor of "music," reverberates with yet another set of hierarchies, including those disciplinary ones meant to denegrate the queerest and unruliest genre that is "performance art." As the introduction to this book made clear, one of the central ways that dominant culture asserts itself is through narratives of capital and progress. As the chapter on *Must* made clear, queer performance refuses heterocapitalist modes of production and reproduction.[12] It comes as no surprise, then, that a person—even a time-based artist and scholar himself—would adopt the voice of dominant culture and dismiss theater and performance art as childish antics in need of discipline and punishment.

Yet something about his repeated utterances "This is my building" and "This is my bathroom" suggests that his speech, actions, and indignant claims to space are about more than disciplinarity, more than gender and sexuality—that perhaps, like the rally and Occupy movement that is unfolding right outside that very building, this professor's claims to space are animated, as well, by the foundational logic of settler colonialism, a logic which was analyzed in detail in the first chapter of this book.

As many Native studies scholars have argued, white settler claims to land have always been intimately connected to the politics of gender and sexuality. For instance, in *When Did Indians Become Straight?*, Mark Rifkin compellingly argues that compulsory heterosexuality and gender normativity in the United States are not Native values but were forcibly produced through acts of rape, torture, genocide, kidnapping, displacement, and "re-education." Andrea Smith (Cherokee) terms this process of indigenous dispossession "conquest"; Scott Morgensen writes about the "unsettling settler desires" that animate it; and Amy Kaplan simply calls it "the anarchy of empire."[13] Call it what you will—this ongoing project of colonization is deeply entwined with the politics of gender and sexuality. In this regard, the professor's preoccupation with the student's reoccupation of the bathroom could also be attributed to not only a discomfort with their (and their teacher's) dissident genders and sexualities but to his settler claim to the space. In other words, that our dissident genders and sexualities would be cause for alarm—an alarm so great it warrants the calling of the police (who will do what, exactly?)—tells us a great deal about the role of sexual and gender policing in the project of "homeland" securitization. Sadly, it also serves as further evidence that the academy is part and parcel of this broader national security state apparatus, while also revealing some of the workings of this apparatus on a local scale.

*In the aftermath of the incident, the music professor begins legal proceedings with the college—threatening to sue on the basis that the presence of transgender students in the bathroom violated his right to privacy. The students attempt to file Title IX grievances—seeking protection from harassment, discrimination, and retaliation on the basis of their gender identities and expressions. I am placed under heightened surveillance. One day, four different deans visit my class, offering to "escort" my students across campus to another building, where our class would be "relocated" for the remainder of the semester. Anticipating their visit, the students circulate an email among themselves. The subject heading is "wear red." It is World AIDS Day, and at this point in the semester, they seem to understand the power of semiotics. I change my outfit six times, in and out of red. The students bring video cameras to class: they seem to understand the power of archives, too. They read an open letter to the deans, which appears in the student newspaper the next day and is emailed to every member of the campus community. The subject heading is "#decolonize bathroom," and the title of the letter is "December 1, 2011, World AIDS Day / Day without Art." They use phrases like "chronic and acute traumas" and "Jim Crow laws," "administrative failings" and "call to action." They refuse to be relocated. The deans back down, cameras rolling. The students are galvanized. I am terrified. The college is scrambling.*

*Next I am asked to supply copies of my syllabus to various members of the college administration. I am called into multiple meetings with members of the upper administration, where I am asked about my teaching philosophy and practices. I am interviewed twice by the Office of Human Resources, where I have to answer leading questions that imply that the purpose of "performance art" is to "provoke" controversy and that queer studies and performance studies are fundamentally "dangerous" disciplines—in other words, questions that point blame at me, my pedagogy, and the undisciplined disciplines and practices in which I am creatively, intellectually, and politically situated. My students are also interviewed by Human Resources and, in a discursive move seemingly lifted from the plot of* Dead Poets Society, *are asked to describe how I put them up to all this (reportedly, they refuse to implicate me—refuse, that is, to throw me, or queer studies, or performance art, under the bus). It went on like this for some months. At one point, I am advised by one dean to apologize to another dean and say that I made an error in judgment—"I was young once, too, and foolish," she says. "Just admit that you were at fault—this will help."*

But it does not help. Because it is structurally necessary that I and the identities, ideologies, and fields of thought that I represent take the blame for the incident and its aftermath. Why was I and not my colleague or the college itself accused of putting the student's "in harm's way"—an accusation that was repeated in various iterations over the course of the year? Because the college must refuse to accept any responsibility, because to assume responsibility would be to consider how this scenario animates broader politics of identity on campus. If this incident were examined, as my students and many of my colleagues insisted it be, as one of trauma and harm; if the tenured professor were cast in a critical light for his speech and actions; if the college considered the various policies—implicit and explicit—that uphold a culture of racism, sexism, and transphobia on campus—we would also have to come to terms with the ways in which, despite claims to the contrary, this "liberal" arts college reproduces the violence of the state. And this was not a claim that this institution was willing to make because its identity rested on its public image and its image of itself as a bastion of liberalism, tolerance, multiculturalism, and inclusion. In other words, the so-called liberalism of the neoliberal university contributes to its role in cycles of systemic violence; its very posturing as a countercultural site forecloses its ability to acknowledge itself as a site and source of violence. As I outlined in the introduction to this book, this is the same tautological argument that the nation-state uses to produce the category of the "terrorist" from which it must then protect itself—a national fantasy of danger projected onto the lives of those deemed eccentric to the nation.

Here I am reminded of Sara Ahmed's essay "The Nonperformativity of Antiracism," in which she deftly articulates the ways in which institutional discourses of antiracism on college campuses actually work to uphold racist ideologies.[14] As Ahmed makes clear, when an institution releases speech acts—in the form of official statements and/or policies on behalf of the institution (e.g., an email signed by the provost about diversity policies on campus)—such speech acts *fail* to do the very thing they claim. Ahmed writes,

> An utterance is performative when it does what it says. . . . The speech acts that commit the university to equality, I suggest, are nonperformatives. They "work" precisely by not bringing about the effects that they name. For Austin, failed performatives are "unhappy": they do not act because the conditions are not in place that are required for the action to succeed (for example, if the person who apologizes is insincere then the apology would be unhappy). In my model of the "nonperformative," the failure of the speech act to do what it says is not a failure of intent or even circumstance, but it is actually what the speech act is doing. In other words, the nonperformative does not "fail to act" because of conditions that are external to the speech act: rather, it "works" *because* it fails to bring about what it names.[15]

In other words, antiracist speech is not coterminous with antiracism, and claims to the contrary elide the incredible amount of material labor required to actually create an antiracist climate on a college campus. In this regard, antiracist discourse is nonperformative in both J. L. Austin's and Judith Butler's sense of the term—it does not *do* anything—and, indeed, it is in fact *counter*-performative, or counterproductive, for it not only fails to act but, in masquerading *as* performative, forecloses real structural change. I agree with Ahmed's formulation, and to it I would add that antisexist, antihomophobic, antitransphobic, or anticissexist discourse operate within similar, and interlocking logics of nonperformativity. This is the double bind of diversity, multiculturalism, and inclusion in neoliberal times—as mere signposts, such discourses effectively *exclude* the very thing they aim (or at least claim) to promote.

*The night before I am nonrenewed due to "budget cuts," I go to see Zell Miller III perform* The Evidence of Silence Broken. *My department chair is there, too, wearing a blue dress. After, I ask her what the agenda for the next day's meeting holds. "We'll just have to wait and see," she replies flatly, her eyes glazed over, her blue dress blowing in the wind. Three administrators are present at the meeting, and the dean of faculty begins by making a joke about my outfit and saying he is usually the first to wear shorts and tie come spring. In a casual and chipper affect, he begins by explaining that they like to do "exit interviews" when faculty's limited terms of appointment have expired; this is business as usual, he says with a smile. Margaret organizes the faculty and staff, who write a letter of dissent to the deans, preparing a statement, as well, which they deliver in person, to no avail. Al Gore comes to campus for the college president's inauguration (the music professor composes the tribute). My students dress up for the event: gay beached whales holding signs that read "An Inconvenient Queer." They stage sit-ins and political funerals, but the semester is nearing an end. I attend their final rally, reading aloud the final passages from Amber Hollibaugh's* My Dangerous Desires. *Afterward, my girlfriend drives me to New York. I have plans to see Peggy, Lois, and*

*Deb's thirty-year retrospective at La MaMa. But I spend the night in New York–Presbyterian with abdominal pains, getting CT scans of my stomach and spleen.*

Before concluding, it is important to pause and acknowledge, retrospectively at least, the ways in which the college has attempted structural change in the years following my departure. Due in large part to the work of the Transgender Policy Committee that I cofounded with a colleague in the film department—the only other openly transgender faculty member at the time—and two trans students, the majority of bathrooms on campus were officially designated all-gender bathrooms by the fall of 2012, with appropriate signage and an email from the college president at the start of the semester, announcing the new policy. There is now a consortium-wide undergraduate certificate program in queer studies, which I helped shepherd through the various stages of administrative approval and which graduated its first cohort of students in the spring of 2012. In 2012, the college also opened a search for its first full-time, tenure-line position in queer studies, completing its hire in 2013. Trans and gender-nonconforming students can now change their names and designate their pronouns through official channels, and the college's website currently includes information for faculty about preferred gender pronouns and a nondiscrimination policy that includes gender identity and expression. Granted, Ahmed's critique as well as my own remain in place, yet it feels important to cite the ways in which this institution—like many others across the nation—are attempting to bring their policies in alignment with the needs and demands of the students and employees, and the stated mission of the college. Additionally, it is worth stating that, while my experience was harrowing to say the least, I am grateful for those relationships forged with my students, many of which continue to this day—including one former student who served as a research assistant on this book itself and who was particularly central in helping me theorize this chapter's claims.

## Cruising Home

I'd like to end where I began this chapter, with a discussion of another course I taught at this college, "Queer Time"—a seminar that, as noted previously, was developed out of my dissertation research and also greatly informed my process of writing this book. I want to (re)turn here as a way of asking, one last time, what performance (and pedagogy) can do in the wake of trauma and violence, particularly those forms of harm that are localized, recent, and, to a certain extent, perhaps even inchoate—those kinds of social experiences that Raymond Williams calls "structures of feeling" because they are still in process, still unfolding, still "in solution," as it were, waiting to be articulated.[16] In the section that follows, I describe a multisite-specific performance that two of my students, Zemora Tevah and Mateo Guadalupe, created together as their final project. Tevah and Guadalupe were not only enrolled in the "Queer Time" class but had also previously taken my "Performing Identity" course (Tevah was the course TA, and Guadalupe had taken the course the year prior and was currently bound up in the bathroom incident and its aftermath in his official capacity, among other things, as one of the founding and active members of the Transgender Policy Committee). In this regard, the performance was created by Tevah and Guadalupe, but part of its efficacy, as I will show, was the ways in which it articulated, for all of us in the audience that April day, something vital and affirming about our collective experience of trauma, its connection to a long history of harm on campus, and its insistence on making those ghosts visible in the present future that is queer performance.

*The night before, we receive an email: "Come dressed as your future utopian self," it reads. (They have just read José Muñoz's* Cruising Utopia, *and the assignment is to make a performance inspired by the book.) To my surprise and delight, most of the students arrive in their highest femme regalia, which is particularly notable given that, in everyday life, most of them present masculine of center. The performers introduce themselves to us as Zemoracle and Cindy Popperz. Zemora Tevah, who usually presents somewhere between tomboy and low-femme dyke, plays Zemoracle—a futuristic brazen femme wrapped in a leopard print shawl with a platinum blond bob, dark sunglasses, and indigo lipstick. She carries a glass Coke bottle as a literal citation to Frank O'Hara's "To Have a Coke with You" and Andy Warhol's* Coca-Cola, *two works that Muñoz describes as aesthetic examples of queer utopian longing.*[17]

*Guadalupe, as Cindy Popperz, is almost unrecognizable to me at first: he generally presents somewhere between-low femme faggot and high-butch dandy. Popperz wears her brunette curls piled high on her head, gathered with a sheer silk scarf that forms a loose knot at the apex of her crown. She wears a sparkly black leotard with a gold shawl wrapped around it. A tattoo peaks out beneath her pink brassiere strap—a line from a poem by Sandra Cisneros: "Ay, corazón, tú que sabes de amor?" it reads across her chest (Oh, my heart, what do you know about love?). Oh, my heart, indeed.*

In keeping with the themes of *Cruising Utopia*, Zemoracle and Popperz take us on a tour of "haunted" sites on campus: first, a gendered locker room in the school gym, which two audience members are invited to enter; later, a media carrel in the library, where we hear stories—via sound and video installation—of clandestine gay sex between students; then, the quad, where we are asked to ring the campus bell; last, to the college president's office, where Popperz and Zemoracle recount an incident of institutional racism and antiracist student activism on campus.

This multisite-specific performance enacts a multiplicity of slips in time and space, publicly and performatively "claiming" the past and future of this campus as queer: not only the locker room, the library, the quad, and the president's office, but all those spaces in between through which we, as a class, are led by Popperz and Zemoracle, making a spectacle of our queerly gendered selves in public—making, that is, a *world* in which we refuse to be made small. In this regard, their performance enacts the project of queer worldmaking which Muñoz outlines in *Disidentifications* and *Cruising Utopia*—namely, the idea that queerness is felt experience, both located within and exceeding the present moment, often taking shape as a longing for a past and/or a future not bound by current structures of the state. As Muñoz himself puts it:

> Queer is not yet here. We are not yet queer. . . . Queerness is a longing that propels us onward, beyond romances of the negative and toiling in the present. Queerness is that thing that lets us feel that this world is not enough, that indeed something is missing. Often we can glimpse the worlds proposed and promised by queerness in the realm of the aesthetic. The aesthetic, especially the queer aesthetic, frequently contains blueprints and schemata of a forward-dawning futurity. . . . Queerness is essentially about the rejection of a here and now and an insistence on potentiality or concrete possibility for another world.[18]

Like utopia (no-place), like Williams's structure of feeling previously cited, like performance itself, "queer" is *in solution*—a feeling and a doing in the present, toward a future (or a past), not reducible to identity. When, for instance, Popperz and Zemoracle (and the rest of us) show up to the performance as high femmes, it "works" precisely because we recognize the misogyny that animates our current and past experiences of oppression on campus and elsewhere, and because we desire something else—"another world." The fact that this group of students—very few of whom perform as femme in their everyday lives—would claim that identity as their future utopian selves also says a great deal about their dreams and imaginings of utopia, and the commensurability of queer femmes and queer feminisms with that dream.

Similarly, when Popperz and Zemoracle lead us into the gendered locker room site, it functions as a sliding signifier across geographies and temporalities of resistance. Of course, it cites the events of the fall, and the gendered bathroom that became a flashpoint—a perfect storm, as it were—of always already circulating anxieties about gender and belonging, and, as I have argued, also race, class, sexuality, and nation. This site-specific performance in the locker room also cites yet another site-specific performance—the one my prior students staged as *their* final project in "Performing Identity," and to which many of the members of "Queer Time" were audience members. It went something like this:

*December 2011. The urinal had been transformed into a makeshift altar space: dildos, glitter, rosary beads, crystals, and moon water. On the mirrors, written in lipstick, were two quotations: To the left, from* Borderlands/La Frontera, *"Homophobia: Fear of Going Home.—Gloria Anzaldúa." To the right, "Transphobia: Fear of Transformation.—Beast." Beast, one of the students who created the performance, invited the audience to sing: "Dear friends, queer friends, let me tell you how I feel. You have given me such pleasure. I love you so." As they led us in rounds, another student invited us to the altar one by one, dipping our hands in the moon water, speaking aloud something we wished to say to "toxic masculinity," casting the water down the drain with a melodious, synchronized flush. I remember saying something like, "I recognize your suffering, and I forgive you."*

To return to a site of trauma and do something else with it is, as I have been arguing throughout the book, an act of hope in a culture of harm. It is a mode of claiming experience in the wake of violence, a methodology for feeling it fully as well as differently, a process through which artists and spectators refuse a linear logic that insists that the present and future be determined by histories of past injury and violence.

It is my contention that this performance worked to reclaim the harmful narrative that cast the students and me as outlaws, by enacting a rightful belonging in time and place. When we reach the president's office, for instance, Popperz plays an audio recording that recalls an action that students of color performed outside the president's office several years back, in response to racist remarks the previous president had made. At one point earlier in the performance, Zemoracle and Popperz had given us each stickers, and, as we listen to the recording outside the office, somebody fixes one to the sign outside the president's office. "THIS SPACE IS QUEER," it reads in handwritten caps: blue ink on white sticker on black sign.

Similarly, Zemoracle and Popperz instruct us to gather at the center of campus and ring the campus bell—an act that carries its own haunted logic: students are to ring their bell when they complete their requirements for graduation and, so the legend goes, anyone who rings it early will be cursed a failure, never to graduate. A student pulls the rope, and the sound reverberates across the campus: "THIS SPACE IS QUEER." In one sense, these moments could be read as gestures of "reclamation," a kind of taking back of space(s) that have made outsiders of us. But there is something about the way in which Cindy Popperz and Zemoracle gayly shepherded us across the campus, resignifying sites of memory and violence as ones of countermemory and resistance; something about the way that we all knew it was so temporary, this queer world we were making together (so temporary, in fact, that it was about to fall apart); something about the way that for thirty or so minutes we hovered together a bit above reality, as if in a waking dream—that did something more, or different, than mere "reclamation." Muñoz offers a blueprint for "cruising utopia," and this performance seems to engage as well as exceed the terms of his project. Their performance offers us a blueprint for not only cruising utopia but also what I would like to call "cruising home."

*Queerness as Horizon* (2012). Riko Fluchel. Performance created and performed by Zemora Tevah and Mateo Guadalupe. Courtesy of Riko Fluchel.

With this turn of phrase, "cruising home," I mean to name a discursive framework for the queer art of making temporary, utopian worlds together in the cracks and crevices of the state apparatus. This is perhaps one way in which non-Native queer and trans folks can reconcile a desire for belonging in a culture that wishes to spit us out—with the complexities of home-making in a settler colonial nation-state that may or may not be ours to *call* home. Past haunted, present precarious, future not guaranteed—yet full with desire and with hope for repair.

As we are heading back to our classroom, into the setting sun, the TA snaps one final picture: Popperz and Zemoracle, backs turned, heading into the horizon. I do not remember seeing this then, but I know it happened because I have the picture. I have the picture because the TA posted it to his Facebook wall nine months later, on the occasion of the untimely death of José Muñoz. When he posts it, he titles it "Queerness as Horizon."

## Postscript

*December 12, 2014. I arrange to meet Margaret and Marla at that café on the corner of Fourth and Washington Square. Walking down from Grand*

*Millions March* (2014). Margaret Cerullo. Street protest, New York City, with Jaclyn Pryor, Mia Rybeck, Shewit Zerai, and Praxedes Quintana (Haverford College). Courtesy of Margaret Cerullo.

*Central, I start to see the signs: #EricGarner and #MichaelBrown, #MillionsMarch and #ShutItDown. We make our way through the masses, Marla charging in front. I am looking for kara, I know she is here—Margaret said it herself. Not five minutes into the march, we start running into people we know, which catches us all by surprise. There are hundreds of thousands, they say, all of us packed in like sardines through the streets of New York, how could the timing be right? The first person we see is the music professor, standing on the sidelines with his wife. With no sense of irony, Margaret says to him, "You know Jaclyn Pryor, am I right?" I smile and say, "Yes, we do; we've met." Later, we run into our former students—they have graduated now: time has passed. Then I run into my current students from my new job at Haverford College—the ones in my "Cruising Home: Queer Kinship in Theory and Practice" course, who have taken the bus from Philadelphia for the march. I am proud and excited to introduce them to Margaret. She pulls out her iPhone and we huddle for a pic. The next day, I receive an email: the subject heading is "Photo from demo." I open the attachment and read the sign they are holding, which I had not noticed the day before:* "REVOLUTION IS NOT A ONE TIME EVENT," *it says. And I think: yes, yes, yes. And: that is it, that is it, that is it.*

## Epilogue

✦

# I Want to Play Airplane, or, It All Comes Back

SMALL ALISON:
Daddy!
Hey, Daddy, come here, okay? I need you.
What are you doing? I said come here.
You need to do what I tell you to do.
Listen to me.
Daddy!
Come here! Hey, right here! Right now!
You're making me mad!
Listen to me.
Listen to me.
Listen to me . . .
I want to play airplane.
I want to play airplane.
I want to play airplane!
I wanna put my arms out and fly . . .
Like the Red Baron in the Sopwith Camel!
No wait, like Superman!
Up in the sky!
Till I can see all of Pennsylvania . . .

—Lisa Kron and Jeanine Tesori, *Fun Home*

History hurts, but not only.

—Lauren Berlant, *Cruel Optimism*

September 10, 2016. One day shy of the fifteen-year anniversary of September 11, 2001, I make a last-minute decision and hop the morning train from Philadelphia to New York's Penn Station. *Fun Home* is closing after its eighteen-month run at Broadway's Circle on the Square, and for a variety of reasons having to do with love and loss, I have not yet seen this hit lesbian musical—although I know it well. I've read (and taught) Alison Bechdel's graphic novel upon which it is based, I've listened to the original cast album, and I've watched and rewatched YouTube clips of eleven-year-old Sydney Lucas singing "Ring of Keys" at the 2015 Tony Awards—where *Fun Home* swept the house with five awards, including best performance by an actor in a leading role, best book, best original score, best direction, and best new musical, as well as a 2014 Pulitzer Prize nomination for best drama.

Rumored to have ended prematurely in the wake of the success of Broadway's *Hamilton*, *Fun Home*—created by playwright Lisa Kron (*2.5 Minute Ride*, *Well*) and composer Jeanine Tesori (*Caroline, or Change*)—is on the surface a coming-out/coming-of-age story about a lesbian teen and her closeted gay father in rural Pennsylvania in the 1970s. Based on cartoonist Alison Bechdel's (*Dykes to Watch Out For*) own life, *Fun Home* charts the uncanny ways that these two queer lives come together and come apart over the course of Alison's life—culminating in Bruce's suicide by oncoming bread truck after his daughter comes out as a lesbian and he is publicly outed as gay. But it's also a play about time and time travel, history and memory, and the ways in which stories get constructed, represented, rearranged, and retold.

"Small Alison" opens the show with the musical number "It All Comes Back," demanding that her father "play airplane" and lift her—belly down, arms out—up in the sky with the bottom of his feet. But this opening song also gestures to the larger themes of history in general, and historical materialism, in particular, that *Fun Home* interrogates and, of course, have been the subject of this book: namely, the proposition that it is possible to fly high, to see all of space and all of time from the vantage point of the present—to be, that is, "like Superman."

As Alison fantasizes about seeing "all of Pennsylvania," her song is abruptly cut short by her father's first line, "Hey! Gimme a hand," as he hauls a cardboard box on stage. In the first of many scenes of father-daughter pedagogy that fuel the plot of the show, Bruce—who has just found this box in a neighbor's barn—teaches his then ten-year-old daughter how to sort trash from treasure, singing praises to the Irish linen and tarnished silver he finds inside, the latter of which he describes as "So beautiful, / So fine / This has traveled continents to get here, / And crossed an ocean of time." The number ends with forty-three-year-old Big Alison (Beth Malone) talking back in time to her now-dead father, explaining that she has held onto his stuff and to his memory for so many years: "You think cartoons are silly," she asserts. "But I draw cartoons, and I need real things to draw from, 'cause I don't trust memory."

Here Big Alison is gesturing toward a later moment in history and in the performance, in which an angry Bruce attempts to teach his precocious child how to draw like a "real" artist. Our hearts break along with Alison's as well as her mother, Helen's, who witnesses the scene, as Bruce ruthlessly critiques a map of their family history that she has made for school—one that defies the rules of perspectival space and linear time. And we are comforted when Alison refuses her father's lesson, singing, "Maps show you what is simple and true / Try laying out a bird's-eye view / Not what he told you, just what you see / What do you know that's not your dad's mythology?" Like Alison, we know that her messy, rhizomatic drawing—much like the graphic novel and lesbian musical in which she finds herself—captures the *feeling* of history better than any "real" art could ever do.

Throughout the performance, Big Alison watches, comments, and sometimes participates in the flashback scenes played by Small and Medium Alison, which form the core of the play's plot. In the delightful "Changing My Major," for instance, Big Alison looks on as the awkward and brilliant Medium Alison (Emily Skeggs) has sex, and has sex with a woman, for the first time in her dorm room at Oberlin—insisting that she is changing her major to "sex with Joan"; in the tour de force "Ring of Keys," Big Alison curiously watches her younger self as she discovers nascent desire for and identification with "an old-school butch" delivery woman at a Pennsylvania diner. She sings, "Your swagger and your bearing / And the just-right clothes you're wearing / Your short hair and your dungarees / And your lace-up boots. / And your keys oh / Your ring of keys. / I know you. I know you. I know you." This number is particularly salient, as it follows yet another moment of failed (normative gender) pedagogy on the part of Alison's father—in which he insists that she put a barrette back in her hair, arguing that it will keep the hair out of her eyes—to which Small Alison defiantly retorts, "so would a crew-cut," refusing the norms of gender and sexuality alongside those of narrative and history.

And when Bruce takes Alison and her two little brothers to New York City for the Fourth of July (bicentennial) weekend of 1976, Little Alison awakens just as her father is departing their borrowed Greenwich Village apartment to cruise at the piers. To send his daughter back to sleep so he can safely slip out the door, he sings a strange, sad, and prescient lullaby titled "Pony Girl": "Pony girl ride, ride away. / I knew you'd break my heart someday. / Some folks get the call to go, / some folks are bound to stay."

In Bechdel's graphic novel, she remembers and rewrites this trip to New York as part of the larger history of the early HIV/AIDS epidemic: "If he'd lived into those early years of AIDS, I tell myself, I might have lost him anyway, and in a more painful and protracted fashion. Indeed, in that scenario, I might have lost my mother, too" (195). In citing Randy Shilts's *And the Band Played On*, a (controversial but important) book about the early years of the epidemic, she continues:

> July 4, 1976
>
> New York Harbor
>
> Tall sails scraped the deep purple night as rockets burst, flared, and flourished red, white, and blue over the stoic Statue of Liberty. The whole world was watching, it seemed; the whole world was there.

> Ships from fifty-five nations had poured sailors into Manhattan to join the throngs, counted in the millions, who watched the greatest pyrotechnic extravaganza ever mounted, all for America's 200th birthday party. Deep into the morning, bars all over the city were crammed with sailors, New York City hosted the greatest party ever known, everybody agreed later. The guests had come from all over the world. This was the part epidemiologists would later note, when they stayed up late at night and the conversation drifted toward where it had started and when. They would remember that glorious night in New York Harbor, all those sailors, and recall: From all over the world they came to New York. (195)

No sooner does Bechdel overlay her father's queer history onto official medical and colonial history of the nation and the world than she undoes it. She writes, "[O]r maybe I am trying to render my senseless personal loss [of my father by suicide] by linking it, however posthumously, to a more coherent narrative. A narrative of injustice, of sexual shame and fear, of life considered expendable" (196).

Watching this scene in *Fun Home*—Bruce's three children peering out the window as Fourth of July sparks fly high—just prior to their father's attempted escape on the down-low—I am reminded of José Muñoz's account in *Cruising Utopia* of the 1969 Stonewall rebellion in New York City, in which he argues that history is only historical in hindsight. As discussed in the previous chapter, at the time of the uprising, it was just some queers and queens bashing back on a hot summer night in June. Like Bruce, they had no way of knowing that they were entering the hole, and whole, of history.

After the show ends, I hightail it to the box office. I want to know if there are any tickets left for the evening's closing performance. They've just had a cancellation: there are two seats for sale. I buy one and wonder who will get the final (golden) ticket.

I have four hours, so I decide to head east to the river. I pass a grand cathedral, where they are just beginning to clean up after what appears to be a public memorial for firefighters who died in the World Trade Center collapse. At first, I think I am at the Cathedral of St. John the Divine, but I realize that that's impossible because St. John is in Morningside Heights. For a moment, I remember Bryn's memorial there a few months prior; how Sarah Schulman said she died of poverty; how Gaines's face was ashen and his head shaven, and how I remember thinking that he looked like Gogol in *The Namesake*.

At the East River, I look south at the hole in the sky; at the graffiti on the steps: "fucc [*sic*] donald trump"; and across the river to Roosevelt Island, where the land comes to a fine point as an enormous gray monument carries the eyes to its vanishing point. This monument, which I don't believe I had ever seen, reminds me of the cover of Michael Taussig's book, *Walter*

*Benjamin's Grave*, and I turn to the man sitting next to me, smoking a cigar, to ask him what it is. "It's a Louis Kahn memorial, I think," he says with some confidence. I later learn that it's Kahn's homage to the "four freedoms" that FDR articulated in his famous State of the Union address in 1941: speech, worship, want, and fear, forever monumentalized in granite and grass.

Moments before the eight P.M. curtain, a trans person in their early twenties files into the seat next to me. They have a giant *Fun Home* poster that they tuck between our seats. I introduce myself and they tell me that their name is Terra; how their friend called to say that there was one ticket left; how they "were supposed to be delivering pizzas tonight" but got fired and drove straight from rural Pennsylvania to the Circle in the Square; how this is the luckiest day of their life.

After the show's finale, "Flying Away," in which all three Alisons sing to one another and Small Alison gets to play airplane one last time, Bechdel, Kron, and Tesori, as well as performers from earlier moments in the show's run, join the current cast on stage for a wild standing ovation and several encore performances. Alison Bechdel hugs her doppel, Big Alison, as Kron takes the *mick*—thanking Bechdel for her brilliant novel, and insisting it's only right that Bechdel get the last word. She thanks the creative team for treating her work and her life with such care, saying "it felt very much like love." Terra's friend takes our picture together in front of the giant, yellow *Fun Home* sign in the lobby: two queer lives that have come together and will come apart over the course of a day.

Back at Penn Station, I realize that I've missed the last train back to Philadelphia. The next is not until three in the morning. I inquire about getting a hotel for the night, but it's too expensive for what was meant to be a quick trip. I think about calling a friend, but I realize I've left my phone in Philadelphia. I lie down on the steps of the architectural wonder that is the James Farley Post Office, across the street from the station. As I am falling asleep, I remember I haven't mailed my September rent. I remember that poem by Merle Feld—about Miriam and her brother Moses at Sinai, which I taped to my white windowpane that framed my view of sugar maples, and the quiet traffic on College Street. I remember how I had put it there so I would remember the "holy" in time. I remember Rebecca mapping my family tree on the bus ride up to New York City—our six-month anniversary trip. I remember my shoes getting wet in the snow on our way to see *Big Love*. I remember my dream about Clark Park one (now three) year(s) before that, and what my acupuncturist later said about energy traveling faster than bodies. I am awoken by the sound of a homeless man screaming—he's talking to himself from the top of the post office steps. I sit up. I check the time. The clock has turned: 9/11 in New York City.

I sleep most of the ride home, occasionally staring out the windows as the train scrapes the deep purple night. I think of my book, of how I might end it—this book about travel and time.

What is left to say is this: I want to believe in repair after trauma, in making whole what has been smashed. I want to pass through the hole of time, and arrive someplace queer and new. I want a bird's-eye view of history, not what is simple and true. I want to play airplane. Like Superman, up in the sky. Like Daedalus and Icarus, but different. Until it all comes back. Until it all comes back. Until it all comes back, I am going to put my arms out and fly.

# NOTES

## Preface

1. Mauthausen-Gusen concentration camp in upper Austria was one of many Nazi labor/extermination camps that imprisoned female sex slaves who were forced to have sex with male inmates and Nazi workers. Other such camps included Ravensbrück, Dachau, Buchenwald, and Sachsenhausen in Germany, and Auschwitz in Poland. See Sonja M. Hedgepeth and Rochelle G. Saidel, *Sexual Violence against Jewish Women during the Holocaust* (Waltham, Mass.: Brandeis University Press, 2010).

2. *The Maelstrom* is an experimental documentary assembled from found home movies chronicling a Dutch-Jewish family in the years leading up to their deportation during the Holocaust. See *The Maelstrom: A Family Chronicle*, directed by Péter Forgács (1997; DVD, Lumen Film, 2005).

## Introduction

1. I borrow this idea from Carolyn Dinshaw, who argues that, within literary works, different histories can rub up against each other, or "touch," in the mind of the reader. See Carolyn Dinshaw, *Getting Medieval: Sexualities and Communities, Pre- and Postmodern* (Durham, N.C.: Duke University Press, 1999).

2. See Deborah Paredez, *Selenidad: Selena, Latinos, and the Performance of Memory* (Durham, N.C.: Duke University Press, 2009); Jill Lane, "Hemispheric Reenactments," lecture at the University of Texas at Austin, March 5, 2010; Diana Taylor, *The Archive and the Repertoire: Performing Cultural Memory in the Americas* (Durham, N.C.: Duke University Press, 2003); Marvin A. Carlson, *The Haunted Stage: The Theatre as Memory Machine* (Ann Arbor: University of Michigan Press, 2001); Peggy Phelan, *Mourning Sex: Performing Public Memories* (London: Routledge, 1997); Elin Diamond, ed., *Performance and Cultural Politics* (New York: Routledge, 1996); Joseph R. Roach, *Cities of the Dead: Circum-Atlantic Performance* (New York: Columbia University Press, 1996); Richard Schechner, *Between Theater and Anthropology* (Philadelphia: University of Pennsylvania Press, 1985); Rebecca Schneider, *Performing Remains: Art and War in Times of Theatrical Enactment* (New York: Routledge, 2011).

3. Jack Halberstam, *In a Queer Time and Place: Transgender Bodies, Subcultural Lives* (New York: New York University Press, 2005), 7.

4. Ibid., 1.

5. Ibid., 1.

6. Judith Butler, "Global Violence, Sexual Politics," in *Queer Ideas: The David R. Kessler Lectures in Lesbian and Gay Studies* (New York: Feminist Press at the City University of New York, 2003), 199–214.

7. On the banality of trauma, see Ann Cvetkovich, *An Archive of Feelings: Trauma, Sexuality, and Lesbian Public Cultures* (Durham, N.C.: Duke University Press, 2003), especially her chapter "The Everyday Life of Queer Trauma."

8. Jill Stauffer, *Ethical Loneliness: The Injustice of Not Being Heard* (New York: Columbia University Press, 2015), 1.

9. For more on microaggressions and affective life, see Claudia Rankine's extraordinary mixed-genre book, *Citizen*. Claudia Rankine, *Citizen: An American Lyric* (Minneapolis: Graywolf, 2014).

10. David Eng, *The Feeling of Kinship: Queer Liberalism and the Racialization of Intimacy* (Durham, N.C.: Duke University Press, 2010), 168.

11. Rea Tajiri, dir., *History and Memory: For Akiko and Takashige* (New York: Women Make Movies, 1991).

12. Eng, *The Feeling of Kinship*, 219.

13. Ibid., 169.

14. Cathy Caruth, *Unclaimed Experience: Trauma, Narrative, and History* (Baltimore: Johns Hopkins University Press, 1996), 3–4.

15. Stauffer uses the phrase "listen well" throughout her book.

16. Walter Benjamin, "Theses on the Philosophy of History," in *Illuminations* (New York: Harcourt, Brace and World, 1968), 257.

17. "Another world is possible" is the slogan of the World Social Forum, which was first held in São Paulo, Brazil, in 2001. The chant "We are unstoppable, another world is possible" has been picked up by various social justice movements.

18. Peggy Phelan, *Unmarked: The Politics of Performance* (London: Routledge, 1993), 1.

19. Diamond, *Performance and Cultural Politics*, 1.

20. Jord/ana Rosenberg, "Gender Trouble on Mother's Day," *Avidly*, May 9, 2014, http://avidly.lareviewofbooks.org/2014/05/09/gender-trouble-on-mothers-day/.

21. Elizabeth Freeman, "Time Binds, or, Erotohistoriography," *Social Text* 23, nos. 3–4 (2005): 57; emphasis mine. For more recent scholarship on queer temporalities, see E. L. McCallum and Mikko Tuhkanen, eds. *Queer Times, Queer Becomings* (Albany: SUNY Press, 2011); Ramón H. Rivera-Servera, *Performing Queer Latinidad: Dance, Sexuality, Politics* (Ann Arbor: University of Michigan Press, 2012); Sara Warner, *Acts of Gaiety: LGBT Performance and the Politics of Pleasure* (Ann Arbor: University of Michigan Press, 2012); and Juana María Rodríguez, *Sexual Futures, Queer Gestures, and Other Latina Longings* (New York: NYU Press, 2014).

22. Benjamin, "Theses on the Philosophy of History," 257.

23. Ibid.

24. Ann Reynolds, *Robert Smithson: Learning from New Jersey and Elsewhere* (Cambridge, Mass.: MIT Press, 2003), xiii.

25. Michael Warner, *Fear of a Queer Planet: Queer Politics and Social Theory* (Minneapolis: University of Minnesota Press, 1993), xxi; emphasis mine.

26. Ibid., vii–xxvii.

27. David L. Eng, Jack Halberstam, and José Esteban Muñoz, introduction to "What's Queer about Queer Studies Now?," special issue, *Social Text* 23, nos. 3–4 (2005): 1–2.

28. Roderick Ferguson, *Aberrations in Black: Toward a Queer of Color Critique* (Minneapolis: University of Minnesota Press, 2003).

29. Puar is building on claims made by Miranda Joseph. See Miranda Joseph, *Against the Romance of Community* (Minneapolis: University of Minnesota Press, 2002).

30. Freeman, "Time Binds, or Erotohistoriography," 59.

31. See Robert McRuer, *Crip Theory: Cultural Signs of Queerness and Disability* (New York: New York University Press, 2006).

32. Scott Lauria Morgensen, *Spaces between Us: Queer Settler Colonialism and Indigenous Decolonization* (Minneapolis: University of Minnesota Press, 2011), 109.

33. Michael Warner, *The Trouble with Normal: Sex, Politics, and the Ethics of Queer Life* (New York: Free Press, 1999).

34. Lee Edelman, *No Future: Queer Theory and the Death Drive* (Durham, N.C.: Duke University Press, 2004), 2.

35. Elizabeth Freeman, introduction to "Queer Temporalities," special issue, *GLQ: A Journal of Lesbian and Gay Studies* 13, no. 2-3 (2007): 167. See also Cathy J. Cohen, *Boundaries of Blackness: AIDS and the Breakdown of Black Politics* (Chicago: University of Chicago Press, 1999), and José Esteban Muñoz, "Thinking beyond Antirelationality and Antiutopianism in Queer Critique," *PMLA* 121 (2006): 825–26.

36. Heather Love traces this history in compelling detail. See Love's introduction to *Feeling Backward: Loss and the Politics of Queer History* (Cambridge, Mass.: Harvard University Press, 2007).

37. Ann Cvetkovich, *Depression: A Public Feeling* (Durham, N.C.: Duke University Press, 2012). See also Lauren Berlant, *Cruel Optimism* (Durham, N.C.: Duke University Press, 2011).

38. Jill Dolan, *Utopia in Performance: Finding Hope at the Theater* (Ann Arbor: University of Michigan Press, 2005), 54.

39. Gary Younge, "The Unbearable Whiteness of the American Left," *The Nation*, April 23, 2014, https://www.thenation.com/article/unbearable-whiteness-american-left/.

40. Sekou Sundiata, "Thinking Out Loud: Democracy, Imagination and Peeps of Color" (keynote address, "NEA 40 Symposium," Austin, Tex., October 29, 2005).

41. Ibid., 6.

42. Ta-Nehesi Coates's recent essay offers a compelling history of the relationship between the rise of Barack Obama and the white nationalisms that arose in the aftermath. See Coates, "My President Was Black," *The Atlantic*, January/February 2017, https://www.theatlantic.com/magazine/archive/2017/01/my-president-was-black/508793/?utm_source=fbb.

43. See Lisa Duggan, *The Twilight of Equality: Neoliberalism, Cultural Politics, and the Attack on Democracy* (Boston: Beacon, 2003).

44. Jasbir K. Puar, *Terrorist Assemblages: Homonationalism in Queer Times* (Durham, N.C.: Duke University Press, 2007), xix.

45. Ibid., xviii.

46. Anne Anlin Cheng, *The Melancholy of Race* (Oxford: Oxford University Press, 2001), x.

47. See Kay Turner, "September 11: The Burden of the Ephemeral," *Western Folklore* 68 (2009): 155–208.

48. See Homi Bhabha, "Of Mimicry and Man," in *The Location of Culture* (London: Routledge, 1994).

49. Diana Taylor et al., "A Forum on Theatre and Tragedy in the Wake of September 11, 2001," *Theatre Journal* 54, no. 1 (2002): 96.

50. Butler, "Global Violence, Sexual Politics," 202.

51. Ibid., 205.

52. Puar, *Terrorist Assemblages*, i.

53. My analysis is framed by David Eng's scholarship on the case. See Eng, *The Feeling of Kinship*, 23–57.

54. Amber Hollibaugh, *My Dangerous Desires: A Queer Girl Dreaming Her Way Home* (Durham, N.C.: Duke University Press, 2000), 265.

55. Donna Payne, Human Rights Campaign, "Envisioning an Inclusive World: The Importance of the Gay Civil Rights Movement," *Dream of a Nation*, newsletter, 2010, http://dreamofanation.org/img/Human-Rights-Campaign.pdf.

56. Margaret R. Somers, *Genealogies of Citizenship: Markets, Statelessness, and the Right to Have Rights* (Cambridge: Cambridge University Press, 2008).

57. Gayatri Chakravorty Spivak, *The Spivak Reader: Selected Works of Gayatri Chakravorty Spivak*, ed. Donna Landry and Gerald M. MacLean (New York: Routledge, 1996).

58. Eng, *The Feeling of Kinship*, x.

59. The debate about gay marriage within LGBTQ academic and popular discourse is extensive. See Cathy Cohen, "Punks, Bulldaggers, and Welfare Queens," *GLQ: A Journal of Lesbian and Gay Studies* 3, no. 4 (1997): 437–65; Marlon M. Bailey, Priya Kandaswamy, and Mattie Udora Richardson, "Is Gay Marriage Racist?," in *Against Equality: Queer Revolution, Not Mere Inclusion*, ed. Ryan Conrad (Chico, Calif.: AK Press, 2014); Yasmin Nair, "Gay Marriage Hurts My Breasts," in Conrad, *Against Equality*. See also Tom Boellstorff's extraordinary essay on gay marriage and queer time, "When Marriage Falls: Queer Coincidences in Straight Time," *GLQ* 12, nos. 2–3 (2007): 228.

60. Eng, *The Feeling of Kinship*, 29.

61. This comment was made during the Q&A after Michelle Tea's keynote. See "How Not to Be a Queer Douchebag," keynote address, "Five College Queer Gender and Sexuality Conference," Hampshire College, Amherst, Mass., March 5, 2011.

62. Michael Kimmel, "Gay Bashing Is About Masculinity," *Ms. Magazine*, October 2010; emphasis in the original.

63. Poet and activist-academic Nikki López commented on the tragic irony of the bar's name in her speech at the Orlando vigil in Philadelphia, Pa., June 13, 2016.

64. Lindsay Reckson, "Hands Up," *Avidly*, December 11, 2014, http://avidly.lareviewofbooks.org/2014/12/11/hands-up/.

65. Ibid.

66. Alison Kafer, *Feminist, Queer, Crip* (Bloomington: Indiana University Press, 2013), 33.

67. See Reynolds, *Robert Smithson*; Michel de Certeau, *The Practice of Everyday Life* (Berkeley: University of California Press, 1988); Gilles Deleuze, *Difference and Repetition*, trans. Paul Patton (New York: Columbia University Press, 1994); Michel Foucault, *Archaeology of Knowledge*, trans. A. M. Sheridan

Smith (New York: Routledge, 2002); Carolyn Steedman, *Dust: The Archive and Cultural History* (New Brunswick, N.J.: Rutgers University Press, 2002); Derrida, *Archive Fever: A Freudian Impression* (Chicago: University of Chicago Press, 1996); Maurice Halbwachs, *On Collective Memory,* ed. and trans. Lewis A. Coser (Chicago: University of Chicago Press, 1992); Carlo Ginzburg, *Clues, Myths, and the Historical Method* (Baltimore: Johns Hopkins University Press, 1989).

68. I borrow the phrase "irrevocable tie" from Alexander, who writes of the "irrevocable tie between citizenship and heterosexuality." See *Pedagogies*, x.

69. Steedman, *Dust*, 3.

70. Blau writes, "When we speak of what Stanislavski called Presence in acting, we must also speak of its Absence, the dimensionality of time through the actor, the fact that he who is performing can die there in front of your eyes; is in fact doing so. Of all the performing arts, the theater stinks most of mortality." See Herbert Blau, *Take Up the Bodies: Theater at the Vanishing Point* (Urbana: University of Illinois Press, 1982), 83.

71. Generally, when referring to this country as a nation-state, I use the term "United States." When referring to it as a social imaginary, I call it "America." I use the term "United States" when referring to the actual nation-state in part to distinguish the nation from *ideas* of nation. It is also an antiexceptionalist move to redress the fact that multiple countries comprise the Americas.

72. See also Cheng, *The Melancholy of Race.*

73. See Alexander, *Pedagogies*; Kathleen Stewart, *Ordinary Affects* (Durham, N.C.: Duke University Press, 2007); Cvetkovich, *An Archive of Feelings*; David L. Eng and David Kazanjian, eds., *Loss: The Politics of Mourning* (Berkeley: University of California Press, 2003); Cheng, *The Melancholy of Race*; Avery Gordon, *Ghostly Matters: Haunting and the Sociological Imagination* (Minneapolis: University of Minnesota Press, 1997).

74. Gordon, *Ghostly Matters*, 3.

75. Michel Foucault, *The History of Sexuality, Vol. 1: An Introduction* (New York: Vintage, 1990), 86.

76. Gordon, *Ghostly Matters*, 16.

77. Combahee River Collective, *The Combahee River Collective Statement: Black Feminist Organizing in the Seventies and Eighties* (Albany, N.Y.: Kitchen Table: Women of Color Press, 1986), 274.

78. Freeman makes a similar point in "Time Binds," 3.

79. I borrow the term "settled knowledge" from Butler, "Global Violence, Sexual Politics."

80. See M. Jacqui Alexander, *Pedagogies of Crossing: Meditation on Feminism, Sexual Politics, Memory, and the Sacred* (Durham, N.C.: Duke University Press, 2005).

81. Michel Foucault, *"Society Must Be Defended": Lectures at the Collège de France, 1975–76* (London: Penguin, 2003), 7.

82. José Esteban Muñoz, *Disidentifications: Queers of Color and the Performance of Politics* (Minneapolis: University of Minnesota Press, 1999), 5.

83. See Paul Bonin-Rodriguez, *Performing Policy: How Contemporary Politics and Cultural Programs Redefined U.S. Artists for the Twenty-first Century* (New York: Palgrave, 2015).

84. Carlson and Strom were partners in life and art for two decades, and were at the time of making *Geyser Land*.

85. See Peggy Shaw, *A Menopausal Gentleman: The Solo Performances of Peggy Shaw*, ed. Jill Dolan (Ann Arbor: University of Michigan Press, 2011), 100.

86. David Román, Diana Taylor, Sue-Ellen Case, Jill Dolan, and Lisa Duggan each contributed at the highest level of giving under the moniker "Queer Family." Incentives for giving, or "perks," included digital production photographs culled from Shaw's body of work and provided in part by the Hemispheric Institute of Performance and Politics at NYU. I organized this fundraiser in collaboration with kara lynch and Suzy Willson. Of note, other "Queer Family" donors included a collective of over a dozen queer and feminist artists and activists who pooled their resources to contribute at the highest level, under the joint moniker "I've Got All My Sisters with Me." Such forms of collective action serve as example of the kind of queer and feminist organizing that this project promotes, transcending and circumventing traditional forms of kinship and support. See https://www.indiegogo.com/projects/peggy-shaw-pension-fund.

87. Paul Bonin-Rodriguez, Jill Dolan, and Jaclyn Pryor, "Colleague-Criticism: Performance, Writing, and Queer Collegiality," *Liminalities: A Journal of Performance Studies* 5, no. 1: (2009): 1–2.

88. See David Román, *Acts of Intervention: Performance, Gay Culture, and AIDS*, (Bloomington: Indiana University Press, 1998), 152.

89. Rosaldo quoted in Jan Cohen-Cruz, *Local Acts: Community-Based Performance in the United States* (New Brunswick, N.J.: Rutgers University Press, 2005).

90. Bonin-Rodriguez, Dolan, and Pryor, "Colleague-Criticism," 3–4.

91. Ibid., 4.

92. Omi Osun Joni L. Jones, "Performance Ethnography: The Role of Embodiment in Cultural Authenticity," *Theatre Topics* 12, no. 1 (2002): 1–15.

93. Carolyn Steedman, *Landscape for a Good Woman: A Story of Two Lives* (London: Virago, 1986), 21.

94. Carlson has used the device of the *tableau vivant* in previous work. See Ann Carlson, *Night Light*.

95. Schechner, *Between Theater and Anthropology*, 36.

96. Judith Butler, "Performative Acts and Gender Constitution," *Theatre Journal* 40, no. 4 (1988): 270–82.

97. Phelan, *Unmarked*.

98. Steedman, *Dust*, 7.

99. I first heard the term "reperformance" in reference to the MOMA's retrospective on New York–based Yugoslavian performance artist Marina Abramović, *The Artist Is Present*. Over the course of seven hundred hours (two and a half months), Abramović and collaborators "reperformed" her entire body of work.

100. See Andrea Smith, "Queer Theory and Native Studies: The Heteronormativity of Settler Colonialism," *GLQ: A Journal of Gay and Lesbian Studies* 16, no. 1 (2010): 41–68.

## Chapter 1

1. Citing Steedman, I am building on her as well as Jacques Derrida's notion of "archive fever," which I discuss at more length in the introduction to this book. See Steedman, *Dust*; Derrida, *Archive Fever*.

2. Dolan devotes a chapter of her book *Utopia in Performance* to discussing the politics of temporality as they relate to Carlson's solo performance, *Blanket.*

3. See folklorist Maggie Holtzberg's diary account describing the process of making a film documenting the traditions of gandy dancers. Maggie Holtzberg, "The Making of the Film: A Diary Account of the Making of *Gandy Dancers*," *Folkstreams.net*, www.folkstreams.net/context, 205.

4. In chapter 4, I offer a more complete analysis of repetition as a norm-producing cultural mechanism as well as its potential for subversion.

5. The first recorded use of standard time was with the Great Western Railway (1840) in the United Kingdom, when different local times were synchronized and a single, "standard" time was applied. Thank you to Zemora Tevah for bringing this history to my attention.

6. I describe the performance as beginning in Livingston and ending in Bozeman. However, *Geyser Land* offered two different ticket options: audiences could board at either depot and travel in either direction. My choice to read from Livingston to Bozeman is informed by my reception experience and framed by the project website, which narrates the performance in the order in which I describe it.

7. Wendy Perron, "A Performance Runs through It," *New York Times*, August 10, 2003.

8. David E. Nye, *Narratives and Spaces: Technology and the Construction of American Culture* (New York: Columbia University Press, 1997), 3.

9. Ibid., 5.

10. Ibid., 25.

11. Amy Kaplan, *Anarchy of Empire in the Making of U.S. Culture* (Cambridge, Mass.: Harvard University Press, 2002), 34; emphasis in the original.

12. Here I riff on Augusto Boal's notion of the spect-actor. See *Theatre of the Oppressed* (New York: Theatre Communications Group, 1993).

13. Ann Carlson, personal correspondence with author, December 10, 2009.

14. Andrea Smith, lecture, University of Texas at Austin, November 17, 2009; emphasis in the original.

15. Ibid. See Smith, "Queer Theory and Native Studies," 50.

16. See Barbara Kirshenblatt-Gimblett, *Destination Culture: Tourism, Museums, and Heritage* (Los Angeles and Berkeley: University of California Press, 1998).

17. Dwight Conquergood, "Performing as a Moral Act: Ethical Dimensions of the Ethnography of Performance," *Literature in Performance* 5, no. 2 (1985): 7.

18. Diana Taylor, *Disappearing Acts: Spectacles of Gender and Nationality in Argentina's "Dirty War"* (Durham, N.C.: Duke University Press, 1997).

See also Taylor, *The Archive and the Repertoire*, 244.

19. I borrow the phrase "ghosting the buffalo" from Strom, which she uses in her interview with the *New York Times*. See Wendy Perron, "A Performance Runs through It," *New York Times*, August 10, 2003.

20. My notion of archives as material things that people "use" as opposed to merely "keep" is informed by art historian Ann Reynolds who makes a similar point in her discussion of Robert Smithson's private archive. See Ann Reynolds, "Culture as a Way of Seeing," in *Robert Smithson.*

21. Catherine Lord, "Track Marks," in *Carlson/Strom: New Performance Video*, exhibition catalogue (Lincoln, Mass.: deCordova Sculpture Park and Museum, 2009), 8.

22. My notion of a cultural scenario is informed by Taylor: "The scenario includes features well theorized in literary analysis, such as narrative and plot, but demands that we also pay attention to milieux and corporeal behaviors such as gestures, attitudes, and tones not reducible to language. Simultaneously *setup* and *action*, scenarios frame and activate social dramas." I will return to a discussion of cultural scenarios in chapter 4. Taylor, *The Archive and the Repertoire,* 28.

23. I borrow the phrase "lure of the local" from Lippard. See Lucy R. Lippard, *The Lure of the Local: Senses of Place in a Multicentered Society* (New York: New Press, 1997).

24. See Philip J. Deloria, *Playing Indian* (New Haven, Conn.: Yale University Press, 1998), 3.

25. Eric Lott, *Love and Theft: Blackface Minstrelsy and the American Working Class* (New York: Oxford University Press, 1993), 41.

26. Benjamin, "Theses on the Philosophy of History," 256.

27. Roland Barthes, *Camera Lucida: Reflections on Photography* (New York: Hill and Wang, 1981), 65.

28. See also Deloria, *Playing Indian.*

29. See E. Patrick Johnson, *Appropriating Blackness: Performance and the Politics of Authenticity* (Durham, N.C.: Duke University Press, 2003); Muñoz, *Disidentifications*; and Frances Negrón-Muntañer, *Boricua Pop: Puerto Ricans and the Latinization of American Culture* (New York: New York University Press, 2004), especially "Jennifer's Butt."

30. I borrow the term "fictive ethnicity" from Hyun-Joo Lee, "Staging 'Fictive' Ethnicity: Asian American Performance after the Immigration and Nationality Act of 1965" (Ph.D. diss., New York University, 2009).

31. See the project website, created by Mary Ellen Strom in collaboration with Morgan Schwartz, www.geyserland.org.

32. See Butler, "Performative Acts and Gender Constitution."

## Chapter 2

1. Here Freeman is describing Hillary Brougher's film *The Sticky Fingers of Time* (Culver City, Calif.: Strand Releasing, 1997).

2. I learned the term "tranzie" from activist and educator Tones Smith, who used the term as a trans-positive colloquial alternative to the derogatory term "trannie."

3. *Must* was produced under the auspices of the English Department's Edinburgh Fringe After-Festival Series, which brings shows from the summer festival in the United Kingdom to the Five College consortium in Western Massachusetts. The 2011 After Festival was curated by Jenny Spencer, director of the University of Massachusetts Edinburgh Fringe Festival summer abroad program.

4. The Five College consortium includes Amherst College, Hampshire College, Mount Holyoke College, Smith College, and the University of Massachusetts–Amherst.

5. The meaning of "genderqueer" varies, but the term generally refers to people who identify as doing their gender in nonnormative, queer ways.

6. For a more detailed account of the relationship between Shaw's work and feminist, lesbian, and queer politics, see, for instance, Sue-Ellen Case, *Split*

*Britches: Lesbian Practice / Feminist Performance* (London: Routledge, 1996); Jill Dolan, *Presence and Desire: Essays on Gender, Sexuality, Performance* (Ann Arbor: University of Michigan Press, 1993) and *The Feminist Spectator as Critic* (Ann Arbor, Mich.: UMI Research Press, 1988); and Charlotte Canning, *Feminist Theaters in the U.S.A.: Staging Women's Experience* (New York: Routledge, 1995).

7. Peggy Shaw, *You're Just Like My Father*, performance, Hampshire College, Amherst, Mass., 1994.

8. *You're Just Like My Father* was previously published in Holly Hughes and David Román, eds., *O Solo Homo: The New Queer Performance* (New York: Grove, 1998).

9. See Taylor, *The Archive and the Repertoire.*

10. See Martin Bauml Duberman, Martha Vicinus, and George Chauncey, *Hidden from History: Reclaiming the Gay and Lesbian Past* (New York: Plume, 1990).

11. For more on transfemininity, see Julia Serano, *Whipping Girl: A Transsexual Woman on Sexism and the Scapegoating of Femininity* (New York: Seal, 2007); Kate Bornstein, *Gender Outlaw: On Men, Women, and the Rest of Us* (New York: Routledge, 1994); Bernstein Sycamore, *Nobody Passes: Rejecting the Rules of Gender and Conformity* (Emeryville, Calif.: Seal, 2006); Susan Stryker, *Transgender History* (Berkeley, Calif.: Seal, 2008); Gabeba Baderoon, "Gender within Gender," *Feminist Studies* 37, no. 2 (2011): 390–416, www.jstor.org/stable/23069910; as well as the special issue of *GLQ* edited by Susan Stryker, "The Transgender Issue," *GLQ: A Journal of Lesbian and Gay Studies* 4, no. 2 (1998). Thank you to Michelle Rowley for her feedback on an earlier draft of this chapter.

12. At the time of this writing, a handful of women's colleges have updated their admissions policies to include trans women and those who fall outside the gender binary, including Mills, Scripps, Mount Holyoke, Bryn Mawr, Simmons, and Wellesley.

13. Shaw, *A Menopausal Gentleman.*

14. I borrow the term "the present future" of queer from Valerie Traub, "The Present Future of Lesbian Historiography," in *A Companion to Lesbian, Gay, Bisexual, Transgender, and Queer Studies* (New York: Wiley-Blackwell, 2007).

15. Ann Daly, *Critical Gestures: Writings on Dance and Culture* (Middletown, Conn.: Wesleyan University Press, 2002), xvi.

16. Again, see Dolan, Bonin-Rodriguez, and Pryor, "Colleague-Criticism."

17. Taylor, *The Archive and the Repertoire*, 2.

18. Unless otherwise noted, all citations to Shaw's plays are from *A Menopausal Gentleman: The Solo Performance of Peggy Shaw*, ed. Jill Dolan. I assisted Dolan in editing this manuscript. See Shaw, *A Menopausal Gentleman*, 15–16.

19. Binding involves flattening one's chest with either elastic bandages or chest binders.

20. See Simone de Beauvoir, *The Second Sex* (1949; rpt., New York: Alfred A. Knopf, 2010).

21. See Joan Nestle, *A Restricted Country*, 3rd ed. (San Francisco: Cleis, 2003).

22. Hollibaugh, *My Dangerous Desires*, 396.

23. Shaw, *A Menopausal Gentleman*, 59.

24. Moraga, for instance, used the phrase "the disappearance of butches" in her 2010 lecture at the University of Massachusetts Stonewall Center. Moraga was challenged by several members of the audience and promised to revise her manuscript before publication, which she did. See Cherríe L. Moraga, *A Xicana Codex of Changing Consciousness* (Durham, N.C.: Duke University Press, 2011), especially "On Keeping Queer Queer." On "paranoid readings," see Eve Kosofsky Sedgwick, "Paranoid Readings and Reparative Readings," in *Touching Feeling: Affect, Pedagogy, Performativity* (Durham, N.C.: Duke University Press, 2003).

25. Artist-activist Kate Bornstein uses this expression. See *Gender Outlaw*.

26. Schechner, *Between Theater and Anthropology*, 36.

27. See Taylor, *Disappearing Acts*. See also "You Are Here: H.I.J.O.S. and the DNA of Performance," in *The Archive and the Repertoire*, 161–89.

28. See Halberstam, *In a Queer Time and Place*.

29. Harvey Young offers an excellent analysis of lynching as an American performative. See "The Black Body as Souvenir in American Lynching," *Theatre Journal* 57, no. 4 (2005): 639–57.

30. Carolyn Dinshaw, Lochrie Karma, and Menon Madhavi, "Queering History," *PMLA* 121, no. 3 (2006): 837–39.

31. Dean Spade, "Mutilating Gender," in *The Transgender Studies Reader* (New York: Routledge, 2006), 319.

32. See also Dean Spade, *Normal Life: Administrative Violence, Critical Trans Politics, and the Limits of Law* (Durham, N.C.: Duke University Press, 2015), and filmmaker Jules Rosskam's experimental film which is inspired by Spade's 2006 essay. See Rosskam, *against a trans narrative* (Chicago: Video Data Bank, 2008).

33. Shaw insists that her stroke was "Mama's fault"—Mama being Ellen Stewart, longtime artistic director of LaMama Theatre in New York's East Village who passed the same day as Shaw and Weaver's *Lost Lounge* performance. "She was trying to take me with her," Shaw said, before adding, "I'm serious" (Peggy Shaw, conversation with artist, August 25, 2011).

34. See Sue-Ellen Case, "Toward a Butch/Femme Aesthetic," in *The Lesbian and Gay Studies Reader*, ed. Henry Abelove, Michele A. Barale, and David M. Halperin (New York: Routledge, 1993).

35. Shaw, *A Menopausal Gentleman*, 85.

36. Shaw and Weaver are no longer lovers, though Shaw maintains that they are still partners both in life and art. Peggy Shaw, personal correspondence with author, August 25, 2011.

37. See *To My Chagrin*, performance, Jump-Start Performance Company, San Antonio, Tex., October 2001.

38. Shaw, *A Menopausal Gentleman*, 156.

39. According to Shaw, the fictive "you" that she has lost was inspired by the loss of her mother as well as the mother of Suzy Willson, Shaw's lover and *Must* collaborator. (Peggy Shaw, personal correspondence with author, August 25, 2011). When I saw the performance, I read the "you" as a lover, and my analysis here reflects my reception experience.

40. Shaw, *A Menopausal Gentleman*, 155.

41. See Cynthia Moss, *Elephant Memories: Thirteen Years in the Life of an Elephant Family* (Chicago: University of Chicago Press, 2000).

42. Shaw, *A Menopausal Gentleman*, 140.
43. Ibid., 130.
44. Dolan, *Utopia in Performance*, 54.
45. Louis Althusser, "Ideology and Ideological State Apparatuses," in *Lenin and Philosophy and Other Essays* (New York: Monthly Review Press, 2001).
46. Liz Lerman, personal correspondence with author, March 2004.
47. Freeman, "Time Binds, or, Erotohistoriography," 60.
48. When Shaw performs *Must*, she usually has a live band accompaniment that plays music throughout the show. They were not able to travel with Shaw for the Amherst production.
49. Shaw, *A Menopausal Gentleman*, 54.
50. Ibid., 152.
51. Ibid., 140.
52. Ibid., 141.
53. In Greek mythology, Gaia is the personification of (Mother) Earth. Thank you to my student Ryan Malloy for articulating this connection between Shaw and Gaia.
54. Dolan, introduction to Shaw, *A Menopausal Gentleman*, 33. See Monique Wittig, *The Straight Mind and Other Essays* (Boston: Beacon, 1992).
55. Shaw, *A Menopausal Gentleman*, 142.
56. Ibid., 146.
57. Joseph Chaikin, *Struck Dumb*, performance, directed by Robert Woodruff, Los Angeles, 1988; Deb Margolin, *3 Seconds in the Key*, performance, New York, 2001; Robbie McCauley, *Sugar*, performance, Boston, 2012.
58. Peggy Shaw, *Ruff*, performance, directed by Lois Weaver, New York, 2011.
59. *Must* was created under the auspices of Clod Ensemble's Performing Medicine project, "a programme of courses, workshops and events which use the arts to provide training to medical students and practicing health professionals." See Performing Medicine, www.clodensemble.com/medicine.htm.
60. For more on butch feelings, see Cvetkovich, *An Archive of Feelings*; Cherríe Moraga, *Loving in the War Years: Lo que nunca pasó por sus labios* (Boston: South End, 1983); Gloria Anzaldúa, *Borderlands/La Frontera;* Nestle, *A Restricted Country;* and Newton, "My Butch Career: A Memoir," in *Queer Ideas: The Kessler Lectures in Lesbian and Gay Studies* (New York: Feminist Press at CUNY, 2003), 81–98.
61. Bonnie Barringer, "When Butches Cry," in *The Persistent Desire: A Femme-Butch Reader*, ed. Joan Nestle (New York: Alyson, 1992), 109.
62. Dolan, *Utopia in Performance*, 54.
63. Shaw, *A Menopausal Gentleman*, 145.
64. Ibid.
65. Ibid., emphasis in the original.
66. Ibid.
67. Ibid., 159.
68. Ibid., 144.
69. Ibid., 145.
70. Dolan qtd. in Shaw, *A Menopausal Gentleman*.
71. Myriam Gurba, *Wish You Were Me* (Portland, Ore.: Future Tense, 2011), 39.

72. Andrea Lawlor, "Position Paper on Cell Phones," in *Position Papers* (Amherst, Mass.: Factory Hollow, 2016).

73. See Amos Mac and Zachary Drucker, *Translady Fanzine*, 2011, www.transladyfanzine.com; and Amos Mac and and Rocco Kayiatos, eds., *Original Plumbing: Trans Male Quarterly* (San Francisco: self-published, 2011).

74. Dolan makes a similar point about the outline of Ann Carlson's body searing to her retina in the final moments of *Blanket*. See Dolan, *Utopia in Performance*, 149.

75. David Román makes a similar remark about the need to write in his essay "November 1, 1992." See Román, *Acts of Intervention*.

## Chapter 3

1. *Here Is New York: A Democracy of Photographs* is now archived on the web. Its curators write, "The causes and effects of the events of 9/11/2001 are by no means clear, and will not be for a very long time. What is clear, though, is this: in order to restore our sense of equilibrium as a nation, as a city, and particularly as a community, we need to develop a new way of looking at and thinking about history, as well as a way of making sense of all of the images which continue to haunt us." See www.hereisnewyork.org.

2. Eng and Kazanjian, *Loss*, 2.

3. On "thanatography," see Philippe Dubois, *L'acte photographique et autres essais* (Brussels: Editions Labor, 1990). See also Phelan, *Mourning Sex*.

4. See, for example, Rothko's *White over Red* (1957) and *Orange and Yellow* (1956).

5. German composer Karlheinz Stockhausen famously got in trouble for similarly aestheticizing 9/11, calling the attacks on the World Trade Center "the biggest work of art that is possible in the whole cosmos [creating] something in one act [that] we couldn't even dream of in music. . . . People practice like crazy for 10 years, totally fanatically, for a concert, and then die. . . . You have people who are so concentrated on one performance, and then 5,000 people are dispatched into eternity, in a single moment. I couldn't do that. In comparison with that, we're nothing as composers." His comments were made on September 17, 2001, at a press conference in Hamburg, Germany. The controversy is chronicled in the *New York Times*. See Anthony Tommasini, "Music: The Devil Made Him Do It," *New York Times*, September 30, 2001.

6. Cvetkovich and Pelligrini make a similar point, about war being declared on emotions, in their introduction to *The Scholar and Feminist Online*. I assisted in editing this special issue, "Public Sentiments," *Scholar and Feminist Online* 2, no. 1 (2003).

7. See Deleuze, *Difference and Repetition*.

8. Anne Bogart, *A Director Prepares: Seven Essays on Art and Theatre* (London: Routledge, 2001), 45.

9. I borrow the phrase "not quite white" from Bhabha, "Of Mimicry and Man."

10. For a persuasive argument about the role of sports and leisure in the performance of whiteness and American belonging, see Neil Foley, "Becoming Hispanic: Mexican Americans and the Faustian Pact with Whiteness," in *Reflexiones: New Directions in Mexican American Studies*, ed. Neil Foley (Austin: University of Texas Press, 1998).

11. My thinking about retrospective memories is informed by Steedman's notion of "retrospective labeling," which she outlines in her book *Landscape for a Good Woman*. Steedman argues that memories "[take] on meaning [only] later." The present, that is, is the "interpretive device" which we sift through, make sense, and make meaning of the past. Steedman, *Landscape for a Good Woman,* 28.

12. See Lane, "Hemispheric Reenactments," lecture at the University of Texas at Austin, March 5, 2010.

13. Butler, "Performative Acts and Gender Constitution."

14. Butler's observations about repetition as a structuring structure of social life are resonant with French sociologist Pierre Bourdieu's notion of *habitus*. Butler's notion of the subversive potential of repetition with a difference is also reminiscent of playwright Suzan-Lori Parks's notion of "rep and rev," short for "repetition and revision," which applies the jazz-like aesthetic of "riffing" to playwriting. Pierre Bourdieu, *Field of Cultural Production: Essays on Art and Literature* (New York: Columbia University Press, 1993). See Suzan-Lori Parks, "Elements of Style," in *The America Play and Other Works* (New York: Theatre Communications Group, 1994). For more on the politics of jazz aesthetics as applied to performance, see Omi Osun Joni L. Jones, Lisa Moore, and Sharon Bridgforth, eds., *Experiments in a Jazz Aesthetic: Art, Activism, Academia, and the Austin Project* (Austin: University of Texas Press, 2010). (I was a member of the Austin Project between 2005 and 2006, and my writing is included in the anthology.) See also Omi Osun Joni L. Jones, *Theatrical Jazz: Performance, Àṣẹ, and the Power of the Present Moment* (Columbus: Ohio State University, 2015). Jones was a mentor to me at the University of Texas, as was Bridgforth, and key interlocutors in earlier stages of writing this book.

15. In 2004 and 2005, the performance began in a lecture hall at the University of Texas at Austin.

16. Alyssa Harad, "Following the Ghosts," http://austin360blogs.com, accessed April 24, 2006.

17. Taylor, *The Archive and the Repertoire*, 28.

18. Ibid.

19. Ibid., 32.

20. Lauren Berlant makes a similar point. See *The Queen of America Goes to Washington City: Essays on Sex and Citizenship* (Durham, N.C.: Duke University Press, 1997).

21. Butler, "Performative Acts and Gender Constitution," 277.

22. See Victor Turner, *The Anthropology of Performance* (London: PAJ, 1988) and *From Ritual to Theatre: The Human Seriousness of Play* (New York: Performing Arts Journal Publications, 1982); Schechner, *Between Theater and Anthropology*; and Dolan, *Utopia in Performance*.

23. See Dolan, *Feminist Spectator as Critic*, as well as Dolan's current blog, thefeministspectator.com.

24. Bonin-Rodriguez, Dolan, and Pryor, "Colleague-Criticism," 12.

25. See Robert Fairies, "Hyde Park Again Awash in Wonders," *Austin Chronicle*, April 9, 2010, www.austinchronicle.com/arts/2010-04-09/990566/.

26. Robert Fairies, "All over Creation: Does Size Matter When It Comes to Art?," *Austin Chronicle*, August 16, 2013. www.austinchronicle.com/arts/2013-08-16/all-over-creation-upscale/.

27. Harley Erdman, *Staging the Jew: The Performance of an American Ethnicity* (New Brunswick, N.J.: Rutgers University Press, 1997), 26. For a discussion of "exteriority" as it relates to race, see also Edward W. Said, *Orientalism* (New York: Vintage Books, 1979).

28. Ibid., 11.

29. Bonin-Rodriguez, Dolan, and Pryor, "Colleague-Criticism," 13.

30. Again, I borrow the phrase "repetition and revision" from Parks, "The Elements of Style."

31. Meredith Monk, "Archaeology of an Artist," lecture, Mount Holyoke College, April 28, 2011.

32. Stewart, *Ordinary Affects*, 45, 47, 79, 15, 10.

33. Paredez, *Selenidad*, 192.

34. Puar, *Terrorist Assemblages*, 125–26.

35. Over the course of the seven-year run, I cast a variety of actors in these roles. The woman was played by a Latina actress for five of the seven years; the man who appears twice was always played by a white actor; the other man was played by an African American actor for the final three years of the production and a white man in previous years. None of them reported being harassed, although it is important to note that the scene takes place in a relatively secluded pocket of the neighborhood.

36. See Michael Warner and Lauren Berlant, "Sex in Public," *Critical Inquiry* 24, no. 2 (1998): 547–66. 68. On orientalism, see Said, *Orientalism*. On intersections of queer, Asian, and performance, see Eng-Beng Lim, *Brown Boys and Rice Queens: Spellbinding Performance in the Asias* (New York: New York University Press, 2014); Martin F. Manalansan, *Global Divas: Filipino Gay Men in the Diaspora* (Durham, N.C.: Duke University Press, 2003); Tan Hoang Nguyen, *A View from the Bottom: Asian American Masculinity and Sexuality Representation* (Durham, N.C.: Duke University Press, 2014).

37. Benjamin, "Theses on the Philosophy of History," 257.

38. José Esteban Muñoz, "Feeling Brown: Ethnicity and Affect in Ricardo Bracho's *The Sweetest Hangover* (and Other STDs)," *Theatre Journal* 52, no. 1 (2000): 68.

39. I discuss the racism and homophobia structuring academic environments such as the University of Texas in my essay "Passing/Out in Texas: The Challenges of Progressive Pedagogy in Neoliberal Climates," *Theatre Topics* 16, no. 1 (2006): 65–84.

40. Zoviet France's "Something Spooked the Horses," on the CD *Decriminalisation of Country Music* (Charrm, 2001).Thanks to Andee Scott for bringing this music to my attention in 2004.

41. In 2010, Austin started an annually repeating, corporate-sponsored event called "Lemonade Day." Its aim is to "teach young people how to start their very own business." I was not aware of this connection when making the work. See www.austin.lemonadeday.org. Thanks to Deborah Paredez for bringing this to my attention.

42. See Raymond Williams, *Marxism and Literature* (New York: Oxford University Press, 1978), especially "Structures of Feeling," 128–35; Stewart, *Ordinary Affects*, 44.

43. See also Michael T. Taussig, *The Nervous System* (New York: Routledge, 1992).

44. Rosalyn Deutsche, *Hiroshima after Iraq: Three Studies in Art and War* (New York: Columbia University Press, 2011), 15–16; emphasis in the original.

45. Mike Agresta, "Austinist Reviews: Floodlines 2008," *Austinist*, April 23, 2008, http://austinist.com/2008/04/23/austinist_revie_16.php.

46. Thank you to Deborah Paredez for suggesting the connection between the performance and *Lot's Wife*. Paredez served as my dissertation adviser and offered extensive feedback on earlier drafts of this and other chapters. See Paredez, "Wife's Disaster Manual," *Lot's Wife Series* (unpublished, 2001).

47. Aimee Zivin, correspondence with the author, April 11, 2010.

48. Jaclyn Pryor, *floodlines*, site-specific performance, 2004–2010.

49. My notion of pilgrimage is informed by Becker's argument that the return pilgrimage is always different from the approach because the witness has been transformed by the experience. I was fortunate to hear Becker talk at the University of Texas in the final stages of creating *floodlines*, and my decision to have the processional retrace its route was inspired by her remarks. See Carol Becker, "Pilgrimage to My Lai: Social Memory and the Making of Art," *Art Journal* 62, no. 51 (2003): 51–65.

50. Phelan, *Mourning Sex*, 4.

51. Kay Edwards, correspondence with the author, April 11, 2010.

52. Bonin-Rodriguez, Dolan, and Pryor, "Colleague-Criticism."

53. Barbara Chisholm, "*Floodlines*: I Was in Hyde Park, but It Wasn't Hyde Park," *Austin Chronicle*, April 3, 2009, www.austinchronicle.com/arts/2009-04-03/762444/.

54. Fairies, "Hyde Park Again Awash in Wonders."

55. Harad, "Following the Ghosts."

### Chapter 4

1. Jill Dolan, *Geographies of Learning: Theory and Practice, Activism and Performance* (Middletown, Conn.: Wesleyan University Press, 2001), 118.

2. Halberstam, *In a Queer Time and Place*, 7–8.

3. Here I am riffing on the title of my previous essay about pedagogy and queer politics. See Pryor, "Passing/Out in Texas."

4. For more on the fragility of whiteness, heterosexuality, and able-bodiedness, see the introduction, "Compulsory Able-Bodiedness and Queer Crip Existence," in McRuer, *Crip Theory*.

5. José Esteban Muñoz, *Cruising Utopia: The Then and There of Queer Futurity* (New York: New York University Press, 2009), 22.

6. Harsha Walia, lecture, Haverford Mellon Symposium: "Anarchism, Decolonization, and Radical Democracy," Haverford College, March 27, 2015.

7. Ferguson, *Aberrations in Black*.

8. See Young, "The Black Body as Souvenir."

9. J. Kēhaulani Kauanui, lecture, Haverford Mellon Symposium: "Anarchism, Decolonization, and Radical Democracy," Haverford College, March 27, 2015.

10. Angela Davis, lecture, "Angela Davis Speaks!," Northern Arizona University, April 24, 2013.

11. See Alisa Solomon and Framji Minwalla, eds., *The Queerest Art: Essays on Lesbian and Gay Theater* (New York: New York University Press, 2002).

12. Phelan makes a similar point in *Mourning Sex*. See her introduction, "This Book's Body."

13. See Mark Rifkin, *When Did Indians Become Straight? Kinship, the History of Sexuality, and Native Sovereignty* (New York: New York University Press, 2011); Andrea Smith, *Conquest: Sexual Violence and American Indian Genocide* (Cambridge, Mass.: South End Press, 2005); Morgensen, *Spaces between Us*; Kaplan, *Anarchy of Empire*. Thank you to Liza Minno for bringing these works to my attention.

14. Thank you to Ollie Schwartz for bringing this essay to my attention.

15. Sara Ahmed, "The Nonperformativity of Antiracism," *Meridians: Feminism, Race, Transnationalism* 7, no. 1 (2006): 104–5.

16. Williams, *Marxism and Literature*, 132–34.

17. Thank you to Riko Fluchel for sharing his thesis with me; much of his theorizing informs my own. See "Behoming [*sic*] the Impossible: Queer World-Making in the Filipin@ Diaspora" (Division III thesis, Hampshire College, Amherst, Mass., 2013).

18. Muñoz, *Cruising Utopia*, 1.

### Epilogue

Epigraph: Thank you to my student Sonia Copple for bringing the passage from *Cruel Optimism* to my attention.

BIBLIOGRAPHY


Abelove, Henry, Michele A. Barale, and David M. Halperin, eds. *The Lesbian and Gay Studies Reader.* New York: Routledge, 1993.

Agresta, Mike. "Austinist Reviews: Floodlines 2008." *Austinist*, April 23, 2008. http://austinist.com/2008/04/23/austinist_revie_16.php.

Ahmed, Sara. "The Nonperformativity of Antiracism." *Meridians: Feminism, Race, Transnationalism* 7, no. 1 (2006): 104–5.

Alexander, M. Jacqui. *Pedagogies of Crossing: Meditations on Feminism, Sexual Politics, Memory, and the Sacred.* Durham, N.C.: Duke University Press, 2005.

———. "Site of Memory: The Atlantic and Other Crossings." Lecture. University of Texas at Austin, 2008.

Althusser, Louis. "Ideology and Ideological State Apparatuses." In *Lenin and Philosophy and Other Essays.* New York: Monthly Review Press, 2001.

Anderson, Benedict R. *Imagined Communities: Reflections on the Origin and Spread of Nationalism.* Rev. ed. London: Verso, 2006.

Anzaldúa, Gloria. *Borderlands/La Frontera: The New Mestiza.* San Francisco: Spinster/Aunt Lute, 1987.

Austin, J. L. *How to Do Things with Words.* Oxford: Clarendon, 1962.

Baderoon, Gabeba. "Gender within Gender." *Feminist Studies* 37, no. 2 (2011): 390–416. www.jstor.org/stable/23069910.

Bailey, Marlon M., Priya Kandaswamy, and Mattie Udora Richardson. "Is Gay Marriage Racist?" In *Against Equality: Queer Revolution, Not Mere Inclusion*, edited by Ryan Conrad. Chico, Calif.: AK Press, 2014.

Barringer, Bonnie. "When Butches Cry." In *The Persistent Desire: A Femme-Butch Reader*, edited by Joan Nestle. New York: Alyson, 1992.

Barthes, Roland. *Camera Lucida: Reflections on Photography.* New York: Hill and Wang, 1981.

Bechdel, Alison. *Fun Home: A Tragicomic.* New York: Mariner Books, 2007.

Becker, Carol. "Pilgrimage to My Lai: Social Memory and the Making of Art." *Art Journal* 62, no. 51 (2003): 51–65.

Benjamin, Walter. "Theses on the Philosophy of History." In *Illuminations.* New York: Harcourt, Brace and World, 1968.

Berlant, Lauren. *Cruel Optimism.* Durham, N.C.: Duke University Press, 2011.

———. *The Queen of America Goes to Washington City: Essays on Sex and Citizenship.* Durham, N.C.: Duke University Press, 1997.

Bhabha, Homi K. "Of Mimicry and Man." In *The Location of Culture.* London: Routledge, 1994.

Blau, Herbert. *Take Up the Bodies: Theater at the Vanishing Point.* Urbana: University of Illinois Press, 1982.

Boal, Augusto. *Theatre of the Oppressed*. New York: Theatre Communications Group, 1993.

Boellstorff, Tom. "When Marriage Falls: Queer Coincidences in Straight Time." *GLQ* 12, nos. 2–3 (2007).

Bogart, Anne. *A Director Prepares: Seven Essays on Art and Theatre*. London: Routledge, 2001.

Bonin-Rodriguez, Paul. *Performing Policy: How Contemporary Politics and Cultural Programs Redefined U.S. Artists for the Twenty-First Century*. New York: Palgrave, 2015.

Bonin-Rodriguez, Paul, Jill Dolan, and Jaclyn Pryor. "Colleague-Criticism: Performance, Writing, and Queer Collegiality." *Liminalities: A Journal of Performance Studies* 5, no. 1 (2009).

Bornstein, Kate. *Gender Outlaw: On Men, Women, and the Rest of Us*. New York: Routledge, 1994.

Bourdieu, Pierre. *Field of Cultural Production: Essays on Art and Literature*. New York: Columbia University Press, 1993.

Brougher, Hillary, dir. *The Sticky Fingers of Time*. Culver City, Calif.: Strand Releasing, 1997.

Butler, Judith. "Global Violence, Sexual Politics." In *Queer Ideas: The David R. Kessler Lectures in Lesbian and Gay Studies*, 199–214. New York: Feminist Press at the City University of New York, 2003.

———. "Performative Acts and Gender Constitution: An Essay in Phenomenology and Feminist Theory." *Theatre Journal* 40, no. 4 (1988): 270–82.

Canning, Charlotte. *Feminist Theaters in the U.S.A.: Staging Women's Experience*. New York: Routledge, 1995.

Carlson, Ann. *Night Light*. Performance. New York and Chicago, 2000.

Carlson/Strom. *Geyser Land*. Performance. Livingston/Bozeman, Mt., 2003.

———. *Meadowlark*. Video installation. DeCordova Museum, Lincoln, Mass., 2009.

———. *New Performance Video*. Video installation. Curated by Catherine Lord. DeCordova Museum, Lincoln, Mass., 2009.

Carlson, Marvin A. *The Haunted Stage: The Theatre as Memory Machine*. Ann Arbor: University of Michigan Press, 2001.

Caruth, Cathy. *Unclaimed Experience: Trauma, Narrative, and History*. Baltimore: Johns Hopkins University Press, 1996.

Case, Sue-Ellen. *Performing Feminisms: Feminist Critical Theory and Theatre*. Baltimore: Johns Hopkins University Press, 1990.

———. *Split Britches: Lesbian Practice / Feminist Performance*. London: Routledge, 1996.

———. "Toward a Butch/Femme Aesthetic." In *The Lesbian and Gay Studies Reader*, edited by Henry Abelove, Michele A. Barale, and David M. Halperin. New York: Routledge, 1993.

Cerullo, Margaret. Speech at Occupy/Decolonize Teach-In. Amherst, Mass., 2011.

Chaikin, Joseph. *Struck Dumb*. Performance. Directed by Robert Woodruff. Los Angeles, 1988.

Cheng, Anne Anlin. *The Melancholy of Race*. Oxford: Oxford University Press, 2001.

Chisholm, Barbara. "*Floodlines*: I Was in Hyde Park, but It Wasn't Hyde Park." *Austin Chronicle*. April 3, 2009. www.austinchronicle.com/arts/2009-04-03/762444/.

Coates, Ta-Nehisi. "My President Was Black." *The Atlantic*. January/February 2017. https://www.theatlantic.com/magazine/archive/2017/01/my-president-was-black/508793/?utm_source=fbb.

Cohen, Cathy J. *Boundaries of Blackness: AIDS and the Breakdown of Black Politics*. Chicago: University of Chicago Press, 1999.

———. "Punks, Bulldaggers, and Welfare Queens." *GLQ: A Journal of Lesbian and Gay Studies* 3, no. 4 (1997): 437–65.

Cohen-Cruz, Jan. *Local Acts: Community-Based Performance in the United States*. New Brunswick, N.J.: Rutgers University Press, 2005.

Combahee River Collective. *The Combahee River Collective Statement: Black Feminist Organizing in the Seventies and Eighties*. Albany, N.Y.: Kitchen Table: Women of Color Press, 1986.

Conquergood, Dwight. "Performing as a Moral Act: Ethical Dimensions of the Ethnography of Performance." *Literature in Performance* 5, no. 2 (1985): 1–13.

Conrad, Ryan, ed. *Against Equality: Queer Revolution, Not Mere Inclusion*. Chico, Calif.: AK Press, 2014.

Crimp, Douglas. *Melancholy and Moralism: Essays on AIDS and Queer Politics*. Cambridge, Mass.: MIT Press, 2002.

Cruz, Arnaldo, and Martin F. Manalansan, eds. *Queer Globalizations: Citizenship and the Afterlife of Colonialism*. New York: New York University Press, 2002.

Cvetkovich, Ann. *An Archive of Feelings: Trauma, Sexuality, and Lesbian Public Cultures*. Durham, N.C.: Duke University Press, 2003.

———. *Depression: A Public Feeling*. Durham, N.C.: Duke University Press, 2012.

Cvetkovich, Ann, and Ann Pelligrini. "Public Sentiments." *Scholar and Feminist Online* 2, no. 1 (2003).

Daly, Ann. *Critical Gestures: Writings on Dance and Culture*. Middletown, Conn.: Wesleyan University Press, 2002.

Davis, Angela. "Angela Davis Speaks!" Lecture. Northern Arizona University, April 24, 2013.

de Beauvoir, Simone. *The Second Sex*. 1949. Reprint, New York: Alfred A. Knopf, 2010.

de Certeau, Michel. *The Practice of Everyday Life*. Berkeley: University of California Press, 1988.

Delany, Samuel. *Times Square Red, Times Square Blue*. New York: New York University Press, 1999.

Deleuze, Gilles. *Difference and Repetition*. Translated by Paul Patton. New York: Columbia University Press, 1994.

Deloria, Philip J. *Playing Indian*. New Haven, Conn.: Yale University Press, 1998.

Derrida, Jacques. *Archive Fever: A Freudian Impression*. Chicago: University of Chicago Press, 1996.

Deutsche, Rosalyn. *Hiroshima after Iraq: Three Studies in Art and War*. New York: Columbia University Press, 2011.

Diamond, Elin, ed. *Performance and Cultural Politics*. New York: Routledge, 1996.

———. *Unmaking Mimesis: Essays on Feminism and Theater*. London: Routledge, 1997.

Dinshaw, Carolyn. *Getting Medieval: Sexualities and Communities, Pre- and Postmodern*. Durham, N.C.: Duke University Press, 1999.

Dinshaw, Carolyn, Lochrie Karma, and Menon Madhavi. "Queering History." *PMLA* 121, no. 3 (2006): 837–39.

Dolan, Jill. *The Feminist Spectator as Critic*. Ann Arbor, Mich.: UMI Research Press, 1988.

———. *Geographies of Learning: Theory and Practice, Activism and Performance*. Middletown, Conn.: Wesleyan University Press, 2001.

———. *Presence and Desire: Essays on Gender, Sexuality, Performance*. Ann Arbor: University of Michigan Press, 1993.

———. *Utopia in Performance: Finding Hope at the Theater*. Ann Arbor: University of Michigan Press, 2005.

Duberman, Martin Bauml, Martha Vicinus, and George Chauncey. *Hidden from History: Reclaiming the Gay and Lesbian Past*. New York: Plume, 1990.

Dubois, Philippe. *L'acte photographique et autres essais*. Brussels: Editions Labor, 1990.

Duggan, Lisa. *The Twilight of Equality: Neoliberalism, Cultural Politics, and the Attack on Democracy*. Boston: Beacon, 2003.

Edelman, Lee. *No Future: Queer Theory and the Death Drive*. Durham, N.C.: Duke University Press, 2004.

Eng, David. *The Feeling of Kinship: Queer Liberalism and the Racialization of Intimacy*. Durham, N.C.: Duke University Press, 2010.

Eng, David L., Jack Halberstam, and José Esteban Muñoz. Introduction to "What's Queer about Queer Studies Now?" special issue, *Social Text* 23, nos. 3–4 (2005): 1–17.

Eng, David L., and David Kazanjian, eds. *Loss: The Politics of Mourning*. Berkeley: University of California Press, 2003.

Erdman, Harley. *Staging the Jew: The Performance of an American Ethnicity*. New Brunswick, N.J.: Rutgers University Press, 1997.

Fairies, Robert. "All over Creation: Does Size Matter When It Comes to Art?" *Austin Chronicle*. 2013. www.austinchronicle.com/arts/2013-08-16/all-over-creation-upscale/.

———. "Hyde Park Again Awash in Wonders." *Austin Chronicle*. April 9, 2010. www.austinchronicle.com/arts/2010-04-09/990566/.

Ferguson, Roderick. *Aberrations in Black: Toward a Queer of Color Critique*. Minneapolis: University of Minnesota Press, 2003.

Fluchel, Riko. "Behoming [*sic*] the Impossible: Queer World-Making in the Filipin@ Diaspora." Division III thesis, Hampshire College, Amherst, Mass., 2013.

Foley, Neil. "Becoming Hispanic: Mexican Americans and the Faustian Pact with Whiteness." In *Reflexiones: New Directions in Mexican American Studies*, edited by Neil Foley. Austin: University of Texas Press, 1998.

Forgács, Péter, dir. *The Maelstrom: A Family Chronicle*. 1997. DVD, Lumen Film, 2005.

Foucault, Michel. *Archaeology of Knowledge*. Translated by A. M. Sheridan Smith. New York: Routledge, 2002.

———. *The History of Sexuality*, Vol. 1: *An Introduction*. New York: Vintage, 1990.

———. *Discipline and Punish: The Birth of the Prison*. Translated by Alan Sheridan. New York: Pantheon, 1977.

———. *"Society Must Be Defended": Lectures at the Collège de France, 1975–76*. London: Penguin, 2003.

Freeman, Elizabeth. Introduction to "Queer Temporalities," special issue, *GLQ: A Journal of Lesbian and Gay Studies* 17, no. 1 (2011).

———. *Time Binds: Queer Temporalities, Queer Histories*. Durham, N.C.: Duke University Press, 2010.

———. "Time Binds, or, Erotohistoriography." *Social Text* 23, nos. 3–4 (2005): 57–68.

Gallop, Jane. *Anecdotal Theory*. Durham, N.C.: Duke University Press, 2002.

Ginzburg, Carlo. *Clues, Myths, and the Historical Method*. Baltimore: Johns Hopkins University Press, 1989.

Gopinath, Gayatri. *Impossible Desires: Queer Diasporas and South Asian Public Cultures*. Durham, N.C.: Duke University Press, 2005.

Gordon, Avery. *Ghostly Matters: Haunting and the Sociological Imagination*. Minneapolis: University of Minnesota Press, 1997.

Gurba, Myriam. *Wish You Were Me*. Portland, Ore.: Future Tense, 2011.

Halberstam, Jack. *In a Queer Time and Place: Transgender Bodies, Subcultural Lives*. New York: New York University Press, 2005.

———. *The Queer Art of Failure*. Durham, N.C.: Duke University Press, 2011.

Halbwachs, Maurice. *On Collective Memory*. Edited and translated by Lewis A. Coser. Chicago: University of Chicago Press, 1992.

Harad, Alyssa. "Following the Ghosts." http://austin360blogs.com, posted April 27, 2006.

Hedgepeth, Sonja M., and Rochelle G. Saidel. *Sexual Violence against Jewish Women during the Holocaust*. Waltham, Mass.: Brandeis University Press, 2010.

Hollibaugh, Amber. *My Dangerous Desires: A Queer Girl Dreaming Her Way Home*. Durham, N.C.: Duke University Press, 2000.

Holtzberg, Maggie. "The Making of the Film: A Diary Account of the Making of Gandy Dancers." *Folkstreams.net*. Accessed August 17, 2006.

Hughes, Holly, and David Román, eds. *O Solo Homo: The New Queer Performance*. New York: Grove, 1998.

Jameson, Fredric. *The Political Unconscious: Narrative as a Socially Symbolic Act*. Ithaca, N.Y.: Cornell University Press, 1981.

Johnson, E. Patrick. *Appropriating Blackness: Performance and the Politics of Authenticity*. Durham, N.C.: Duke University Press, 2003.

Jones, Omi Osun Joni L. "Performance Ethnography: The Role of Embodiment in Cultural Authenticity." *Theatre Topics* 12, no. 1 (2002): 1–15.

———. *Theatrical Jazz: Performance, Àṣẹ, and the Power of the Present Moment*. Columbus: Ohio State University Press, 2015.

Jones, Omi Osun Joni L., Lisa Moore, and Sharon Bridgforth, eds. *Experiments in a Jazz Aesthetic: Art, Activism, Academia, and the Austin Project*. Austin: University of Texas Press, 2010.

Joseph, Miranda. *Against the Romance of Community*. Minneapolis: University of Minnesota Press, 2002.

Kafer, Alison. *Feminist, Queer, Crip*. Bloomington: Indiana University Press, 2013.

Kaplan, Amy. *Anarchy of Empire in the Making of U.S. Culture*. Cambridge, Mass.: Harvard University Press, 2002.

Kauanui, J. Kēhaulani. Lecture at Haverford Mellon Symposium: "Anarchism, Decolonization, and Radical Democracy," Haverford College, March 27, 2015.

Kimmel, Michael. "Gay Bashing is About Masculinity." *Ms. Magazine*, October 2010.

Kirshenblatt-Gimblett, Barbara. *Destination Culture: Tourism, Museums, and Heritage*. Los Angeles and Berkeley: University of California Press, 1998.

Kron, Lisa and Jeanine Tesori, *Fun Home*. Performance. Directed by Sam Gold. Broadway Circle in the Square, New York City, September 10, 2016.

Kushner, Tony. *Angels in America*. London: Nick Hern, 2007.

Lane, Jill. "Hemispheric Reenactments." Lecture, University of Texas at Austin, March 5, 2010.

Lawlor, Andrea. "Position Paper on Cell Phones." In *Position Papers*. Amherst, Mass.: Factory Hollow, 2016.

Lee, Hyun-Joo. "Staging 'Fictive' Ethnicity: Asian American Performance after the Immigration and Nationality Act of 1965." Ph.D. diss. New York University, 2009.

Levins Morales, Aurora. *Kindling: Writings on the Body*. Cambridge: Palabrera Press, 2013.

Lim, Eng-Beng. *Brown Boys and Rice Queens: Spellbinding Performance in the Asias*. New York: New York University Press, 2014.

Lippard, Lucy R. *The Lure of the Local: Senses of Place in a Multicentered Society*. New York: New Press, 1997.

López, Nikki. Speech at Orlando Vigil. Philadelphia, June 13, 2016.

Lord, Catherine. "Track Marks." In *Carlson/Strom: New Performance Video*. Exhibition catalogue. Lincoln, Mass.: DeCordova Museum and Sculpture Park, 2009.

Lott, Eric. *Love and Theft: Blackface Minstrelsy and the American Working Class*. New York: Oxford University Press, 2013.

Love, Heather. *Feeling Backward: Loss and the Politics of Queer History*. Cambridge, Mass.: Harvard University Press, 2007.

lynch, kara. *invisible—the archivist's vault*. Site-specific performance. Greenfield, Mass., 2011.

Mac, Amos, and Zachary Drucker. *Translady Fanzine*. 2011.

Mac, Amos, and Rocco Kayiatos. *Original Plumbing: Trans Male Quarterly*. San Francisco: self-published, 2011.

Manalansan, Martin F. *Global Divas: Filipino Gay Men in the Diaspora*. Durham, N.C.: Duke University Press, 2003.

Margolin, Deb. *3 Seconds in the Key*. Performance. New York, 2001.

McCallum, E.L. and Mikko Tuhkanen, eds. *Queer Times, Queer Becomings*. Albany: SUNY Press, 2011.

McCauley, Robbie. *Sugar*. Performance. Boston, 2012.

McRuer, Robert. *Crip Theory: Cultural Signs of Queerness and Disability*. New York: New York University Press, 2006.

Monk, Meredith. “Archaeology of an Artist.” Lecture. Mount Holyoke College, April 28, 2011.

———. *Juice: A Theatre Cantata in Three Installments*. Site-specific performance. 1969.

Moraga, Cherríe. “Still Loving in the Still War Years: On Keeping Queer Queer.” Keynote address. LGBT Stonewall Center, University of Massachusetts, Amherst, October 5, 2010.

———. *Loving in the War Years: Lo que nunca pasó por sus labios*. Boston: South End, 1983.

———. *A Xicana Codex of Changing Consciousness*. Durham, N.C.: Duke University Press, 2011.

Morgensen, Scott Lauria. *Spaces between Us: Queer Settler Colonialism and Indigenous Decolonization*. Minneapolis: University of Minnesota Press, 2011.

Moss, Cynthia. *Elephant Memories: Thirteen Years in the Life of an Elephant Family*. Chicago: University of Chicago Press, 2000.

Muñoz, José Esteban. *Cruising Utopia: The Then and There of Queer Futurity*. New York: New York University Press, 2009.

———. *Disidentifications: Queers of Color and the Performance of Politics*. Minneapolis: University of Minnesota Press, 1999.

———. “Feeling Brown: Ethnicity and Affect in Ricardo Bracho’s *The Sweetest Hangover* (and Other STDs).” *Theatre Journal* 52, no. 1 (2000).

———. “Thinking beyond Antirelationality and Antiutopianism in Queer Critique.” *PMLA* 121 (2006): 825–26.

Negrón-Muntañer, Frances. *Boricua Pop: Puerto Ricans and the Latinization of American Culture*. New York: New York University Press, 2004.

Nestle, Joan. *A Restricted Country*. 3rd ed. San Francisco: Cleis, 2003.

Newton, Esther. “My Butch Career: A Memoir.” In *Queer Ideas: The Kessler Lectures in Lesbian and Gay Studies*, 81–98. New York: Feminist Press at CUNY, 2003.

Nguyen, Tan Hoang. *A View from the Bottom: Asian American Masculinity and Sexual Representation*. Durham, N.C.: Duke University Press, 2014.

Nye, David E. *Narratives and Spaces: Technology and the Construction of American Culture*. New York: Columbia University Press, 1997.

Paredez, Deborah. *Selenidad: Selena, Latinos, and the Performance of Memory*. Durham, N.C.: Duke University Press, 2009.

———. “Wife’s Disaster Manual.” *Lot’s Wife Series*. Unpublished, 2001.

Parks, Suzan-Lori. *The America Play and Other Works*. New York: Theatre Communications Group, 1994.

Payne, Donna. Human Rights Campaign. “Envisioning an Inclusive World: The Importance of the Gay Civil Rights Movement.” *Dream of a Nation* (newsletter), 2010. http://dreamofanation.org/img/Human-Rights-Campaign.pdf.

Perron, Wendy. “A Performance Runs through It.” *New York Times*, August 10, 2003.

Phelan, Peggy. *Mourning Sex: Performing Public Memories*. London: Routledge, 1997.

———. *Unmarked: The Politics of Performance*. London: Routledge, 1993.

Pryor, Jaclyn. *floodlines*. Site-specific performance. 2004–2010.

———. "Passing/Out in Texas: The Challenges of Progressive Pedagogy in Neoliberal Climates." *Theatre Topics* 16, no. 1 (2006): 65–84.

Puar, Jasbir K. *Terrorist Assemblages: Homonationalism in Queer Times*. Durham, N.C.: Duke University Press, 2007.

Rankine, Claudia. *Citizen: An American Lyric*. Minneapolis: Graywolf, 2014.

Reckson, Lindsay. "Hands Up." *Avidly*. December 11, 2014. http://avidly.lareviewofbooks.org/2014/12/11/hands-up/.

Reddy, Chandon. "Asian Diasporas, Neoliberalism, and Family: Reviewing the Case for Homosexual Asylum in the Context of Family Rights." *Social Text* 23, nos. 3–4 (2005): 101–19.

Reynolds, Ann. *Robert Smithson: Learning from New Jersey and Elsewhere*. Cambridge, Mass.: MIT Press, 2003.

Rifkin, Mark. *When Did Indians Become Straight? Kinship, the History of Sexuality, and Native Sovereignty*. New York: New York University Press, 2011.

Rivera-Servera, Ramón H. *Performing Queer Latinidad: Dance, Sexuality, Politics*. Ann Arbor: University of Michigan Press, 2012.

Roach, Joseph R. *Cities of the Dead: Circum-Atlantic Performance*. New York: Columbia University Press, 1996.

Rodríguez, Juana María. *Sexual Futures, Queer Gestures, and Other Latina Longings*. New York: NYU Press, 2014.

Román, David. *Acts of Intervention: Performance, Gay Culture, and AIDS*. Bloomington: Indiana University Press, 1998.

Rosenberg, Jord/ana. "Gender Trouble on Mother's Day." *Avidly*. 2014. http://avidly.lareviewofbooks.org/2014/05/09/gender-trouble-on-mothers-day/.

Rosskam, Jules, dir. *against a trans narrative*. Chicago: Video Data Bank, 2008.

Said, Edward W. *Orientalism*. New York: Vintage Books, 1979.

Savage, Dan. *It Gets Better: Coming Out, Overcoming Bullying, and Creating a Life Worth Living*. New York: Dutton, 2011.

Schechner, Richard. *Between Theater and Anthropology*. Philadelphia: University of Pennsylvania Press, 1985.

Schneider, Rebecca. *Performing Remains: Art and War in Times of Theatrical Enactment*. New York: Routledge, 2011.

Sedgwick, Eve Kosofsky. *Touching Feeling: Affect, Pedagogy, Performativity*. Durham, N.C.: Duke University Press, 2003.

Serano, Julia. *Whipping Girl: A Transsexual Woman on Sexism and the Scapegoating of Femininity*. New York: Seal, 2007.

Shaw, Peggy. *A Menopausal Gentleman: The Solo Performances of Peggy Shaw*. Edited by Jill Dolan. Ann Arbor: University of Michigan, 2011.

———. *Menopausal Gentleman*. Performance. Dixon Place, New York City, 1997.

———. *Must: The Inside Story*. Directed by Suzy Willson. University of Massachusetts–Amherst, April 5, 2011.

———. *Ruff*. Performance. Directed by Lois Weaver. Dixon Place, New York City, 2012.

———. *To My Chagrin*. Performance. Jump-Start Performance Company. San Antonio, Tex., October 2001.

———. *You're Just Like My Father*. Performance. Hampshire College, Amherst, Mass., 1994.

Smith, Andrea. *Conquest: Sexual Violence and American Indian Genocide*. Cambridge, Mass.: South End, 2005.

———. Lecture. University of Texas at Austin, November 17, 2009.

———. "Queer Theory and Native Studies: The Heteronormativity of Settler Colonialism." *GLQ: A Journal of Gay and Lesbian Studies* 16, no. 1 (2010): 41–68.

Snediker, Michael D. *Queer Optimism: Lyric Personhood and Other Felicitous Persuasions*. Minneapolis: University of Minnesota Press, 2009.

Solomon, Alisa, and Martin Duberman. *Queer Ideas: The Kessler Lectures in Lesbian and Gay Studies*. New York: Feminist Press at CUNY, 2003.

Solomon, Alisa, and Framji Minwalla, eds. *The Queerest Art: Essays on Lesbian and Gay Theater*. New York: New York University Press, 2002.

Somers, Margaret R. *Genealogies of Citizenship: Markets, Statelessness, and the Right to Have Rights*. Cambridge: Cambridge University Press, 2008.

Spade, Dean. "Mutilating Gender." *The Transgender Studies Reader*, 315–22. New York: Routledge, 2006.

———. *Normal Life: Administrative Violence, Critical Trans Politics, and the Limits of Law*. Durham, N.C.: Duke University Press, 2015.

Spivak, Gayatri Chakravorty. "Can the Subaltern Speak? Speculations on Widow Sacrifice." *Wedge* 7–8 (1985): 120–30.

———. *The Spivak Reader: Selected Works of Gayatri Chakravorty Spivak*. Edited by Donna Landry and Gerald M. MacLean. New York: Routledge, 1996.

Stauffer, Jill. *Ethical Loneliness: The Injustice of Not Being Heard*. New York: Columbia University Press, 2015.

Steedman, Carolyn. *Dust: The Archive and Cultural History*. New Brunswick, N.J.: Rutgers University Press, 2002.

———. *Landscape for a Good Woman: A Story of Two Lives*. London: Virago, 1986.

Stewart, Kathleen. *Ordinary Affects*. Durham, N.C.: Duke University Press, 2007.

Strom, Mary Ellen. *Geyser Land Web Project*. www.geyserland.com.

Stryker, Susan. *Transgender History*. Berkeley, Calif.: Seal, 2008.

———, ed. "The Transgender Issue," special issue, *GLQ: A Journal of Lesbian and Gay Studies* 4, no. 2 (1998).

Sundiata, Sekou. "Thinking Out Loud: Democracy, Imagination and Peeps of Color." Keynote address. "NEA 40 Symposium," University of Texas at Austin, October 29, 2005.

Sycamore, Bernstein. *Nobody Passes: Rejecting the Rules of Gender and Conformity*. Emeryville, Calif.: Seal, 2006.

Tajiri, Rea, dir. *History and Memory: For Akiko and Takashige*. New York: Women Make Movies, 1991.

Taussig, Michael T. *The Nervous System*. New York: Routledge, 1992.

Taylor, Diana. *The Archive and the Repertoire: Performing Cultural Memory in the Americas*. Durham, N.C.: Duke University Press, 2003.

———. *Disappearing Acts: Spectacles of Gender and Nationalism in Argentina's "Dirty War."* Durham, N.C.: Duke University Press, 1997.

Taylor, Diana, et al. "A Forum on Theatre and Tragedy in the Wake of September 11, 2001." *Theatre Journal* 54, no. 1 (2002): 95–138.

Tea, Michelle. "How Not to Be a Queer Douchebag." Keynote address. "Five College Queer Gender and Sexuality Conference," Hampshire College, Amherst, Mass., March 5, 2011.

Tommasini, Anthony. "Music: The Devil Made Him Do It." *New York Times*, September 30, 2001.

Traub, Valerie. "The Present Future of Lesbian Historiography." In *A Companion to Lesbian, Gay, Bisexual, Transgender, and Queer Studies*, 124–45. New York: Wiley-Blackwell, 2007.

Turner, Kay. "September 11: The Burden of the Ephemeral." *Western Folklore* 68 (2009): 155–208.

Turner, Victor. *The Anthropology of Performance*. London: PAJ, 1988.

———. *From Ritual to Theatre: The Human Seriousness of Play*. New York: Performing Arts Journal Publications, 1982.

Warner, Michael. *Fear of a Queer Planet: Queer Politics and Social Theory*. Minneapolis: University of Minnesota Press, 1993.

———. *The Trouble with Normal: Sex, Politics, and the Ethics of Queer Life*. New York: Free Press, 1999.

Warner, Michael and Lauren Berlant. "Sex in Public." *Critical Inquiry* 24, no. 2 (1998): 547–66. 68.

Warner, Sara. *Acts of Gaiety: LGBT Performance and the Politics of Pleasure*. Ann Arbor: University of Michigan Press, 2012.

Williams, Raymond. *Marxism and Literature*. New York: Oxford University Press, 1978.

Wittig, Monique. *The Straight Mind and Other Essays*. Boston: Beacon, 1992.

Young, Harvey. "The Black Body as Souvenir in American Lynching." *Theatre Journal* 57, no. 4 (2005): 639–57.

Younge, Gary. "The Unbearable Whiteness of the American Left." *The Nation*. April 24, 2014. https://www.thenation.com/article/unbearable-whiteness-american-left/.

# INDEX

Page numbers in **boldface** refer to illustrations.